"THE BEST DETECTIVE FICTION
BEING WRITTEN. . .

Add a stinging social commentary . . . A Celinesque
journey into darkness, and we have an Andrew
Vachss, one of our most important writers."

Martha Grimes

"A sleuth who lives not just on society's edge, but on
its underbelly. . . . Strong, gritty, gut-bucket stuff, so
unsparing and vivid that it makes you wince. Vachss
knows the turf and writes with a sneering
bravado. . . . Burke prowls the city with a seething,
angry, almost psychotic voice appropriate to the devils
he deals with. . . . Vachss is good, his Burke books
first-rate."

Chicago Tribune

"Move over Hammett and Chandler, you've got
company. . . . An absolute original . . . Andrew Vachss
has become a cult favorite, and for good reason."

Cosmopolitan

"Burke is the ultimate creature of the streets. . . . The
best character in years!"

Dallas Times Herald

"Fans of Vachss's stylized mix of sentiment and rock-
hard-boiled action and prose won't be disappointed."

The Kirkus Reviews

BLOSSOM

Andrew Vachss

IVY BOOKS • NEW YORK

Ivy Books
Published by Ballantine Books
Copyright © 1990 by Andrew Vachss

Library of Congress Catalog Card Number: 89-43394

ISBN 0-8041- 0751-3

This edition published by arrangement by Alfred A. Knopf, Inc.

Manufactured in the United States of America

First Ballantine Book Edition: July 1991

FOR ANDREW MITCHELL

born: October 19, 1985
unearthed: September 6, 1989

you never had a good day on this earth
sleep now, child

BLOSSOM

1

THE SUN DROPPED on the far side of the Hudson River like it knew what was coming.

I turned off the West Side Highway at Thirtieth Street, cruising east toward Tenth Avenue. Glanced at the photograph taped to my dashboard. Marilyn, her name was. Fourteen years old, her father said. Chubby, round-faced little girl, smiling at the camera, standing next to a Bon Jovi poster in her pink ruffled bedroom.

Marilyn ran away from home. Ran herself straight to Hell. I didn't know what she was before she caught the bus that dropped her into Port Authority, but I knew what she was now.

Raw meat on the streets. A pimp's prey as soon as her feet hit the sidewalk.

She'd be out here somewhere, chasing money.

Me too.

Marilyn wouldn't be working the commuters heading home through the Lincoln Tunnel. The hard-core tunnel bunnies would take her the way a Cuisinart took vegetables. A girl that young should be working indoors, but she hadn't turned up. Only one place left.

I fluttered my hand in a "get down" gesture but Max the Silent was way ahead of me, puddling himself into a pool of shadow in the back seat.

You can't make more than a couple of passes at any one

1

block. The working girls know all about comparison shoppers. I stopped for a light on Twelfth. The Prof was at his post, his tiny body in a wheelchair, a Styrofoam begging cup jingling coins in his hand. He caught my eye. Nodded his head. Pointed up the block with a finger held at his waist.

You couldn't miss her. Babyfat spilling out all around the borders of the red hot pants, nervously plucking at her white halter top. Face unreadable behind the thick makeup. Hair piled on top of her head to make her look taller. Wobbling on spike heels in the heat waves the retreating sun left behind on the pavement. She was leaning against a long low building with some other girls. Cattle waiting for the prod.

My eyes flicked to the I-beam girder on the corner. Something moving in the shadows. Her pimp? No, one of the triple-threat street skells: clean your windshield, sell you a vial of crack, or slash at your face while another snatched at your wallet. Whatever pays.

I slowed the Plymouth to a crawl. Empty parking lot to my right. A black girl detached herself from the lineup, cut diagonally across the block toward me, streetlights glinting off her high cheekbones, crack-lust in her dead eyes.

"Want to give me a ride, honey? Change your luck?"

"Not tonight," I said, my eyes over her shoulder.

"She underage, man. Jailbait, big time."

I lit a cigarette. Shook my head. The black girl stepped aside. Walked away, switching her hips out of habit. Her other habit. AIDS and crack—racing to see which would take her down first.

Marilyn came over. Tentative. "You want to party?" Watching my face. Wanting me to say no. Not wanting me to. Lost.

"How much?" I asked, so she wouldn't spook.

"Fifty for me, ten for the room."

"What do I get for the fifty?"

Her eyes were somewhere else. "You get me. For a half hour. Okay?"

"Okay."

She walked around the front of the car, her head down. Resigned.

She got in the car knees first, the way a young girl does. Closed the door. "Take a left at the corner," she said, fumbling in her purse for a cigarette. I knew where she wanted me to go—one of the shadowy deserted parking lots on West Twenty-fifth. In case I wanted to save the ten bucks for the room. She looked up as I drove through the green light, heading for Ninth. "Hey . . . I said . . ."

"Forget it, Marilyn." Using her name so she wouldn't think I had violence on my mind. Her pimp would have warned her about men who wanted to hurt her for fun. He'd tell her this was all about business. Beat it into her if she didn't understand. Beat her again to make sure.

"Who're you?" Everything in her voice running together in a sad-scared baby-blend.

"It's not important. Your father said you ran away, so . . ."

"You're taking me back there."

"Yeah."

She snatched at the door handle. Jiggled it. Hard. No go. Looked at my face. She knew. Started to cry.

She didn't look up until I pulled in behind Lily's joint. Max flowed out of the back seat. I lit a smoke, waiting.

"This isn't my home."

I didn't answer her.

Lily came back with Max, her long black hair bouncing in the night breeze. She opened the passenger door, said, "Hi, Marilyn," and held out her hand. The kid took it. They always do. Lily would keep her for a while, talk to her, see what happened, and why. Then, if it was okay, the little girl would make a call and her father would come in and get her. If it wasn't okay, Lily knew what to do.

I've been doing this for a long time. Cruising the cesspool flowing around Times Square, trolling for runaways. Sometimes the pimp is around when I work—that's why Max was along.

I used to bring them straight back where they came from. Now I know better.

It's a new game, but the same old rules—her father had paid me up front.

⑪2

I LEFT MAX at Lily's. His woman, Immaculata, worked there too. They'd go home together. The Prof's home was in the streets. I went home alone.

Pansy's huge head loomed out of the darkness as I entered my office. Her ice-water eyes were glad to see me—disappointed that I was alone. A Neapolitan mastiff, she runs about 140 pounds. In the office shadows she looked like a muscular oil slick. I took out two hot dogs I had wrapped in napkins from my coat pocket. The beast curled into a sitting position, slobber erupting out both sides of her jaws, waiting. I gave it a few seconds. Finally said, "Speak!" and tossed the whole mess at her. It disappeared. She gave me her usual "Where's the rest of it?" look and finally ambled over to her favorite corner where she's worn the Astroturf carpet down to the original cement.

"You want to go out?" I asked. She was indifferent, but walked over to the back door out of habit. I watched her clamber up the fire escape to the roof. Her yard was all concrete.

Like mine was once.

⫼ 3

IN THE STREET the next morning, I dialed the pay phone in the back of Mama Wong's restaurant. My number—the only one anyone has for me. Mama answered the way she always does.

"Gardens."

"It's me."

"You come in, okay?"

"Now?"

"Yes. Front door, okay?"

I hung up. Pulled off the highway, heading east for Chinatown. Past the tiny triangular park at the back of Federal Plaza. Watched an ancient Chinese lead two middle-aged women through an elaborate Tai Chi, oblivious to the bench-covering winos.

The white dragon tapestry stood alone in the front window of Mama's joint. Whatever was waiting inside wasn't the law and it wasn't trouble.

I parked the Plymouth in the back, right under the Chinese characters neatly printed on the alley wall. I didn't bother to lock the car—I couldn't read Chinese but I knew what the sign meant. Max the Silent marking his territory.

The blank-faced steel door at the back of Mama's opened just a crack. I couldn't see inside. They could see me. The door closed. I walked through the alley to the street, turned the corner. Bells tinkled as I opened the front door. A red light would flash in the kitchen at the same time.

Mama was at her altar. The cash register. She bowed her head slightly, motioned me to her as I returned her greeting. I glanced toward the back. A woman was in my booth, facing away from me. Dark chestnut hair spilled over the back of the blue vinyl cushions.

"For me?" I asked Mama.

"Woman come in yesterday. Just ask for Burke. Say her name Rebecca."

I shrugged. It didn't ring any bells. Even alarm bells.

"Woman say she wait for you. I tell her, maybe you not come in long time. She say she come back. I tell her to wait, okay?"

"She's been here ever since?"

"In basement."

"She carrying anything?"

"Just message."

"That's it?"

Mama bowed. "You talk to her?"

"Yeah."

I walked over to the back. Sat down across from the stranger.

A slim woman, small face framed by the thick chestnut hair, dominated by big dark eyes, hard straight-cut cheekbones. No makeup. Her lips were thin, dry. Polish half flaked off her nails, roughened hands. Hands that had been in dirt, dishwater, diapers. One of Mama's waiters leaned over, put a pitcher of ice water and two glasses on the table. Replaced the overflowing ashtray. Caught my eye. I shook my head slightly. I still didn't know her.

"You want to talk to me?" I asked the woman.

"I want to talk to Burke."

"That's me."

"How would I know?"

"Why would I care if you know?"

"I'm Virgil's wife," she said, watching my face.

"Who's Virgil?"

"If you're Burke, you know."

"You having a good time, lady? You got nothing better to do?"

Her voice was hard coal, from a deep vein. "I got to know. I'm on my own here. My man's in trouble. He said to find his brother. Told me where to go. I couldn't call on the phone. He said it would be hard. Said you'd be hard. Ask me what you want first . . . get it over with."

"Who's Virgil?"

"If you're Burke, he's your old cellmate."

"What's his trouble?"

"Prove it to me first," she said, watching.

"Virgil went down for a homicide. Manslaughter. He stabbed . . ."

"I know about Virgil. I want to talk to Burke."

"You want the secret code?"

"Don't mock me. I have to be sure. These Chinese people, they kept me here. Searched my pocketbook. I don't care. If you're not him, tell me what I have to do to meet him. Whatever it takes."

"I'm Burke. Didn't Virgil describe me?"

Her smile didn't show her teeth. "Lots of men ain't so good-looking. That don't narrow it down much."

"Virgil's no Cary Grant himself."

"My husband is a handsome man," she said. Like she was telling a moron what day it was.

"Virgil I knew, he was a quiet man. Hillbilly. Didn't do much talking. He came to Chicago when the work ran out back where he came from. His woman followed him. A freak from her hometown followed her. Freak got himself diced and sliced. I spent a long time getting him ready for the Parole Board, then the fool blew it when they asked him why he stabbed the man. Virgil told them the guy just needed killing. You remember that?"

"I remember that. I had to wait another six months for him."

"He had a long, straight scar on the inside of his right forearm. Chainsaw kicked back on him when he was a kid. Wrote a letter to his woman every damn day. He could play the piano like his hands were magic."

"Still can."

"You believe I know him?"

"Yes. But I don't know you. Virgil said you'd tell me a name. He said to ask you . . . the most dangerous man alive . . . he said there'd only be one answer. And Burke would know it."

I lit a smoke. Watched her face through the flame from the wooden match. "Wesley," I said. Whispering his name. Feeling the chill from the grave.

She nodded. Let out a long breath. "It's you. Burke." She fumbled in her purse, found a cigarette. I lit it for her. "Virgil's your brother . . ." making it a question.

"Yes," I said, making it clear. She was asking about commitment, not genetics.

She dragged on her cigarette, shoulders slumping against the back of the booth. "Thank the Lord."

4

I FELT MAMA behind me. I dropped my left shoulder slightly. She came around to the table, standing between me and Virgil's woman.

"This is Rebecca, Mama. My brother's wife."

Mama bowed. "You want soup?"

I nodded the question at Rebecca. "Yes, please," she said.

Mama's face was composed, eyes watchful. "You not eat anything all this time. Very hungry, yes?"

"I think I must be . . . never thought about it."

One of Mama's waiters appeared, wearing his white jacket loose to give easy access to the shoulder holster. Mama said something to him in Cantonese. He left as quietly as he had appeared.

"Everything okay?" she asked.

"It's okay, Mama."

The waiter brought a steaming tureen of hot and sour soup. Mama used the ladle carefully, filling my bowl, then Rebecca's.

"Eat first," she ordered, walking back to her register.

"Take small sips," I told Rebecca. It was too late. She snorted a harsh breath out her nose, dropped her spoon.

"Whoa! What *is* this?"

"It's Mama's soup. She makes the stock herself, adds whatever's around from the kitchen. It's good for you."

"Tastes like medicine."

"Give it another shot. Small sips, okay?"

"Okay." A tiny smile played at her lips.

She was hungry. The waiter brought a plate of dry noodles. She watched as I sprinkled a handful over the top of the soup. Did the same. The bowl emptied. I held up the ladle. She nodded. I filled her bowl again. I could feel Mama's approval from across the room. Two dots of color flowered on Rebecca's cheekbones. She was a tough woman—Mama's soup isn't an appetizer.

The waiter took the bowls away. Returned the ashtray. I lit her smoke. Lit my own. "Tell me," I said.

"After Virgil got out, we left Uptown. Moved out of Chicago. To Hammond, then to Merrillville. It's just over the line. In Indiana."

"I know where it is."

"He got work. In the mill. Things were good, Burke. I had a little girl. Virginia. She's almost ten now. And a little boy. He's called Virgil too, like his daddy. Virgil's a good man. You know that. Worked doubles when the mill was really pumping. When they cut back, he got this regular gig, playing the piano at a club in Chicago. We got a house. Ours. Not rented or nothing. Never did go back to Kentucky, get us some ground like we planned."

Get us some ground—own some land of their own. Never happen here. I dragged deep on my cigarette. Waiting for her to find the rhythm, tell me the truth.

"I got a cousin. Second cousin, really. My cousin Mildred's boy. Lloyd. He got himself in some foolishness back home. Drinking, cutting school, stealing cars for fun. Like kids do, you know?"

I nodded.

"Anyway, Mildred asked me, could Lloyd come up and stay with us for a while? He don't have no father, Mildred figured maybe Virgil'd settle him down some. We got room.

I asked Virgil. My man, he didn't say a word. I wanted it, it was okay with him. That's the way he is.''

I remembered. On the yard, me moving on a group of blacks who'd surrounded a new kid, wishing I had the shank I kept in my cell. Feeling Virgil move right behind me. Never having to look back—I was covered. I knew the way he is. He wasn't raised in juvenile joints like me, but he played by the same rules. Stand up or stand aside.

She lit a smoke from the butt of her first one. "Lloyd came to live with us. I got him into the high school. He was okay. Kind of kept to himself. Stayed in his room. Virgil got him a little part-time job at the 7-Eleven. He was saving for a car. Lloyd, he was real nice to our kids. Virginia really liked him. Like he was an older brother. I worried 'cause he never had him a girlfriend or nothing, but Virgil, he said a man grows at his own pace, not to fuss about it. Said I was so worried he'd take Lloyd over to one of the cathouses in Cal City. Wait downstairs for him. I told Virgil, he brings my cousin's boy to a whorehouse, he'd better find himself a motel room 'cause he wouldn't be sleeping in his own bed.'' Another thin-lipped smile. "I guess that cured me, though. Anyway, things were okay. Then it happened. There's this place where all the teen-agers go to park. Like a lovers' lane? Out by the dunes. The cops found this young man and his girl. Shot all to pieces. The papers said it was a crazy sniper. Bullet holes all over the car. They started this big investigation.'' Her eyes sneered a coal miner's sarcastic respect for any investigation conducted by the government.

I waited for the rest of it.

"They were still poking around when it happened again. Not a mile away. Two more. Teenagers, the papers said. Just babies, really. Anyway, one of the kids at the school must of said something about Lloyd 'cause the cops came around. Virgil told them he was the boy's father, they could talk to him, they wanted to know anything. Cops asked, could they look in the boy's room? Virgil told 'em get a warrant. One of the cops, this big black detective, he spoke real soft. Made a lot of sense. The other guy with him, skinny, nasty man, he was real hostile. Said they'd checked, found Virgil had a record. He and Virgil, they nearly got into it right in my living room. The black cop, he told the other guy to wait outside and cool off. Sat in my living room, drinking my coffee, talking to Virgil, telling us he didn't give a damn about maybe finding some marijuana in the boy's room, not to worry. Virgil wouldn't move. You know how he is—like a mountain mule. Lloyd, he tried to say something to the cop, but Virgil told him to keep his mouth shut. Then there was a knock on the door. It was the skinny cop. He had a warrant in his hand. The black cop must of told him to go and get it. While he kept us occupied with his talk.

"Virgil got mad. The way he gets. Quiet-mad. The black cop, he took out his gun, told Virgil they was gonna search Lloyd's room. They found a rifle. An old bolt-action .22. We didn't even know he had one. And some magazines. Filthy magazines . . . and a camouflage suit . . . you know, like that Rambo wears. They arrested Lloyd. Took him down to the juvenile place in Crown Point.

"We got him a lawyer. The papers said they got the sniper. I went to visit Lloyd. He was scared to death, Burke. They had to put him in a room by himself, all the other boys threatening him and all. I asked him straight out. He said he didn't do it. But he wouldn't look me in the face. Virgil said that don't mean nothing, the boy was probably 'shamed behind those magazines in his room and all.

"The night it happened, Lloyd was out somewhere. We thought he was working, but it turned out that was his night off. He told the cops he was just off walking by himself. So he got no alibi. The lawyer said it didn't look good for him. We was still waiting on the bullet tests . . . the ballistics or whatever they call it . . . we got to go to court. The judge wouldn't set no bail. No bail at all. Remand, they called it. Then the bullet tests came back. And it wasn't from that rifle they found in Lloyd's room. That wasn't the murder weapon. So their case, it didn't look so good anymore.

"We went back to court. This time, the judge made the bail. He set fifty thousand dollars on the boy. Virgil and I, we talked it over. We put up our house, and he came home with us.

"Lloyd, he couldn't go back to school, with all this hanging over his head. Just a couple of weeks left anyway. Virgil told him to stay in the house until the trial. He couldn't go back home—the judge said he couldn't leave the state. Then one of the boys at school, he told the cops how he and some other kids used to sneak around at night in the lovers' lane. Just to watch the other kids going at it, you know? He said Lloyd used to go with them. He said, one time, Lloyd was real angry for some reason. Like he was mad at the girls. The papers got ahold of it. That was enough for the cops. The black detective, he called. Told Virgil to bring Lloyd back to court again. They were going to revoke his bail."

She lit another smoke. "That's when Virgil run. He told me where he was goin'. Took Lloyd with him. He told me to find you."

"Find me and do what?"

"He said he had a question. Only you would know the answer. That's what he wants you to do. Answer the question."

"And then?"

"And then he'll know what to do."

"The cops are looking for him?"

"Every cop in the state, seems like. They got a warrant for Virgil too. Aiding and abetting a fugitive, the black cop said."

"How'd you get here?"

"I did what Virgil said. Took a plane to New York. Took

a cab to Manhattan and then I called the number. I spoke to a Chinese woman. The woman who's sitting over there right now. She asked me to tell her where I was calling from. Pay phone. Told me to just wait there. Some Chinese men came up in a car, took me here. Then I just waited."

"You know the question Virgil wants answered?"

"No. But I know you'll know the answer. Virgil said so."

"Where is he?"

"You'd never find it. I'll have to show you."

"No good. The cops'll be watching. Just tell me. Slow and careful."

It took her a long time. I made her tell me again. "You don't speak to Virgil?"

"No. He figured the phones'd be tapped."

"Okay. I'll go and see him."

"Now?"

"Soon. You go on back. I'll find him."

She grabbed my eyes with hers. "I know you will. And now I know you're Burke for real."

"How d'you know?"

"You didn't write anything down."

☙ 5

REBECCA WENT ALONG with two of Mama's thugs. They'd take her to the airport. She didn't look back.

Virgil would be okay wherever he was. He wasn't trained like I was, but I'd schooled him good, all that time we'd spent together in the cell after lights-out. He wouldn't make any rookie mistakes. He called, and I'd come to him. But I had to clear the slate first.

◗◗ 6

EARLY SATURDAY MORNING. I found the Prof at work. He was hunched over the tabloids in a restaurant booth in the DMZ, a block past Times Square, listening to Olivia. She's a heavy-built black lady, works as a cleaning woman, cook, hospital orderly . . . whatever rich people need. She plays stupid but she doesn't even come close. And she's got camera eyes.

He felt me close in, whispered something to Olivia. She slid out of the booth, eyes down.

"Remember Virgil?" I asked the little man.

"The ridge runner? Sure."

"He got himself a major beef. Out in Indiana. I got to go see about him."

"You doing social work now?"

"He's one of us."

"Yeah, you're singing my song, but you're singing it wrong. My man's a stone citizen, Burke. He picked his home, let him go it alone."

The Prof could never forgive anyone who'd rather work than steal. People like that, they couldn't be trusted.

"I got to do it."

"Yeah. You always *got* to do it. That white trash holding any cash?"

"It's not like that."

"Never is, seems like. You went to school, but you still play the fool. A rhino ain't a racehorse."

"What's that mean?"

"Means you can't operate outside, bro'. The city, the streets. Even the jailhouse. You know all that, right? But you can't pay your bills in the hills. You got a subway complexion, son. And you smell like concrete. You ain't gonna fool nobody. You can't even buy yourself heat out there, turns out you need it."

"So I'll live by my wits."

"That what they call being half safe?"

"I know what I'm doing."

The little man ignored me. The way he always does when he's on a scent. "What you want to mess with all those beady-eyed, inbred Bible-thumping farmers?"

"Virgil was with us," I told him.

"*Was* was yesterday. This ain't. The straight track never goes back."

"I'm not asking you to come along."

"That's right. Be crazy by your ownself. You know how to work it. Lay in the cut, work the shadows. Talk loud and you draw a crowd."

"Okay."

The Prof snorted his disgust. "I ain't your parole officer, bro'. Why you reporting in?"

"Backup."

The little man nodded. "You need a loan, pick up the phone."

"The Mole, okay?"

"I'll give him a play. Once a day."

"Thanks, Prof."

He extended one hand to the counter, helped himself to

my cigarettes, pocketing the pack as he lit one. Nodded his head and went back to his hustle.

‖ 7

I HAD ONE more job to wrap up before I left the city. The call had come in a few weeks ago and I'd been dancing with the freak ever since. He'd called a few times. Always the same thing: told Mama he had some information he wanted to sell. About a missing kid. He wouldn't leave a callback number. Wouldn't say when he'd call again. Wouldn't drop the kid's name.

Mama reads phone voices the way some Gypsies read palms. She'd been screening my blind dates ever since the first call, years and years ago. When I thought I could scam my way through this junkyard of a life. "Twisted man," she'd said. Voices came through the phone wire to Mama's filter all the time. Dope dealers, gunrunners, porno merchants, mercenaries and missionaries, cops and gangsters. They all knew where to find me.

They thought.

If Mama said the man was twisted, he'd bounce every needle on a psychiatrist's scale.

One night, I'd been there when he called. In the basement with Max. Mama called me to the phone. I picked it up.

"Okay. Talk to me."

"This is Burke?"

"Yeah."

"I got something." A young man's voice. "Something I want to sell."

I let him feel the silence. Feel what was in it. Waited.

"A missing kid. I know where he is. What's it worth?"

"To who?"

"That's not my problem. That's yours. You make the connection, get the cash. And we'll trade."

"Trade for what, pal? Is there some kind of reward out for this kid?"

"No. He's been gone a long time."

"So?"

"So I figure . . . you talk to his people . . . see if they're willing to pay. I don't . . . I can't call them myself. I don't even know where they are."

"Give me a name."

"Not a chance."

"The *kid's* name, pal."

"Oh."

The line went quiet again. I cleared my mind, listened: the freak's bad breathing, wires humming. No background noise. A pay phone, somewhere quiet.

"Jeremiah Brownwell."

"Never heard of him."

"Just check it out. I'll call you back."

8

THERE'S ALL KINDS of registries for missing kids, from federal to local. None of them would tell me what I needed to know to put this together. I called the cops.

The postcards show the Brooklyn Bridge from the top. From the bottom, it wouldn't attract any tourists. There's an opening at ground level along Frankfort Street just past Archway Seven. Big enough for a football game. A long time ago, they rented out the space. You can still see what's left of the faded signs: Leather Hides, Newsprint, Packing and Crating. One Police Plaza to the north, high-rise co-ops to the south.

Four in the afternoon, the moist heat working overtime. The streets would overflow with yuppie traffic in a short while, heading for South Street Seaport bistros to unwind, cool down after a hard day worshiping the greed-god. When it got dark, the urban-punk killing machines would become sociopathic clots in the city's bloodstream, preparing themselves to defend their graffiti-marked territory. Merciless and coarse, their only contribution to society would be as organ-donors.

In this city, race-hatred so thick you could cut it with a knife. Some tried.

I waited on the abandoned loading dock, playing the tapes again in my head. There's supposed to be a kid inside every adult. When women talk about men being little boys inside,

they say it with a loving, indulgent chuckle. Or they sneer. I
knew the little boy I'd been—I didn't ever want to see him
again.

The car was the color of city dust. It bumped its way onto
the concrete apron. The front doors opened and the cops
rolled out. McGowan and Morales. NYPD Runaway Squad.
They strolled over to where I was waiting, McGowan tall and
thick, hat pushed back on his head, cigar in one hand, Irish
smile on his mobile face. Morales was a flat-faced thuggish
pit bull—more testosterone than brains. If he was a shark,
he'd be a hammerhead.

I dropped to the ground, leaned against the loading dock
as they approached.

"You okay?" McGowan asked in that honey-laced voice
that had charmed little street girls and terrorized pimps for
twenty years.

I nodded, watching Morales. We'd gone a few rounds
awhile back, then touched gloves when it was over. He
wouldn't turn on me for no reason, but he'd never need a
very good one.

"Is it for real?" I asked.

McGowan puffed on his cigar. "Jeremiah Brownwell was
reported missing almost five years ago. He was seven then.
With his mother at a shopping mall in Westchester. Just vanished. No ransom demand. Not a trace."

"So it was in the papers?"

"Yeah." Reading my thoughts. "Anyone could've picked
it up."

"Was there ever a reward posted?"

"Not that I know of. It was before all this missing children
stuff in the media. The kid's parents hired a PI and he put
the word around. That's all. The kid's picture was in the
paper."

"He won't look like that now. If it's him."

"No."

Morales leaned forward, chest out, forehead thrusting. Like he was getting ready to butt the bridge of my nose into my skull. "What's the deal? What's the motherfucker want?"

"Cash."

"Where d'you come in?"

"He wants me to see if the kid's parents will put up the money. Make a switch."

"What's ours?"

I ignored him. "You speak to the kid's folks?"

McGowan took over. "Yeah. They'd pay. Something. What they have. It's not all that much."

"If it's him . . . he's not going to be the same kid."

McGowan's face was grim. "I know."

"They *still* want him?"

"They want what they lost, Burke."

"Nobody ever gets that back."

McGowan didn't say anything after that. Morales' ball-bearing eyes shifted in their fleshy sockets. "The fuck that called you. It's extortion, right?"

"I'm not a lawyer."

"A lawyer's not what that guy needs."

McGowan shot his partner a chill-out look. Like asking a fire hydrant to run the hundred-yard dash.

"They got any sure way to identify the kid?" I asked.

"Pictures, stuff like that. Things only the kid would know. Name of his dog, his first-grade teacher . . . you know."

"Yeah. The freak . . . the one who called me . . . he says he wants ten large."

"They can do that."

"No questions asked?"

"No."

"Win or lose?"

"Yes."

"Let's take a shot."

"That's one thing we can't do," McGowan said, a restraining hand on his partner's forearm. Morales had flunked Probable Cause at the Police Academy—his idea of civil rights was a warning shot.

"I'll give you a call," I said.

Ⅶ 9

THE FREAK KEPT dancing. It took another few days to calm him down. I let him pick the place. A gay bar off Christopher Street. He told me what he'd be wearing, what he looked like. When he'd be there. "Bring the cash," he said. Hard guy.

Vincent's apartment was on West Street. The outside looked like a set from *Miami Vice*. Glass brick, blue-enameled steel tubing wrapped around each little terrace. I stood so the video monitor would pick up my face, pressed the buzzer.

Inside it was turn-of-the-century England. Vincent's twin pug dogs yapped at my heels until I sat down on the dark paisley couch. He's a big man, maybe six and a half feet, close to three hundred pounds. Long thick sandy hair combed straight back from a broad face.

"You know nothing about this person?"

"Just what I told you on the phone," I said.

"He thinks he's safe in a gay bar," Vincent said, two fingers pressed against a cheekbone. "Like he's one of us."

"That's the way I figure it."

"What can I do?"

"I need to talk to him. Not in the bar, okay?"

"You want to take him out of there?"

"Yeah."

"He won't want to go?"

I shrugged.

Vincent rubbed his cheekbone again, thinking. "You did me a favor once. I consider you a friend, you know that. But I can't be part of . . . uh . . . your reputation is . . . I'm not saying I personally believe every silly rumor that jumps off the street, but . . ."

"All I want to do is take him out of there. Without anybody noticing."

"Burke . . ."

"A little boy disappears. Five years later, a young guy calls me, says he knows where he is. Wants to trade him for cash. Scan it for yourself. What's it say to you?"

He wouldn't play. "It's not important. Those . . . creatures . . . they have sex with children and they say such sweet things about it. Fucking a little boy isn't homosexual."

"I know."

"I know you know. Are you saying I owe you? From that business in the Ramble?"

The Ramble is part of Central Park. An outdoor gay bar. One of Vincent's friends got caught there one night by a wolf pack. They left him needing a steel plate in his head. Good citizens, Vincent and his friends went to the cops. The badge-boys found the gang easily enough. Fag-bashers: pitiful freaks, trying to smash what they see in their own mirrors. One got the joint, the rest got probation. Then Vincent came to me. Max went strolling through the Ramble one night. The punks who'd walked out of the courthouse ended up in the same hospital as Vincent's friend. When the cops interviewed them, all they remembered was the pain.

"I don't know what you're talking about."

"I have to make some phone calls," he said.

🔱 10

THE MEET WAS for ten o'clock. The pay phone in the parking lot off the West Side Highway rang at 9:50. Vincent's voice. "He just went in. Alone."

A smog-colored Mercedes sedan pulled up. Vincent's life-partner was in the front seat. "Please don't smoke in the car," he said. Didn't say another word to me, looking straight through the windshield. Dropped me off in front of the bar.

The freak was in a back booth. Short curly brown hair dropped into ringlets over his forehead. Dressed preppie, older than he was. I pegged him for maybe nineteen. Greenish drink in a slim glass in front of him.

"I'm Burke," I said, sliding into the booth across from him.

"You have the money?"

"Sure."

He dry-washed his hands. Noticed what he was doing. Fired a cigarette with a lighter that looked like a silver pencil. "How can we do this?"

"You give me the kid, I give you the money."

"How do I know . . . ?"

"You called *me*, pal."

"If I tell you where he is . . . how do I know I'll get the money?"

I shrugged. "You want to come along when I pick him up?"

24

"I *can't*. That's not the deal."

"Is there a pay phone in this joint?"

"I guess so . . . I'm not sure." He waved his hand. Heavy gold chain on his wrist. Slave bracelet. A waiter came over. Didn't look at me.

"What will you have?"

"A ginger ale. Lots of ice, okay?"

"And for you?" he asked the freak.

"I'm okay. Do you have a pay phone here?"

"In the back. Just past the rest rooms."

"Thanks."

I lit a smoke, waiting. The waiter came back with my drink. A black cherry floated in the ice. All clear. I leaned forward. "We'll go to the pay phone. I'll call a friend of mine. He takes a look. While we wait, okay? He tells me he's spotted the kid . . . where you say he is, I give you the cash."

"Right here?"

"Right here."

"You've got it with you?"

"Sure."

"Show me."

"Not here. Out back. Okay?"

He got up. I followed him. The corridor was shadowy with indirect lighting. Past the rest rooms. No sounds seeped from under the doors—it wasn't that kind of gay bar. The pay phone stood against the wall. I reached in my inside pocket. Took out an envelope. "Count it," I told him. He took it in his hands, opened the flap. He was halfway through the bills before he noticed the pistol in my hand. Blood blanketed his face. Vanished, leaving it chalk-white.

"What is this?"

"Just relax. All I want is . . ."

Max loomed behind him, one seamed-leather hand locked on the back of the freak's neck. Pain took over his eyes, his mouth shot open in a thin squeak. I holstered the pistol, took the envelope from his limp hand. Max pushed the freak ahead of him. I slipped out the back door first, checked the alley where my Plymouth was parked. Empty.

We stepped outside. I heard bolts being slammed home behind us. I popped the trunk on the Plymouth. Wrapped the duct tape around the freak's mouth a few times, lifting the hair off the back of his head so it wouldn't catch. Max slapped the heel of his hand lightly into the freak's stomach. The freak doubled over. I put my lips right against his ear. "We're going for a ride. Nothing's going to happen to you. We wanted you dead, we'd leave you right in this alley. You're riding in the trunk. You make any noise, kick around back there, anything at all, we stop the car and we hurt you. Real, real bad. Now nod your head, tell me you understand."

The freak's head bobbed up and down. The trunk was lined with army blankets next to the fuel cell. Plenty of room. He climbed in without a word. Max and I got into the front seat and took off.

⚡ 11

I USED THE Exact Change lane on the Triboro, grabbed the first exit, and ran parallel to Bruckner Boulevard through the South Bronx to Hunts Point. Turned off at Tiffany, motored past the mini-Attica they call a juvenile detention facility at the corner of Spofford, and turned left, heading for the network of juke joints, topless bars, and salvage yards that make up half the economy of the neighborhood. The other half was transacted in abandoned buildings. They stared with windowless eyes above crack houses doing a booming business on the ground floors.

We drove deeper, past even the bombed-out ruins. Past the meat market that supplies all the city's butcher shops and restaurants, past the battered hulks of railway cars rotting on rusty tracks that run to nowhere. Tawny flashes in the night. Wild dogs, hunting.

Finally we came to the deadfall. A narrow slip of land jutting into the East River, bracketed by mounds of gritty sand from the concrete yards and the entrance road to the garbage facility. I wheeled the Plymouth so it was parallel to the river. Max and I climbed out. Rikers Island was just across the filthy water, but you couldn't see it from where we stood. We opened the trunk. Hauled the freak out, ripping the duct tape from his mouth. He was shaking so hard he had to lean against the car.

"Take a look around," I told him.

A giant German shepherd lay on her side a few feet from us. Dead. Her massive snout buried in a large paper McDonald's bag. Her underbelly was a double row of enlarged, blunted nipples. She'd sent many litters to the wild dog packs before her number came up. A seagull the size of an albatross flapped its wings as it cruised to a gentle stop near the dog. Its razor beak ripped at her flesh, tiny eyes glaring us to keep our distance. Some kind of animal screamed. Sounds like a string of tiny firecrackers closer still.

The freak's chest heaved. He snorted a deep breath through his nose. It told him the truth his eyes wanted to deny.

"This is a graveyard," I said, my voice calm and quiet. "They'd never hear the shots. Never find the body. Got it?"

He nodded.

"You bring something with you? Something to prove you know where the kid is?"

He nodded again.

Max reached inside the freak's jacket. A wallet. Inside, a Polaroid snapshot of a kid. Long straight hair fell down either side of a narrow face. The kid in the picture was wearing blue bathing trunks, standing on a dock, smiling at the camera.

"Tell me something . . . something so I know it's the right kid."

The freak dry-washed his hands. "Monroe found him. A few years ago. In Westchester. He ran away from home."

"I won't ask you again."

"Lucas . . . that's what we call him . . . he told us everything. Just ask me . . . anything . . . I can . . ."

"Tell me what his room looked like—his room at home."

"He had bunk beds. His parents always thought they'd have another kid. Lucas, he said that bed was for his brother, when he came. And he had a whole G.I. Joe collection. All the dolls. And the Transformers. He loved the Transformers."

"He have a TV set in his room?"

"No. He was only allowed to watch television on the weekends. In the morning."

"He have a dog, this kid?"

"Rusty. That was the name of his dog. He cried all the time about Rusty until Monroe got him a dog."

Yes.

I lit a cigarette, feeling Max close, waiting. I handed the freak back the money envelope, feeling every muscle in his body soften as he took it.

"Tell me something," I asked him. "How old were you when Monroe found you?"

He didn't waste time playing. "How did you know?"

"How old?"

"Ten."

"And now you're . . ."

"Seventeen."

"So when you got too old, the only way to stay with Monroe was to bring him someone new, yes?"

His face broke, trembled for control, lost it. I listened to him cry.

"Lucas, he's old enough now, isn't he? And you're out."

He slumped down on the filthy ground near the car, head in his hands. "I could've helped him . . . find someone else."

"Yeah. But Monroe, he's gonna let Lucas do that. And you, you wanted the money for a new start?"

"He never loved me at all!" the freak sobbed.

I squatted down next to him. "Where is he?"

"I'll tell you everything." He started talking, his voice a hiss that he couldn't stop, spewing pus. When he got to the home address, I left Max standing next to him. Pulled the mobile cellular phone from the front seat. A gift from a nujack whose nine-millimeter automatic wasn't as fast as Max's hands. Punched in the number, hit the Send button. McGowan was right there. I gave him the address. "The kid's not going to want to go," I told him.

He sighed into the phone. I cut the connection to McGowan.

I walked back over to the freak. Looked down and let him hear the truth. "You're square now. Somebody did something to you, you did something to somebody else. It's over, okay? You're gonna need a lot of help now, understand? You got some real decisions to make. You'll find some phone numbers in your pocket later. Those people, they can help you, if you want the help. You don't want the help, that's up to you. There's another number. Wolfe, over at City-Wide. You want to testify against Monroe, she'll handle it. Set you up with anything you need. But this other stuff, it's over. You go back to your old ways, you're coming back here. Understand?"

He nodded, watching me from under long eyelashes, trembling slightly.

"You come back here, you're coming back to stay."

I nodded at Max. He did something to the kid's neck. We put him back into the trunk. He'd wake up later with a bad headache and five hundred bucks in his pocket.

⚜ 12

I MET MCGOWAN and Morales early the next morning. At the diner where they hang out. They hadn't been to sleep yet.

"You found him?" I asked.

"Yeah." McGowan's voice was dead.

"Get him home?"

"He said he *was* home. His name is Lucas. A special boy, he told us he was. A special boy. He's a poet. You wanna see his poetry?" He slid a slick magazine across to me. *Boys Who Love* it said on the cover. Picture of a kid sitting astride a BMX dirt bike, sun shining behind him.

"Page twenty-nine," McGowan said.

The poem was entitled "Unicorn." All about little buds needing the pure sunlight of love to bring them to full flower.

"You lock the freak up?" I asked.

"Yeah. He's got his story ready, this Monroe. He found the kid wandering around a shopping center. The kid told him he was being sexually abused at home. This Monroe, he saved the boy. Raised him like his own kid. Spent a fortune on him. Private tutors, the whole works."

"And the kid won't testify, right?"

"Right. We took him home. Saw his mother and father. Looked right through them."

"What's next?"

"Lily talked with him. She says he's 'bonded' to that devil. Harder than deprogramming a kid caught up in one of those cults. Gonna take a long time. We ran it by Wolfe at City-Wide. She says she's got enough to indict Monroe even without the kid.

"And Lucas said there was another kid. Older than him. Layne. Wolfe wanted to know, maybe this Layne, he'd testify against Monroe . . ."

His voice trailed off, making it a question. I shrugged.

"I fucking *told* you," Morales said.

"And the ten grand's gone too?"

"Yeah."

"Wolfe's the best. She was standing by. Got a telephonic search warrant. There was enough stuff in the house . . . pictures and all . . . Monroe goes down for a long time even without the kid's testimony. Wolfe says they can use that DNA fingerprinting, prove this kid is who the parents say he is. She asked if you were in this."

"And you told her . . ."

"No."

It wouldn't fool Wolfe. She wasn't asking McGowan for information, she was sending me a message. The beautiful prosecutor played the game right to the edge of the line, played it too hard for the degenerates to win.

But they kept coming. Tidal waves from a swamp the EPA could never clean up.

Morales ground out his cigarette in the overflowing ashtray. Hard, the way he did everything. "Whatever he gets, it's not enough. Next to him, a rapist's a class act." His eyes held mine, waiting.

"What're you saying?"

"He's not saying nothing," McGowan snapped. "Just frustrated, that's all."

"You think the *federales* will play Let's Make a Deal with this freak?"

"They could. He knows a lot. Networked all over the place. He even had one of those computer programs where you send images over the wire to a laser printer."

"Good." You do enough bragging about where the bodies are buried, you could join the crowd.

Morales weighed in. "Yeah. Fucking great. He drops a pocketful of dimes on his brother freaks, does a few soft years in a federal rest camp, sees one of those whore-psychiatrists, comes out and gets a job in a day-care center or something. Maybe writes a book."

I shrugged.

Morales took it as a challenge. "You think those fucking therapists can fix a freak like him?"

"No. They know what to call it, that's all. Pedophilia. Like it's a disease. They had a disease named after hijackers, maybe I would of gotten past the Parole Board the first time."

Morales wouldn't let it go. "A few years ago, they'd have to lock slime like that away from the regular cons. Not no more. Baby-raping motherfuckers like him need to resist arrest more often."

McGowan shook his head sadly. He got up to leave, Morales trailing in his wake. The cops tossed bills on the table for their breakfast and split. I watched the smoke collect near the ceiling of the diner. Thinking of something Wesley once told me.

Something he once called me.

◊ 13

I WAS AS close to square as I was going to get. I could go on vacation, not worry about the mail piling up on the doorstep.

But a responsible businessman doesn't take a vacation unless his desk is clean. After a half hour of dodging potholes deep enough to have punji sticks at the bottom, the Plymouth poked its anonymous nose off the BQE at Flushing Avenue. Heading through Bedford-Stuyvesant. Some people call it "do or die Bed-Stuy." Those people are called something else. Escapees.

On to Bushwick. A bad piece of pavement even by city standards: if you went down on these streets from less than three gunshot wounds, the hospital would write "natural causes" on the death certificate. Just before the intersection at Marcy Avenue, a three-story shell of a wooden building, blackened timbers forming X-braces, decaying from the ground up. Next to it, an abandoned Chinese take-out joint. Hand-painted sign: House of Wong. Parked in front, a car full of black teenagers, baseball caps turned on their heads so the bills pointed backwards. Waiting for night.

The going rate for three rocks of instant-access cocaine is five bucks. The dealers won't take singles, makes too much bulk in their pockets. The bodegas operate as war-zone currency exchanges: a five-dollar bill costs you six singles.

I crossed Broadway, past a pet store that advertised rabbits. For food. A rooster crowed from somewhere inside one of the blunt-faced buildings.

A Puerto Rican woman strolled by on the sidewalk, wearing a bright orange quasi-silk blouse knotted just below her midriff, neon-yellow spandex bicycle pants with thick black stripes down the sides stretching almost to her knees. Backless white spike heels, no stockings. She was fifteen pounds over the limit for a yuppie aerobics class, but on this street, she was prime cut. She acknowledged the men calling out to her with her lips and her hips, but she never turned her head.

Another couple of blocks. The projects. An olive-skinned little boy was playing with a broken truck in a puddle near a fire hydrant, making it amphibious.

Most of the businesses were war casualties, liquor stores and video rental joints the only survivors.

And the crack houses. Fronted by groups of mini-thugs hoping to grow up to be triggerboys. Watching the escape vehicles slide by, Mercedeses and BMWs, seeing themselves behind the wheel. Ghetto colors slashing the grime, not telling the truth.

Gut-grinding poverty. Sandpaper for the soul.

Pigeons overhead, circling in flocks. Hawks on the ground.

Make enough wrong turns and you're on a no-way street.

A no-brand-name gas station on the corner. It pumped more kilos than gallons. A big dirt-colored junkyard dog was entertaining himself, dropping a blackened tennis ball from his mouth down a paved slope, chasing it once it got rolling. A trio of puppies watched in fascination.

The sign outside said Custom Ironwork. A sample covered the front door. I rang the bell. Door opened. Guy about five feet tall answered. Red Ban-Lon shirt, short sleeves threatened by biceps the size of grapefruits. He either had a pin head or a twenty-inch neck. One dark slash was his full supply of eyebrows. His hands gripped the bars like he could bend them without a welding torch.

"What?"

"Mr. Morton."

"Who wants him?"

"Burke. I got an appointment."

He must have been told in front. In one-syllable words. I stepped back as he shoved the iron gate open, stepped past him as he stood aside.

"Upstairs."

I heard him behind me on the steel steps, breathing hard by the second flight. Bodybuilder.

"In here."

Bars on the windows, gray steel office desk, stacks of army-green file cabinets against the wall. The man behind the desk was younger than I expected. Deep tan, expensive haircut, heavy on the gel. Diamond on one finger, wafer-faced watch on his wrist. Manicure, clear nail polish. White silk shirt, tie pulled down. Suit jacket on a hanger, dangling from a hook on the wall.

"Mr. Morton?"

"Yeah."

"My name is Burke. We have an appointment."

"You got what you're supposed to have?"

"Yes."

He looked sideways at the bodybuilder. "You pat him down?"

"No, boss. I thought you . . ."

Morton glanced across at me, tapping his fingers. "Never mind," he told the bodybuilder in a disgusted voice. To me: "Put it on the table." Hard edge in his voice, looking me right in the eyes. Tough guy, projecting his image.

I had his image: lunch meat, on white bread. I reached in my pocket, laid the thick envelope on the desk.

"You got this straight from him? You look inside?"

"Yeah."

"How come? You don't trust the *senator*?"

"I didn't want to come up short. It wouldn't be respect-ful."

He nodded. "You know how much this costs?"

"I know what he told me. Twenty-five K."

"That's what's in there?" Gesturing at the envelope.

"In hundreds. Used, no consecutives."

"Okay." He took a nine-by-twelve manila envelope from the desk drawer. "You want to look?"

"No."

His head tilted up. "No?"

"I agreed to bring you an envelope, bring him an enve-lope."

"What if this one's empty?"

"It wouldn't be."

"Or else what?"

"You have to ask the man. It's not my business."

He lit a cigarette. "I know you. I know your name. I wouldn't want you to come back if the man was unhappy."

"Sure."

"What's that mean?"

"It means, you know my name, you know I'm not a chump. Like the senator, right? Don't jerk my chain. The pictures are in there. And the negatives. Not because you're worried about me coming back."

"Then why?"

"Only a fucking sucker buys pictures. We both know that. You got more. Or copies of the negatives. Maybe you'll never do anything with them, maybe you will. But it won't be soon."

"That sounds like a threat."

I reached in my pocket. The bodybuilder's mouth-breathing didn't change. He was a side of beef—couldn't guard his own body. I lit a cigarette of my own, blew out the wooden match with the exhale, dropped it on the floor. The manila envelope was fastened with a string wrapped around two red buttons. I untied the string, spilled the pictures on the desk. Eight-by-tens, black&white. Nice lighting, good contrast, fine-grained. Professional setup. The senator flat on his back, a girl riding him, facing the black calf-length socks covering his feet. Camera got both their faces nice and clear. Side-shot of the girl on her knees, mouth full. Long light-colored hair trailing down to her shoulders. Half a dozen others. Different positions. One thing in common: you could always see both faces. I smiled at Morton. "Melissa never seems to get older, does she?"

White splotches flowered under his tan. The hand holding the cigarette trembled.

"I don't know what you're talking about."

I dragged deep on my smoke. "Twenty-five grand. That wouldn't cover your investment, would it? How'd you work it this time? Pay off the clerk, get her a new birth certificate? Register her at some high school? Get her to visit the senator for some term paper?"

His cigarette burned his hand. He snubbed it out in the ashtray, concentrating like it was a hard task.

"Get out of here," he snapped. He wasn't talking to me. The beef left the room—maybe he wasn't so stupid.

The door closed behind him. I didn't turn around. Morton put his hands on the table. "What d'you want?"

"Melissa, she's been running this con forever. She's got to be twenty-two, twenty-three by now. She came to you, right?"

He nodded.

"Yeah, she knows how to work it. The senator, he's getting ready to announce for Congress. Make his big move. How old you tell him she was, fifteen?"

"Sixteen."

"Yeah. It's a nice scam. The twenty-five, that's good-faith money, right? You're a square guy, you turn over the pictures behind an up-front payment, he sends you the rest."

He nodded again.

"I figure it for a hundred large. Minimum. What's your piece?"

"Half."

"How'd she do it? You first?"

He took a deep, shuddering breath. Lit another smoke. "You know the Motor Inn? By the courthouse in Queens?"

"Sure."

"She was working the cocktail lounge. Not a hooker. I took a room there, waited for her until her shift was over. She must of run my plates. Sent me a picture in the mail. Just to show me how it was done."

"She didn't threaten you?"

"No. Said it would be an easy fifty grand. Maybe more, later. If the senator goes higher up the ladder."

This greaseball had about as much chance against Melissa as Charles Manson did of getting work release. I put the pictures back in the envelope. The negatives were in a separate wrapper. "You had a week since I called you. You asked around, checked me out?"

"Yeah."

"So you're not going to be stupid."

"No. Not twice."

"I'll take these to the senator. Far as I'm concerned, my job is over. Understand?"

"You won't tell him?"

"Fuck him. Why should I? You sting a senator, you're on my side of the street."

An oil-slick smile twisted his mouth. He nodded agreement.

I picked up the cash envelope. Stuffed it in my pocket. Got to my feet.

"Hey! You said . . . I was on your side of the street . . ."

"This is the toll," I said.

⫰ 14

SOME GUY WHO knew more about adjectives than he did about the junkyard once wrote that the city never gives up its secrets. But it'll sell them.

I stopped at a light on Hester Street. Two men shambled up to the car, clutching filthy rags—the tools of their trade. Smeared dirt around the windshield, held out their hands to me, palms up. I reached under the seat for my supply of those little booze bottles they give away on airlines. A stewardess I know brings them home from work. Handed them each a bottle. Watched their faces light up as I cut out the middleman.

The newspapers call them ''homeless.'' They don't get it. Today, the Grapes of Wrath come out of a bottle of Night Train.

I left the Plymouth in lower Manhattan. It didn't look like anything worth stealing, but I flipped the switches to make sure. There was twenty-five grand under the front seat.

Tail end of the evening rush hour as I walked down the steps into the subway tunnel. Both branches of the Lexington Avenue line pulled in at the same time. I opted for the 6 train, the local. The only advantage of having a seat on the subway is that your back is covered.

A legless man pulled himself along the floor of the train, his hands covered with tattered mittens. The upper half of his body sat on a flat wooden disc, separated from the cart by a foot-high column. So you could see he wasn't faking it. He rattled the change in his cup, not saying a word. Humans buried their faces in newspapers. I tapped his shoulder as he rolled by. Stuffed a ten-dollar bill in his cup. He pulled it out, looked it over. Locked my eyes.

"Thank you, my brother," he said. Strong, clear voice.

We always know each other, those of us missing some parts.

I got out at Seventy-seventh Street, walked west through the throngs of trendoid ground slugs toward Park Avenue. Found the senator's co-op. Told the doorman my name was Madison. He called up, told me to go ahead. The senator let me in himself.

"We're alone," he said. Like I cared.

His study was just what you'd expect if you read a lot of magazines that never leave the coffee table.

He gestured to a leather chair, took one himself. I lit a smoke. He frowned. "My wife doesn't like smoking . . . I'm afraid there's no ashtrays anywhere in the house."

I took out a metal Sucrets box, popped it open, tapped my cigarette into it. Handed him the envelope.

"Did you look inside?"

"No."

He was a tall, thick-bodied man, graying hair carefully coiffed to hide a receding hairline. Light brown eyes held mine. His famous "anti-corruption stare" the TV cameras liked so much. On me, it was as useful as an appendix. He dropped his eyes, opened the envelope, held the pictures so I couldn't see them. Leafed through them, one by one. I watched his face. Melissa's rightful prey: he'd never want a woman grown enough to judge him.

He put the pictures away. Five to one he wouldn't burn them. "You do good work, Mr. Burke."

"That's what I'm paid for," I reminded him.

"Oh. Yes." He handed me a #10 business envelope. Heavy, cream-colored stock. "You want to count it?"

"I trust you, Senator," I assured him.

He stroked his chin in a gesture so practiced it had become habit. "I never did anything like this before." Meaning deal with thugs like me, not fuck underage girls. "It seems to have worked out well. Perhaps I'll have something for you to do in the future."

"Any time."

"You came highly recommended. I didn't want to deal with . . . you know . . ."

I knew.

"I mean . . . I know how you people work. You have your own code. You'd never talk even if . . ." Reassuring himself. I knew who'd given him my name. Cops have their own code too.

I got up to go. He didn't offer to shake hands. I'd see him again someday. The senator wasn't cut out for crime. He was the kind of man who'd use vanity plates on a getaway car.

◊ 15

THE EXPRESS TOOK me back as far as Fourteenth Street. A little kid squatted at the curb with his pants down, dumping a load while his mother shared a joint with a mush-faced human in a sleeveless dungaree jacket. In New York, the pooper-scooper laws only apply to dogs. On the corner, a guy was handing out leaflets, facing away from me. He fed me one with a deft behind-the-back move, slapping it into my palm like passing the baton in a relay race. I glanced at it. A topless bar. Where We Know How to Treat a Gentleman. I crumpled it up, tossed it at an overflowing garbage can. Missed.

Another leaflet-dealer at the next corner. Look down or look hard. I grabbed his eyes as I closed in, my hands clenched into fists. "Don't look so angry, chief. I saved one for you," he sang out. Fuck it, I took one. Jews for Jesus.

A derelict combed his hair, holding a rearview mirror from a car in one hand, adjusting his look. Fancy running shoes on his feet—you can always pick up a pair in the homeless shelters. The yuppies donate their old models every time a new style comes out. Tax-deductible relevance.

A blissed-out dude with long hair and *Star Trek* eyes sat on a blanket, jet-lagged from time travel. A hand-lettered sign propped up next to him: Wind Chimes. Empty pint bottles of wine all around him. A woman stopped in front of him. Asked, "Where are the wind chimes?" He held up one of the bottles, admiring the play of sunlight on the glass. Tapped it gently with a tiny hammer. The bottle cracked, tinkled as the glass fell onto the blanket. His smile was pharmacological.

Something white under my windshield wiper. As I came closer, I saw it was a business card. A tiny black&white photo of a woman in bra and garter belt, red lipsticked imprint. Dial 555-PAIN slashed across the top. I read the small print. Press (1) Submissive Sarah; (2) Two beautiful bisexual girls; (3) Adventures of Lady Whiplust. Smaller print: $1.50 first minute, $0.50 for each additional minute.

16

NOTHING ON THE all-news station. Pushed the buttons. Found some sports-talk program. So sad to listen to callers desperate to stay on the line, prolong the contact. "Mike, I've got a couple of quick questions, and then a comment, okay?" Not all Dumpster-divers are homeless—the city's a giant cellblock, stuffed with humans who never see each other. As lonely as masturbation.

You make your bed, you have to sleep in it. Some people smoke in theirs.

I opened the newspaper. In the Personals: hand-drawn picture of a little girl, pretty bow in her hair, licking a lollypop. A child's rounded scrawl: "Call me, please." It was signed Bridgette. The phone number said: $3.50 a call, max. Adults Only.

Virgil had called at the right time. New York was always hard, but now it was ugly.

Full of checks that bounced and women who didn't.

A good time to go.

▼ 17

BUT FIRST, I had to see my lawyer. Davidson was in the conference room, surrounded by a mountain of books, arguing with two other guys. One was about my age, the other a rookie.

"But the law clearly says . . ." the young guy was saying.

"Says to who?" Davidson challenged him. "You think the jury's going to be a bunch of smartass law students?"

"But your defense . . . it admits guilt."

The older guy smiled. "He *is* guilty, Denny. But the State has the burden of proof. The cases all hold . . ."

Davidson cut him off. "This isn't a bar exam, kid. Vega shot Suarez. Four fucking times, okay?"

"But if you put him on the stand . . ."

"Yeah, yeah. The DA will bring out that this isn't the first time Vega used a gun on somebody. But my man gets to tell his story."

"Some story."

"Hey! The dead guy, Suarez, he gets into an argument with our guy Vega in the club. Vega slaps him. Suarez walks out. He tells every hombre in the place that he's going home, get his shit, and make a comeback. All right? Couple of hours later, the door opens. Suarez rolls in, puts his hand in his pocket. Our guy shoots first. Self-fucking-defense."

"Suarez didn't have a gun. All he had in his pocket was a knife."

Davidson shrugged. "You threaten a man in a South Bronx social club, you come back inside and reach for your pocket, you're *supposed* to get shot. *That's* the law, kid."

I shook hands with Davidson. Lit a cigarette. It didn't make a dent in the fumes from Davidson's bratwurst-sized cigar. He introduced me around. As Mitchell Sloane, a lawyer he was working with on a Jersey case. With Davidson, confidentiality goes a long way.

He didn't ask the other two guys to leave. Even though his partner knew the score, we talked obliquely. Habit. I asked him if he ever got paid on the last matter we covered and he nodded. Meaning: my credit was good if I got popped again.

The kid stepped out. Came back with another guy. I knew him from the courts. Drug lawyer. Good-looking boy, nice rap. Took his cash in paper bags, put some of it back into his wardrobe. Ruby ring, diamonds around the bezel of his watch. Very stylish.

The new guy ignored me. "You going to handle the Simpson trial?" he asked Davidson in a flea-market voice.

"Yep."

"I got a piece coming."

"How so?"

"Goldstein referred it to you, right?"

Davidson shrugged.

"Simpson came to me too. Same day as Goldstein. I guess he didn't like the fee—so he went shopping."

Davidson raised his eyebrows.

"I quoted him seventy-five. Too rich for his blood—he went for the lower-priced spread—that's how Goldstein got called."

"So you figure . . . he doesn't go to Goldstein, I don't get the case?"

"That's about it." The guy smiled, looking over at me, including me in his slice-of-the-pie bullshit. One lawyer to another.

"How much you figure it's worth?" Davidson asked him.

"Well, Goldstein gloms a third, right? I figure I should . . . How much is he paying you anyway?"

Davidson puffed on his cigar. "A buck and a quarter."

The guy's face went white. "A hundred and twenty-five fucking thousand dollars?"

"Yep."

"Why?"

"That's what I charged him."

The guy sat down, wondering what went wrong with the world. His ruby ring dimmed.

Davidson ignored him, turned to me. "We have something to discuss? Some new matter?"

"No rush," I told him. "I got plenty of time."

We smoked in silence for a minute.

The other guy made a face. "You ought to start working out," he said to Davidson. "Give up those weeds."

"I can kick your ass on the basketball court," Davidson sneered at him.

"Please! You got to be fifty pounds overweight."

"A little bulk's good for you." Davidson truly believes that. His son is two years old—kid looks like a sumo wrestler.

The drug lawyer shot his cuffs, looked at his watch. Total self-absorption was the one commitment he never failed to keep. "I was thinking . . . maybe being married isn't such a bad thing. Ever since I got divorced . . . this AIDS thing . . . really puts a damper on your social life. You ever read the Personal ads . . . like in the *Voice*?"

"No," Davidson said.

"I read them all the time," I told him.

"Yeah? You think it's a good idea?"

"What?"

"Putting an ad in . . . maybe meet something really good?"

I shrugged.

"You ever met anybody you wanted to meet that way?"

"Sure," I said.

Davidson smiled. He knows what I do.

The guy rubbed his chin. "The wording . . . that's tricky. I mean, you don't want to say too much, but . . ."

"I got the ad for you," I told him.

He looked up, waiting.

"Got a pencil?"

He whipped out a fat Mont Blanc pen, like doctors use to write prescriptions.

"Take this down: Woman wanted. Disease-free. Self-lubricating. Short attention span."

His face went blotchy-red. Davidson raised his hand above his head. His silent partner looked up from a law book, slapped him a high-five. The drug lawyer gave me what he thought was a hard look and walked out.

I ground out my smoke. Handed Davidson a business card. Mitchell Sloane. Private Investments. Address, phone number, fax number too. Clean engraved printing, very classy. The address and the numbers were Davidson's.

"I need a corporation formed," I told him. "Just like it says on the card."

"How long is this corporation going to be in business?"

"A month, maybe two. No more."

"You need a sign on the door?"

"I thought, maybe a nice brass plaque."

"Un-huh. And the phones?"

"The number on the card, I can bounce it to anywhere I want. Say to one of your dead-end lines?"

"I'll have Glenda pick it up during business hours. You want a tape on the machine for evenings and weekends?"

"Yeah."

He spread his palm out before me. Five. I counted out the cash.

"It's done," he said. "Glenda will sweep the tapes every morning when she comes in, okay?"

"Okay. You licensed to practice in Indiana?"

"I'll get a local guy to do the paperwork," he said. Davidson took cases all over the country.

We shook hands. He was dictating the incorporation memo as I walked out the door.

⚓ 18

BACK AT THE office, I tried to hustle Pansy into a vacation at the Mole's junkyard. She acted like she didn't know what I was talking about, so I let her out to her roof while I fixed her a snack. A half gallon of honey vanilla ice cream with a couple of handfuls of graham crackers mixed in. It was waiting for her when she ambled downstairs. Lasted about as long as a politician's promise. It would end up being worth the same too. The beast prowled a step behind me as I went through the place throwing everything I'd need into an airline-size bag.

It's easy enough to beat the scanners they use in the security corridors at the airport, but I was traveling clean.

A handful of loose change spilled on the floor. Pansy snarfed at it experimentally. I let her play with the coins. I wouldn't even tell a dog to drop a dime.

⑩ 19

TERRY OPENED THE gate for me at the junkyard. It seemed like he was bigger every time I saw him. He wouldn't have a kid's body much longer. His eyes hadn't been a child's even when I found him. When he was for rent on the streets.

The dog pack swirled around Terry, growling and snapping, eyes down. Waiting. Simba bounced into the circle, his ears up, tail rigid as a flagpole behind him. "Simbawitz!" I greeted the beast. He ignored me, eyes pinning Pansy. The Neapolitan watched him from her higher perch, calm as stone if you didn't know her. But I saw the hair on the back of her neck bristle and felt her tail swish rhythmically against my leg. Terry jumped on the hood of the Plymouth and I pressed the gas. Some of the pack yapped after us, but Simba stood rooted, confident that he had faced down the new arrival without bloodshed.

I followed the path Terry pointed out, planted the Plymouth in a spot between two gutted yellow cabs. I gave Pansy the signal and she didn't protest when Terry came close. We walked the rest of the way to the Mole's bunker.

"I'll get him," the kid said, disappearing down the tunnel, leaving me outside with my dog.

"You'll be okay for a couple weeks, girl," I told her. "You've been here before, remember?" She growled an acknowledgment, not bitching about it.

The Mole shambled up to us, seating himself on the cut-down oil drum he uses for a deck chair. Greeted me the same way he answers his phone . . . by waiting for someone to speak.

"Mole, I got to go away for a while. An old buddy of mine got himself in a jackpot in Indiana. You can keep Pansy for me . . . let me leave the Plymouth here too?"

"Okay."

"The Prof will be calling you. Once a day, all right? I need to get a message to him, I'll leave it with you."

"Okay."

"You working on anything?" I asked. Just to give him room—I couldn't understand the stuff he does if I had another life sentence to study it.

"The Mole's teaching me about heavy water," the kid piped up.

"I'm sure your mother will be pleased," I said to the kid, giving the Mole an opening.

"Michelle called you?" he asked.

"Mole, you know the deal. She said she was going to Denmark. That's a name, a name for what she wants done. Not a place. She could be in Europe, could be down to Johns Hopkins in Baltimore. She'll call when she's coming home. You know that."

"I get letters," the kid said. Proudly.

Michelle, the beautiful transsexual hooker. The slickest hustler I ever knew. The woman who made Terry her son. The strange, lovely woman who danced for years with the Mole. Never touching. But she'd never change partners. When I was coming up, I always wanted a big sister. Big sisters, they taught you to dance, told you how to act around girls, stepped into the street for you when it came to that. Showed up on visiting days when you were locked down. Sold whatever they had to pay for lawyers. Little sisters, they were nothing but grief. You had to jump in anyone's face who messed with them. And their girlfriends, by the time

they were old enough for you to play with, your little sister
didn't bring them home after school. They'd get married, get
beat up by their husbands. More work to do. I told Michelle
once she was like a big sister to me, trying to tell her I loved
her the only way I could. All she heard was "big." Like she
was older than me. She told me I was a pig and a guttersnipe,
ground her spike heel into the toe of my shoe and stalked out
of Mama's restaurant. Didn't speak to me for weeks. Until I
got in trouble and she came running.

She'd been threatening to have the operation for years.
"I'm going to lose these spare parts one day, baby. Stop
being trapped. Be myself." We never took it seriously until
she left. I missed her. Terry was patient. The Mole was
breaking up inside. "My biological family" was the only
reference Michelle made to her parents. She was the one who
told me what "family of choice" meant. The Prof knew.
"She don't just know how to say it, bro', she knows how to
play it."

A transsexual who could never have a child. And a solitary
genius who never would. Terry was their child. Snatched
from the night. Blooming in a junkyard.

The Mole drove me over to a gypsy cab joint where I could
catch a ride to the airport. He didn't wave goodbye. If it
wasn't Nazi-hunting, it wasn't on his list.

⚓ 20

I FLEW INTO Midway on a Thursday night, traveling light. Adjusted my watch to Central Time. A city snake shedding its skin, coming into a new season.

The countergirl confirmed my reservation, asked me if I was interested in an upgrade. She made the word sound so orgasmic I went for the optional car phone.

She didn't blink twice at Mitchell Sloane's American Express gold. It wouldn't bounce. I'd had it for years. Charged something every couple of months, paid the bills by check. Sloane was a solid citizen. Had the passport to prove it.

I would rather have paid cash, not left so much paper behind me. But the drug dealers ruined that: paying cash is a red flag to the DEA, and everyone has a phone. I was lousy with cash. New York cash. Enough to live on for years if I went back to my underground ways. After Belle went down, I went crazy. Off the track. I had the bounty money the pimps had paid me to take the Ghost Van off the streets. All the money Belle had been saving for her wedding day. But I went after more. Not for the money—just to be doing something. Cigarettes by the truckload from North Carolina. Cartons of food stamps, sold to bodegas with nothing on their shelves—you can buy TV sets with them in Puerto Rico. Extortion. Rough stuff. Scoring like a madman. Never getting square.

Until a dead man pulled me out of the pit. Wesley.

21

I KNEW WHERE to go. The Lincoln Town Car had a full tank of gas. Clean inside, but not fresh. Like a motel room where they put a sanitation band across the toilet seat.

The road to Indiana smelled like steel and salt. Near the water it smelled like sewage. Near the mills, like rust.

The motel was outside Merrillville, where Virgil had his house. One story, X-shaped. Mid-range: not classy enough for the desk clerk to tell me about their fine restaurant, not raunchy enough to ask me if I wanted anything sent to my room.

I set the door chain, unpacked, clicked on the TV set. I balanced a couple of quarters on the metal doorknob, positioned a glass ashtray on the napless carpet underneath it. Closed my eyes and drifted away.

When I woke up, the Cubs were in the mid-innings of a night game. I went back to sleep.

22

THE NEXT MORNING, I took a long shower. Shaved carefully. Put on the dove-gray summer-weight silk-and-worsted suit Michelle made me buy when we'd both been way ahead after a nice score. White silk shirt, plain dark tie. Black Bally slip-ons, thin gray Concord watch with tiny gold dots on the band, black star sapphire ring. Black aluminum attaché case filled with charts, projections, blueprints, maps. Ready to go.

The freestanding building had space for a dozen cars. Only two slots occupied as I pulled the Lincoln into the lot. Evergreen Real Estate.

Pleasant-faced middle-aged woman at the front desk. "Good morning, sir. Can I help you?"

"Yes, please. I wonder if I could see the manager."

"Certainly, sir. Your name, please?"

"Sloane."

She tapped one of the buttons on her console. "John, a Mr. Sloane to see you." A pause. "Well, I don't *know*, do I?" She gave me a flash-smile, shrugged her ample shoulders. "He'll be right out."

The manager was wearing a light blue seersucker suit, open-necked white shirt underneath. He was a tall man with a dark crewcut just past military length. He extended his hand. "I'm John Humboldt, Mr. Sloane. You wanted to speak with me."

I shook his hand. "Yes, sir, I did. It's about some invest-ments. I wonder if we could talk in . . ."

"Right this way."

He led me back to his office, stepped aside to usher me in first. "Have a seat."

The office walls were paneled in knotty pine, covered with laminated certificates and engraved plaques. Apparently, John Humboldt was a whale of a salesman.

I handed him the Mitchell Sloane business card. "I'm in the area to check out some potential sites. I have a number of clients . . . a consortium of investors with cash . . . who want to get in on the ground floor."

He scratched his head, doing the country boy act for the city slicker. "Well, that's mighty interesting, Mr. Sloane. But the ground floor of what? I guess you must know heavy industry isn't exactly working overtime lately in these parts."

I lit a cigarette, my face telegraphing the struggle. Should I trust this man?

Hell, yes.

"Mr. Humboldt, we both know the legislature has just given approval for pari-mutuel racing in this state. For the first time."

"That bill hasn't passed. It was just introduced."

"It'll pass this time," I assured him. "And once it does, they'll need racetracks."

"And you think Lake County . . . ?"

"No doubt in my mind."   .

"I see."

"Sure you do. I'm going to be looking around for ap-propriate sites. Spend a couple of weeks. When I locate something I believe might be appropriate, would you be in a position to make the approach? We don't want anyone knowing about this . . . once they think there's outside money available, you and I both know what'll happen to the price.''

"You can rely on me," Humboldt said, extending his hand again.

"I'm sure. Now, I'll be staying at different places. Low profile, you know? But my office will always know where to reach me. And I'll write the number of the car phone on the back of this business card for you, okay? I'm looking forward to us doing business.''

"Me too." As sincere as any real estate broker ever was.

"I'll be in touch, Mr. Humboldt.''

"Call me John," he said.

▌▌ 23

I SPENT THE rest of the day driving around. Stopping occasionally, making little squibbles in a notebook. Not for me—my eyes photographed what I needed to know. In case somebody decided to take a look inside the real estate speculator's fancy car.

I used a pay phone just off Sixty-first Avenue. Called the number on my business card. Glenda answered, grown woman's professional voice with just an undercurrent of purr. She knew how to do it.

"Mitchell Sloane Enterprises.''

"It's me, Glenda. Any calls?''

"Just one. Hung up when I answered. Probably a wrong number.''

"Probably wasn't." Nice of Humboldt to be so trusting. "I'll give you a call tomorrow."

"Bye-bye."

⚓ 24

EARLY AFTERNOON CAME. The diner was set back from the road, squatting on a rectangular slab of blacktop, near the intersection of U.S. 30 and 41. Couple of miles from the Illinois line. The parking lot was about a third full: pickup trucks with names of businesses painted on the doors, a clay-splattered 4×4, sedans and hardtops. Working cars, working people. The food was either good or cheap.

The joint had wraparound windows. All the booths looked out to the parking lot. Long counter lined with padded stools. The lunchtime crowd was thinning out. I walked through slowly—found a booth near the back.

The waitress was a stocky girl, light brown hair cut in a short bob. She was wearing a plain white uniform with a tiny red apron tied across the front. The skirt was too short and too tight for off-the-rack. She leaned over, both palms flat on the Formica tabletop, plump breasts threatening to pop out of the top piece of her uniform where she'd opened a couple of extra buttons. A little red plaque shimmered on her chest. When she stopped bouncing, I could see what it said. Cyndi.

"Hi! You need a menu?"

"Please."

"Be right back."

I watched her switch away. The sweet rolls in this joint weren't only on the shelves. Seamed stockings. Medium-height white spike heels. Hell of a sacrifice for a waitress to make on her feet all day. If they all dressed like her, the meals had to be lousy.

She was back in a minute, a one-page plastic-covered menu in her hand. I looked it over quickly. The cook must have figured whatever was good enough for Ted Bundy was good enough for food. I slid past the burgers and the chicken to something that looked safer.

"The tuna salad . . . you make it up here?"

"You can get an individual can if you want." She leaned over again, flashed me a smile. Dot of red on an eyetooth from the carmine lipstick. "That's what I do," she said, patting one round hip. "I have to watch my weight."

"That seems like a nice job."

"Waiting tables?"

"Watching your weight."

"Oh, you!" Giggling. At home now. With what she first learned in junior high.

"I'll have the tuna. An order of rye toast. And some ginger ale."

"We serve beer here too. Cold. On tap."

"Not while I'm working."

She scribbled something with her pencil, long fingernails wrapped around the corner of her order pad, the same color as her lipstick. "I haven't seen you before. You're new in town?"

"Just passing through for a couple of weeks."

"You said you were working. I mean, nobody comes here for a *vacation*."

"I'm looking over some property."

"Oh. Are you one of those developers?"

"Sort of. I . . ."

"Hey, Cyndi. Shake it up, will ya? You got two blue plates

sitting here!'' A voice barked from somewhere behind the counter.

She leaned forward again, shouted, ''How's this?'' over her shoulder, and wiggled her rump furiously. A line of laughter broke from the counter, working its way around the curve. ''That what you been wanting, Leon?'' Someone laughed. Cyndi's face was lightly flushed. ''The old man's a pain in the butt.''

''You're not worried about losing your job?''

''I *wish*. This place isn't my idea of heaven. I used to work over at the Club Flame, you ever go there?''

''I just got here.''

''It's a topless joint,'' she said, watching my eyes. ''The tips aren't as good here, but at least you don't have guys trying to grab your ass all the time.''

''I guess you have to be comfortable if you're going to do your work.''

''Well, *I'm* not about to spend my life here. Not in this town. I . . .'' She turned as another waitress walked past. A slim woman, lemon-blonde hair tied back with a white ribbon. Her uniform was the same material as Cyndi's, but on her it looked like a nurse's outfit. The hemline was below her knees, white stockings, flat shoes, blouse buttoned to her neck. As she turned, her body-profile was an upside-down question mark. Cyndi put a hand on the blonde woman's arm. ''Blossom honey, could you grab those two blue plates from Leon while I take this man's order?''

''Sure.'' The blonde walked away, shoulders squared. Something buzz-bombed my mind—then it was gone.

''Now what was I saying?'' Cyndi licked her lips like it would help her concentrate.

''You're not about to spend the rest of your life here.''

A smile flashed. ''You listen good, don't you, honey? Yeah. Not here. I like Chicago better. You ever been there?''

''Lots of times.''

"There's where I like to go. Get out of this town . . . like for a weekend, you know?"

"Sure."

"I'll get your order. Think about it."

I lit a cigarette, looked out the window at the traffic.

Cyndi bounced her way back to my booth, unloaded her tray. "Give me a dollar for the jukebox." She smiled. "This place is too quiet."

I handed her a buck.

"What d'you like?"

"Whatever suits you."

"Hmmm . . ." she said. Like she was thinking it over.

The blonde walked past again. "Cyndi, they want you over on four."

"Okay, honey." She caught my eye. "Ain't she something! Poor girl doesn't make nothing in tips. I tried to talk to her, let her know how to work it. She's not much in the boobs department but she's got a sweet little butt on her. I told her there's things you can do to these stupid uniforms . . . like I did. But not Miss Priss. I don't think she likes men, you know what I mean?"

I nodded, sticking a fork into the tuna. I ate slowly, watching the women work. One of those sugar-substitute girl singers came over the jukebox. Some sad song. No juice.

The blonde came past my table, a tray in each hand, nicely balanced. Slender neck, broad, flat nose, thin lips. Ripple of muscle on her forearm. No polish on her nails. Her big eyes flicked at mine, went away. She walked smoothly, the loose skirt not quite hiding what Cyndi worked so hard to advertise. Blossom.

Cyndi came back just as I was lighting a smoke. "Was it okay?"

"Sure."

"You want some dessert?"

"I'll pass this time."

"Then you'll be back, right?"

"This is your regular station, this booth?"

She gave me a little bounce, big smile. "Yeah. Sometimes you get lucky, huh?"

"Sometimes."

"Which one is your car?" she asked, leaning over again, looking out the window.

"The gray one."

"The Lincoln?"

"Yeah."

"Oh, you must be in a *good* business."

"Good enough."

"This one isn't so good. I start at the breakfast shift and work right through to six. That's when I get off."

"I'll remember."

"See that you do, honey." Dropping the check on the table, walking away, giving me a last look at what I'd be missing if I wasn't around at six.

The diner's jukebox was time-warped. Patti LaBelle. "I Sold My Heart to the Junkman."

I left a ten-dollar bill sitting on a four-dollar check.

◊ 25

DARKNESS DROPPED TO meet the steel-mill smog. A blanket you could feel. I showered, changed my clothes. Lay back on the bed, redrawing the map Rebecca had given to me on the ceiling of the motel room.

I looped the Lincoln past the strip bars on the Interstate, watching. Nothing. Pulled over on U.S. 30, got out and checked under the hood. I gave it another half hour, zeroing in so I could feel it if anyone came inside the zone. Still nothing. Anyone following me was better at it than I was.

Time to move. I turned off the highway, found the blue house at the end of the block. The garage was standing closed at the foot of the driveway. I left the Lincoln in the street, slipped on a pair of thin leather gloves, used the key Rebecca had given me, opened the garage. Inside, a late-'70s Chevy sedan, key in the ignition. I started it up, eased it out into the street. Put the Lincoln inside, pulled my airline bag from the front seat, closed the door. Looked back at the house. The lights were on in the front rooms. Rebecca's cousins. I didn't know what she'd told them but I know what they'd tell the cops if anything happened. Nothing.

The Chevy blended into the terrain, at home on the back roads. I followed Rebecca's directions to Cedar Lake. Found Lake Shore Drive. A resort area, mostly summer cottages. I stopped at a bench set into a wooden railing across from a funeral home. Smoked a cigarette and waited. The sign said Scenic Overlook. Told me the lake was 809 acres. Three miles long, a mile and a half wide. Twin flagpoles on either side of the bench. Electricity meter on a pole. I stood at the railing. Somebody had carved Steve & Monica inside a clumsy heart. I traced it with my fingers. Three bikers went by on chopped hogs, no helmets.

Still quiet. Safe.

The house was set on a sloping rise, right next to a railroad overpass. I nosed the Chevy up the dirt road, pulled around to the back. Turned the car around. As soon as I closed the door, the car looked like it'd been there for years, rusting to death.

The house was dark. One back window had been repaired with a cardboard carton and some tape. I peered inside. Bulks of furniture, steady shadows, dirt and dust. Nobody lived there. I took a quarter out of my pocket, holding it between my fingers. Tapped it sharply on the steel door to the cellar. Three fast, three slow. Waited. Did it again. Convict code. We always find a way. A guy who did time on the Coast told me about scooping all the water out of the steel toilets, using the tubing as a communication line to the other blocks. Guys in solitary use a kind of Morse code. Takes a whole day to pass a message along. We played chess through the mail. Used little scraps of mirror to see what's happening down the tier. Hand signals. We'd find a way. And some guys, they'd be in solitary even when they hit the streets.

Three answering taps, spaced the same way. I tapped back, this time six in a row, all quick. The padlock on the storm door was a phony—it rested alongside the rings, not through them. I pulled it open and stepped into the darkness.

Down a flight of concrete steps, feeling my way. When I got down far enough, I reached up, pulled the storm door closed behind me.

I hit the bottom of the steps, put a palm along the wall to guide me. A white burst of light in my face, rooting me where I stood. It snapped off, leaving bright-spangled lights dancing inside my eyelids.

A switch clicked. Soft pool of light in a corner of the basement.

''Thanks for coming, brother.''

Virgil.

☙ 26

HE LOOKED ABOUT the same. Thick black hair, combed back along the sides '50s style, hazel eyes, a long face, pointed jaw, dominated by a falcon's beak for a nose. Indians had visited his grandfather's turf and they hadn't all got themselves shot.

Taller than me, a mountain man's build, the power in the bone, not the muscles. Big hands, thick wrists. The whole package built to survive the mountains and the mines.

Or prison.

He extended his hand, gave mine a brief squeeze, dropped it, and turned to stand next to me. Letting me see it for myself. My eyes adjusted, working in figure-eight loops from the pool of light. Small refrigerator against one wall, two-burner hot plate, canned goods stacked almost to the ceiling. Virgil handed me a flash. I swept the rest of the basement. It was as neat and clean as a lifer's cell. Three army cots, big portable radio with speakers on each side and a carrying handle, a pair of sawhorses with a rough plank across them for a table.

Virgil took the flash from me, pointed it and followed the beam, me right behind. I left my bag on the floor, keeping both hands free. The basement had more than one room. We turned the corner, stepped into a small bathroom. Just a toilet and a drain in the floor for the shower someone had put together out of a length of hose draped over a hook. We walked through to the furnace area. An ancient oil burner squatted, dying of metal fatigue, its plug pulled years ago.

Virgil spoke. "Come on out of there, boy. It's okay."

The door to the oil burner opened from the inside. A kid stepped out, blinking his eyes at the light. A slightly built boy with close-cropped light hair, trembling.

"Uncle Virgil . . ."

Virgil ignored him. "This here's Lloyd," he said to me. "My wife's kin."

The kid watched me like a bird watching a cat. A bird who couldn't fly.

"Get on inside," Virgil said to him, stepping aside so the kid could walk in front of us.

Back in the big room, Virgil nodded toward the left-hand corner. A triangle of packing crates, hubcap on the floor between them. I took a seat. Virgil settled in. "You too," he told the kid.

He nodded his head at the corners of the basement. "This here's the living room. Over there's the kitchen, far side's the bedroom. You already seen the bathroom. Man who owns this house, he's kin of Rebecca's." He said her name the way they do in Appalachia, twanging hard on the first "e," dragging it out.

"Ain't nobody gonna come around. We got electricity for at least another month, until they turn it off. Garbage goes in the plastic bags. We stack 'em back behind the furnace. Got enough food here for a long time. Anybody comes, it's me they find. Lloyd hides himself in the furnace. Reba'll come back for him, it comes to that."

"You going to go quietly?" I asked him.

He saw where I was looking. At the pair of long guns resting against the wall just behind him.

He shrugged. "They don't want me for much of nothing. Helping a bail jumper, that's no kind of time. It just didn't seem natural to hole up without some firepower."

"This an ashtray?" I asked, pointing at the hubcap on the floor.

"Yeah. The basement windows are all boarded up but there's plenty of cracks in them. It clears out pretty good."

I lit a smoke, sneaking a glance at the kid in the flare of the wooden match. He was sitting soft, waiting. Like Terry, when I first rented him from a kiddie pimp. Not exactly like Terry: this boy didn't know why I came. And he did care.

I looked across at Virgil. We'd done time together and he'd passed the test. More than once. The test of time, the test of crime. In my world, no difference. "What's my end?" I asked him.

"I need to know some truth. Reba, she'd'a told you what happened over here, right?"

I nodded.

"First the cops thought it was Lloyd. Then they didn't. Now they back to where they was. It's Lloyd. In their minds. Me, I don't know about this stuff. Freak stuff. But you know them . . ."

Them. Humans who kill for love. Torture for fun. They set fires to watch the flames. Black-glove rapists. Snuff-film directors. Trophy-takers. Baby-fuckers. Pain turns on the switch. Blood lubricates the machinery. Then the power-rush comes. And they do too.

It's not sex. Castrate the freaks and they use broomsticks or Coke bottles.

I've been studying them all my life. Since I was a tiny little kid. They taught me. Nightmare walkers.

Virgil was right. Whoever ventilated those kids in lovers' lane . . .

"I know them," I said in the quiet darkness. The kid couldn't meet my eyes. Or wouldn't.

"You're here to talk to Lloyd. When you're done, you tell me the truth. You'll know. Nobody's better at it than you. I know you did it before. For that lawyer. I remember you telling me about it. Never forget it. That's what I need now.''

I dragged deep on my smoke. ''I'm in.''

Virgil nodded. Turned to the kid. ''Lloyd, this man's my brother. You heard what he said. He's gonna talk to you. You're gonna talk to him. When it's done, I'm gonna know the truth. You got it?''

''Uncle Virgil . . .''

''What?''

''I didn't do it.''

''You didn't do it, my brother will know. Then I'll get something together for you. Whatever it takes. You a member of the family. My wife's cousin. Blood kin. You didn't do it, we're behind you. I risked my house for you. My home. Where my children live. And it looks like I may be going back to jail for a little bit too. That's okay. A man's got no more than his family.''

''Will I have to go to jail?''

''Jail? Boy, you better *pray* you going to jail. Only way you're going inside is you *didn't* do what they say you did.''

''Uncle Virgil,'' the kid's voice was a ribbon of broken glass, drooling out of his slack mouth. ''I don't understand. What do you mean?''

Virgil lit a cigarette of his own. I knew what he was doing. Getting his thoughts together, making sure it came out right. ''Lloyd, you didn't do this . . . my brother tells me you didn't do this . . . then we come up with a plan. Some plans don't work out. And then people go to jail. You have to go to jail, you'll go like a man, you understand? That ain't no big thing. And you'll always have your people. Inside and out. Something waiting for you. Like I had.''

He took another hit on his cigarette, hazel eyes anchored on Lloyd. ''But if you did it . . . if that was you sneaking around killing those kids . . . then I won't shame my wife by letting her know. I won't have kin of mine doing evil like that.''

"I . . ."

"Lloyd, it turns out you did it, you gonna be what they call a fugitive. Only they never gonna catch you, understand?"

"You mean . . . I'm going to run away?"

"No. You did this thing, you not running any farther than this basement."

27

THE BOY SLUMPED forward, covering his face with his hands. Shoulder blades bowed like a broken bird's wings, dry-crying, chest in spasm. But he didn't say a word.

I watched him for a minute. Virgil was granite. I knew he'd kill if he had to—that's how he came to prison. And I knew his word was good.

I looked up. Caught his eye. "Virgil, I'm beat. Just got in from the Coast. This interrogation, it's going to take a long time. How about if I catch some sleep, talk to Lloyd when I get up?"

He got it. "Whatever you say, brother. I could use some sleep myself. We got all the time in the world. Take the first bunk, the one over on the left."

I got up, walked over to the cot. Folded my jacket into a pillow, lay back, closed my eyes.

Virgil smoked another cigarette. "Lloyd," he said, "I need to take a shower before I sack out. I'll talk to you later."

I heard the rush of the shower. Heard the kid get up, light himself a smoke. Heard the hubcap rattle on the cement floor as he ground it out. I rasped a breath through my nose. As many times as the nose had been broken, it was perfect for faking a snore. Virgil took his time, giving the boy every chance to bolt. He didn't go for it. By the time Virgil came back inside, I'd heard the kid's cot creak.

Dead quiet. You could hear crickets chirp, a car pass on the highway. The summer heat didn't penetrate the basement. Faint whiff of diesel fuel on the air.

It was worth the shot. If the kid tried to get out while we were asleep, we'd know.

But if he didn't run, we'd know nothing. Sniper-blasting unsuspecting kids in a parked car wasn't the same as trying to get past Virgil in the dark.

⭐ 28

I LET THE past play on the blank screen of my mind, regulating my breathing, focusing. Getting to the center. Virgil had called the right number—I knew how to do it.

A long time ago, I had this fool dream of being a private eye, working off the books. This young lawyer reached out for me through Davidson. I met them both in the parking lot near the Brooklyn Criminal Court. Davidson made the introductions. Vouched for me. He let the young lawyer speak for himself.

"I represent Roger B. Haynes." Like I should have heard of the guy.

"Eighteen-B," Davidson interrupted. Telling me the

young lawyer was assigned to the case, not privately retained. Any money for me was coming out of his pocket.

"He was arrested for the rape of a little girl. The rape took place right near the Brooklyn Botanic Garden. In broad daylight. The girl ID'd him in a lineup. There's plenty of medicals to prove she'd been raped, but nothing to connect Haynes to it."

"SODDI?" I asked him. Some Other Dude Did it.

"That's what he says," Davidson growled.

"It's true," the kid said. "Haynes was in New Hampshire when it happened. At a flea market. He was buying stock for his store. A dozen people saw him. There's no way he could have driven back in time to commit the rape."

"So what d'you need me for?"

The young lawyer tilted his head at Davidson. "He says you know these people . . . child molesters and all. I thought . . . maybe you could ask around . . . maybe there's one of them working that area."

I shrugged.

"He's got priors," Davidson said.

"For what?" I asked the young lawyer.

"The same thing. But that was *years* ago. He did his time. He's even off parole. And he's been discharged from therapy."

"Cured, huh?"

"Yeah, cured. You think it's impossible? Would *you* want to be arrested every time the cops had a hijacking case open?"

Davidson chuckled. "He's got you, Burke."

"He's got a baby-raper."

"You mean you won't help?"

"What do I give a flying fuck if some skinner falls for something he didn't do? Probably didn't pull enough time on his first bit anyway."

Davidson lit his cigar. "It wouldn't shake me up if he went

down either. But if he didn't do this one, it means the guy who did, he's got a free pass.''

I thought it through. "You got any money?" I asked the young lawyer.

"I could go five hundred.''

"For that, I'll talk to your guy. You walk me in there, tell them I'm your assistant or something. I'll talk to him. He's telling the truth, I'll look around for you.''

"How will you know?''

"I'll know," I assured him.

He looked at Davidson. The husky man nodded.

"Okay," the kid said. "When can you go?''

"When can you pay?''

"I'll write you a check right now.''

Davidson thought that was almost as funny as I did.

◊ 29

I LOOKED MORE like a lawyer than the kid did when I met him the next morning on the steps of the Brooklyn House of Detention. The guards let us pass without a question. Getting into jail is always easy.

They brought him down to the Attorneys' Conference Room. He was medium height, nice-looking in an undistinctive way. Powerfully built, well-defined upper body in a white T-shirt. Shook hands firmly, looked me deep in the eye, moving his lips to make sure he got my name right.

"Rodriguez, huh?" He smiled. "You don't look Puerto Rican."

"You don't look like a baby-raper," I said, lighting a cigarette, flicking a glance at his face over my hands cupped around the wooden match.

His expression didn't change, no color flashed on his cheeks. Calm inside himself. He was used to this—a therapy veteran.

The young lawyer pulled his chair away from the table, sat back in a corner, his yellow legal pad open on his lap. My play.

I worked the perimeter, tapping softly at the corners. The way you crack a pane of glass during a burglary—the quieter you go in, the easier you go out.

"You were up in New Hampshire when it happened?"

"Yes. Buying stock for my store at the flea markets."

"What kind of store do you have?"

"I call it Inexplik. Not really antiques, anything people collect. Glass bottles, baseball cards, first editions, dolls, knives, Hummel figurines, commemorative plates, proof sets . . . like that."

"You have anything special in mind you were looking for when you were up there?"

"Well, there's *always* things you look for. I mean, I know what my regular customers want and all. Like Barbie dolls . . . you can always sell them. But you have to keep your eyes open, spot hot items before people know what they're worth. Like those plastic compacts women used to carry around in the '50s. The kind with mirrors on the inside? They come in all shapes and colors. Right now, you can get them for a song, but they're going to be very, very collectible soon."

He folded his hands in front of him on the desk. The nails were bitten to the quick, ragged skin around the sides. He saw where I was looking, folded his hands across his chest.

"Can you still buy handguns up there?" I asked.

"I guess so. I mean, they have them right on the tables. But they're against the law in New York. I wouldn't mess with them. Besides, gun collectors are just a different *breed* from the people I deal with."

He was emphasizing the wrong words, arching an eyebrow when he did—a squid throwing out ink.

"You're not gay." My voice was flat—it wasn't a question.

His mouth smiled like it was a separate part of his face. Not answering like that was the answer.

"Homosexuals don't rape little girls," I said, my voice flat.

"No, they don't," he agreed.

"They don't rape little boys either."

"Huh?"

"Didn't they tell you what *you* were when you had all that therapy?"

His right hand squeezed his left wrist, hard. Muscles twitched along his forearm. "What I *was*."

"Say it."

His eyes were a soft, brooding brown, muddy around the rim where they bled into the white, hard in the tiny circles around the pupils. "A pedophile, that's what they said."

"But you're all better now?"

"I still have feelings . . . but I have something else now. Control. Feelings don't hurt anyone."

"No. They don't, Roger. When you got busted for this, the cops search your house?"

"Yes! They tore the place *apart*."

"Come up empty?"

"Yes, they did. I don't even know what they were looking for."

I lit another smoke, patient. When you work freaks, you

don't feel yourself getting warm. The closer you get to the center, the more you feel the chill. "They search your store too?"

"Yes."

"Nothing?"

"Nothing."

"How about if I take a look myself?"

His Adam's apple bobbed as he swallowed. "What for?"

"Oh, I think I could find something. Maybe something that would crack this case."

"Like what?"

"You deal with collectors, right?"

He nodded, watching.

"And you got a computer somewhere around . . . keep track of the merchandise?"

"Yes."

"Got it crash-coded?"

"How come you . . . ?"

"I got a friend. Real genius with those things. She knows how to get inside, past the crash-codes . . ."

"No!"

"Sure, Roger. You're not making any money selling that flea-market crap, are you? Not *real* money. Like you said, you have to know what your customers want."

He turned to the young lawyer. "Can he *do* this?"

The young lawyer shrugged. "We're just trying to help."

"This is all privileged, right?"

"All privileged," the kid assured him.

"If I did . . . uh, *share* with other collectors, that wouldn't prove anything."

"Nothing at all," I told him. "In fact, it would explain a lot of things. Like how you really make a living. And how come you can make it through the night. We both know you guys never stop. Like you said, feelings don't hurt. Looking at pictures, that don't hurt either."

"That's right. The pictures, they're an . . . *outlet*, you understand? A release valve. Those therapists, they don't understand the need. The drive. I'm my own therapist now. I can look at the pictures, fantasize in my mind." Watching my face. "And get off when I have to, when the drive pressures me. In the institution, they tried to take that away from us. Control our thoughts. Fascists. We had to look at the pictures and then they'd *shock* us. Blast us with electricity. It *hurt*. After a while, I couldn't even get a hard-on when I saw beautiful little pictures."

He was crying, face in his hands. They taught him how to do that inside the walls too. I waited for it to stop.

"It doesn't matter, Roger," I told him, voice low, softcored. "The rape went down at four forty-five in the afternoon. You were spotted just before two at the flea market. It's almost two hundred and fifty miles from there to Brooklyn. No way it could have been you."

He looked up, tears streaking his face. I went on like I'd never stopped. "There's a two-twenty flight out of Keene, New Hampshire. Air New England. Flies to the Marine Air Terminal just past La Guardia. Five minutes from the BQE. Maybe another twenty, thirty minutes to Brooklyn."

He went quiet. I felt the young lawyer stiffen behind me.

"I drove my car up there," he said.

"But you didn't drive it back, did you? One of your freak friends, another *collector*, he did that, right? Then maybe he flew to Boston, where he had another car waiting of his own. You guys trade these little favors, don't you? Like you trade the pictures?"

"You're crazy! You think I raped some little girl in the back of a taxicab?"

"I think you have two cars, Roger. There's the van you use for your business. The one you drove up to New Hampshire. And one you keep for prowling. You drive the car to the Marine Air Terminal, park it in the lot there, take a cab home. Then you drive the van to the flea market. Get yourself seen. Take the plane back here, hop in your car, and go to work.''

I lit another smoke. ''The cops'll find the other car, Roger. They'll check the passenger manifest list for the airline. And they'll find your friend too. It won't be hard.''

''You can't tell them any of this. Attorney-client privilege. You said so.''

''There's something special about kids, isn't there, Roger? That soft, smooth skin. How they got no hair anywhere on their little bodies.''

''Shut up!''

''They'll find that car, Roger. And they'll find the kid's blood in the back seat. You're going inside. Again. For a long fucking time.''

''I'm sick . . . you can't . . .''

''You're a maggot. A maggot down for Rape One. Of a child. With force and violence. And you're a two-time loser. So it's the Bitch for you. Habitual Offender. That's a life top in this state. But look at the good side: they don't do therapy on lifers. You'll be all alone in your cell, and you can paint your freak pictures in your mind all you want. You're done.''

''You can't tell! I know all about it. You can't tell—you'll lose your license.''

''Hey, Roger. *I'll* never tell. But if some smart cop decides to look for that other car of yours, that's just the breaks, huh?''

He came across the table then, reaching for my throat. I jammed the stiffened fingers of my right hand into his diaphragm, shifted my hands to the back of his neck as the breath shot out his mouth, snapped his face hard into the top of the table. By the time I felt the young lawyer's hands reaching around my chest to pull me off I was done.

I was faster then. Smarter now.

▥ 30

I COULDN'T WATCH his eyes, so I listened to his breathing.
Feeling the rhythm, waiting for ragged to go smooth. For
that twilight sleep to settle into REM. That's why they do
surgery past midnight and before dawn—it's when the body
shuts down, goes limp inside. The knife goes in easier.

The luminous dial of my fancy watch said 3:45. The kid
was under, quiet now. I fished a quarter from my pocket,
tapped it softly against the leg of my cot. An answering tap
from Virgil. Awake, and ready. I flexed my upper body,
pulling into a sitting position without using my hands. The
kid didn't stir. Virgil sat up too—I could see his shape in the
darkness. He followed me around the corner to the furnace.
A whispered conversation, and we were ready to work.

▥ 31

GET UP, LLOYD.'' Virgil gripped the kid's shoulders, shook
him gently.

The kid moaned, whimpering something, still half asleep. I wouldn't want his dreams. We let him use the bathroom, throw some cold water on his face. Not saying anything, letting him feel the pressure. When he came back to the main room, we had a straight chair set up. It wouldn't be light for a couple of hours. I sat directly across from the kid, within whispering distance. Virgil was a few feet away, sitting on an angle to us, something dark on his lap.

"Here's the way it works, Lloyd," I told him, neutral-voiced. Working it flexible: soft to hard, hard to soft. First the shell, then the center. "You and I have a talk. About all this stuff that's been going on. And you tell me the truth. You always tell me the truth. About everything. Every single time. You know why?"

"I told the truth, I . . ."

"You know *why*, Lloyd?" Shifting my voice a notch closer to hard. His eyes flicked up to mine, sulky. Dropped. "Because that's the way I'll know, see?" I said. "I find out you lied about one thing . . . *any* thing . . . then you're a liar, understand? And you didn't shoot those kids, did you?"

"No!"

"And that's the truth, isn't it?"

"Yes. I swear."

"Cross your heart and hope to die?"

"Yes!"

"Lloyd," I said, my voice laced with a tinge of sorrow, like it was out of my hands. "That's what you're doing, boy. Don't lie. Don't let me catch you in a lie. No matter what the truth is, tell it to me." I leaned forward. "Nothing's as bad as dying, Lloyd. Anything else, me and Virgil, we could fix it. But don't lie."

"I . . . won't."

I leaned back, lit a smoke, nodding my head to seal the deal. He didn't ask for one. Virgil didn't move.

"You got friends at school?"

"Yes. I mean, maybe . . . not really. Friends. I mean, guys I talk to but . . ."

"But you work alone?"

"At the store?"

"No, Lloyd. When you go out at night. You walk by yourself?"

"Sometimes . . ."

"You look in windows?"

"I'm sorry . . . I'm sorry . . ."

"It's all right, Lloyd. I know about the windows. Nobody ever sees you, huh?"

"No."

"You do that at home too? Before you moved up here?"

"Just a couple of times."

"It's okay. Take it easy. You're telling the truth. Nothing to worry about. You ever take your rifle with you? When you go out walking?"

"No. I never did. I swear."

"You ever let them see you?"

"Who?"

"The women. The women in the windows."

"No. I wouldn't want . . ."

"You ever take it out, play with it . . . while you watch?"

"Nooo. No. I just wanted to . . . *see* them . . . see what they look like . . . just . . ."

"Okay. You were scared . . . when you went out walking?"

"Not . . . scared. Like, uh . . . nervous, you know?"

"I know." Shifting gears—same highway. "Those magazines. The ones the cops found in your room. Where'd you get them?"

"I sent away for them."

"What kind of magazines were they?"

"About . . . women. I . . ."

"There's more of 'em over in the corner—found 'em down

in the basement.'' Virgil's voice. Like saying the milk was in the refrigerator. ''You want to see them?''

''Yeah.''

He got up, came back with a foot-high stack, bound with twine. Dropped it on the floor next to my chair, pulled at the cord. A knot unraveled.

''Lloyd know these were here?'' I asked him.

''Yeah. Never touched them either,'' he said, answering my next question.

I shone my pocket flash on the first one. ''Beauty in Chains.'' Women bound, gagged, blindfolded. In street clothes, some half dressed, some nude. Bent over chairs, standing on tiptoe, hands suspended over their heads, hog-tied. Helpless. Ropes, straps, handcuffs. They were all like that. All the same. Some had the covers pulled off. A few had pages ripped out. Not neatly cut. Jagged edges. Torn.

''How much did these cost?'' I asked Lloyd.

''Twenty-five dollars was the most. Some were fifteen, one was only five.''

In the underbelly of the human heart, dirt isn't cheap.

''You look at these?'' I asked Virgil. Buying time. Something about the magazines. Something past the obvious. The way inside.

''I looked at them.'' His voice was flat, giving nothing away.

I lit another smoke, turning the pages, getting the feel. Lloyd watching me. Waiting for the judgment.

It came to me. ''The pages you ripped out . . . where are they?''

''I threw them away.''

''No you didn't.''

''I *did!* I mean . . . I didn't throw them away exactly . . . I . . . burned them.''

''Where?''

"In the woods. Just past the dunes. I made a campfire. Every time."

"Every time?"

"Every time a new one came . . . with those pictures."

I dragged on my smoke, looking down the white barrel of the cigarette, visually placing the red tip in the center of Lloyd's out-of-focus face. Like the laser-dot from a sniper rifle. Zeroing in. "What was in the pictures, Lloyd? The pictures you burned up."

He made a strangling sound deep in his throat.

I felt Virgil settle into himself. Knowing it was important, not knowing why. Knowing he had to wait. He had a hunter's patience. I had a convict's.

Lloyd felt the weight. "Could I have a smoke?"

"When it's over. What was in the pictures?"

He took short, shallow breaths. The blankets were coming off and he knew it was going to be cold.

"The pictures . . . they were getting hurt."

"The women?"

"Yes. I couldn't look at them."

"Who was hurting them?"

"Men, mostly. Sometimes other women."

"Tell me."

"They beat them. Whipped them. Even . . . c-c-cut them once. Ugly. So ugly . . ."

He was crying. Not a sociopath's tears. Crying for someone else. It felt right. I had to be sure. I probed the wound, watching for the runoff. Clean or dirty. Blood or pus. "You don't like other people in your pictures, Lloyd?"

"Other people . . . ?"

"You can't own the women if there's somebody else there. They wouldn't be all yours."

"All mine? They're not mine. I just wanted to see . . . not be so . . ."

"Afraid?"

"Yes." Sobbing now.

"When they're helpless . . . tied up . . . you can look all you want? Like when they're in the windows?"

"Yes."

I couldn't close the wound until it was clean. The scalpel probed again. "Lloyd, you ever see a dead woman?"

"No."

"Ever want to see one?"

"*No!* God. No. *Dead?*"

I zoned in on his face, going into his skull, reaching out, searching to see if that maggoty little worm of evil was there. My voice was soft, smoothing the road, stroking the beast to full boil. "A dead woman, Lloyd. A dead naked woman. Just lying there. You could do whatever you wanted. She'd be all yours. She'd never say anything. Whatever you wanted to do . . ."

He stumbled from the chair, staggering past me, making wounded-animal sounds. I held up my hand to stop Virgil from going after him.

We heard him hit the floor in the bathroom. Heard the low grunting scream—ripped from his guts like he'd ripped the pictures from his tortured mind. Projectile vomiting, his lungs hitting the top of his throat.

When he got his breath, he used it for crying.

◗ 32

AFTER A WHILE, the crying was over. My work wasn't. I nodded to Virgil. We walked around the concrete corner, found the kid sitting in his own stink, face in his hands. Drained.

"Get on your feet," I told him. "Clean yourself up."

He made noises. Didn't move.

"Now," I told him, voice hard.

"I *can't*."

I turned on the shower full blast. Virgil grabbed the kid under his armpits, hauled him to his feet. I turned the hose on him. He sagged in Virgil's hands. The water hit him clean, ran off foul.

We let him finish the job himself. Waited while he toweled himself off. He came back inside wearing an old red flannel bathrobe. I pointed at the chair. He sat down again.

Virgil tossed him a pack of cigarettes. It landed in the kid's lap. He didn't move, didn't raise his head.

"It's okay, Lloyd," I said, propping him up for what had to come.

"I told the truth." His voice was thin, sad.

"I know. But we're not done. Can you light that cigarette?"

"I don't know." Fumbling in his lap.

"Try."

A wooden match flared in Virgil's hand. He was kneeling

next to the kid, one hand on his shoulder. Lloyd got it going, took a deep drag. Coughed. Took another. The early dawn light seeped in. The boy's skin was transparent, the skull showing through.

"You're scared of women, Lloyd?"

"I . . . think so."

"But you like them?"

"Yes. I do . . . like . . . them. I think I do. But when they talk to me . . ."

"I know. Someone told you they wouldn't like you, didn't they? Someone told you they'd know something about you . . ."

His shoulders shook like he was freezing. Crying again, the cigarette dropping from his hand. Virgil plucked it off the kid's lap, one hand still on his shoulder, trying to send his strength into his wife's cousin. Not knowing why yet, trusting what he felt.

I lit a cigarette of my own. Centering myself, watching the red dots that always danced before my eyes when the freaks played with kids. Remembering. Getting past it. Like I had a long time ago. When I made my choices.

"Who was it, Lloyd?" I asked him. Voice soft, not waiting for the answer. "Your mother's boyfriend? A teacher? The coach? Your uncle?"

I let Virgil's rock-hard core work its way into the boy's guts. Waiting for the anchor to set.

"How did . . . how d'you know?"

"I know who did it. Not his name. But I know him. They're all alike. Listen to me, Lloyd. They're all liars. You told us the truth here. And you're going to beat this. He lied to you. As soon as you tell us everything, I'll start to prove it to you."

"Ain't nobody gonna hurt you, son." Virgil's voice. The kid caught the last word, grabbed at it like a lifeline. He wouldn't have to face the monster alone.

Anymore.

"It was the preacher," he said. "The preacher."

"Yeah. When did it start?"

"When I was nine. Just before I was ten. Just before my birthday. He had model race cars. Radio-controlled. He used to take me to the races. He said, when I was ten, he'd let me steer one in a time trial."

"And your mother, she thought it was great, you spending time with him?"

"She sure did. My real father, I don't know where he is. Mama said the preacher was a good man. I think she liked him herself, you know? Always inviting him over for dinner, saying like he needed a wife to make a home for him and all. He was nice to me. Took me for rides in his car, bought me a baseball glove. Like I was his own son, Mama said."

"How'd it happen? He show you some pictures?"

"Pictures. Little boys, with no clothes on. That's the way it started. He'd let me play with the video games he had in his house if I took my clothes off. I didn't want to do it, but . . . in the pictures, like . . . boys were doing all kinds of things without their clothes on. Like he said. It was a natural thing. For a special treat once, he took me camping, He told me stories, about wolves and bears in the woods. I wasn't scared, but he said he'd better let me in his sleeping bag so I would be okay. It felt . . . weird . . . but . . . he was the preacher and all . . ."

"It's okay."

"He said we had a special love. A special secret love, he said. He said God picked me for him, 'cause I was special. It was a mark, a mark only certain people could see. A mark on me."

"And you couldn't tell anyone . . ."

"Couldn't tell anyone. Couldn't make him stop."

"So you started to get into trouble . . ."

"To make it stop. When I got to be around thirteen, I felt

things inside of me. I thought, maybe they'd put me away someplace, like in one of those juvenile homes . . . and . . . stealing cars . . . riding by myself . . . I felt scared but . . . *good*, you know?''

I knew.

"How'd you know where to buy those magazines?''

"He had them. Not like mine. Bad ones. I copied down the address where he sent away for them.''

Virgil lit a smoke, handed it to Lloyd. The kid dragged on it greedily, blowing it out his nose and mouth at the same time.

"Did the preacher know where your mother sent you?''

"Yeah. He wrote to me. Telling me I'd be back soon and we'd have good times again. He even said maybe he'd come up here to visit me just before school starts in the fall.''

"Those pictures . . . the ones you saved . . . not the ones you ripped out. You thought women could see this mark you have on you?''

"That's what he said. He said they'd always see it. And maybe they'd laugh at me. Or worse. He said women are evil. Nasty, smelly evil things. Down there.''

"But you like them, don't you, Lloyd?''

He nodded.

"You know what that means?''

"No.''

"Listen to me, now. Listen good. It means the preacher was a liar. There's no mark on you. There never was. Women won't hurt you . . . not the ways the preacher said they would. You're a man—you'll be a man. The preacher can't change that.''

"The stuff . . . he made me do . . . I . . . .''

"It doesn't mean anything, Lloyd. Nothing. You want to know about women, you're curious about them. That's *natural*, okay? All young men, they feel like that. Tying them up so they can't hurt you . . . peeking in windows so you can watch without them seeing you . . . you don't need that. There's other ways."

"How?" Spark of desperate hope in his eyes.

"You'll see. Me and Virgil, we'll show you. It'll take some time, but it's going to be all right. *All* right, understand?"

He nodded. Wanting it to be true.

"Lloyd? One of the kids around here, he told the cops they were sneaking around, looking in on parked cars. Remember?"

"Yes. It's true. I was with them."

"And you told the other kids that you hated them . . . that maybe something should happen to them?"

"I didn't mean it. It just . . . hurt so bad. That they could be with girls and I couldn't. The mark . . ."

"The mark is gone, boy. It never was there. It was a lie. And this is the truth. Don't hate women. Don't be afraid of them. *They* never did anything to you."

"I . . ."

"But somebody did, Lloyd. The man who told you about evil . . . that's what *he* was. Understand?"

The kid ground out his cigarette. Hands shaking, but his voice was steady then—hot wire of pain burning. "I hate him," he said.

"That's the first step," I told him.

∅ 33

I PULLED OUT before the full morning light. Switched the Chevy for the Lincoln. Left the stack of magazines in the Chevy's trunk. Rebecca's cousins would know what to do with whatever they found back there.

Back in the motel, I took a shower. Slept until noon.

∅ 34

WHEN I GOT up, I called Glenda. Nobody asking for me.

I put on my prospector's outfit and went into the streets to look around.

Found a pay phone. Dumped in a handful of quarters, dialed the Mole's junkyard. Heard the phone picked up at the other end. The Mole never answered—he just waited.

"It's me. The Prof call in?"

"Every day." It was Terry's voice. Like father, like son.

"Tell him I'm okay. Keep checking, okay?"

"Sure."

I drifted in loops, looking for enough vacant land to build a racetrack on.

After a couple of hours, I realized I'd never get a feel for these streets without some help. I wasn't tuned in—couldn't feel the heat. If there was any.

⦀ 35

IT WAS ALMOST five when I pulled into the parking lot of the diner. I found my way to the booth in the back, lit a smoke, waited.

Blossom came to the table, a menu tucked under one arm, order pad open in her hand.

"What'll it be?"

I looked up just in time to see Cyndi smoothly bump her hip into Blossom, pushing the blonde woman aside. "This is my table, honey," she said, flashing a smile.

"It's *been* your table the past half hour, girl."

"I was on my break. Now shove off, okay?"

Blossom gave her a "watch your step" look and moved away, not looking back.

"Thought I'd see you last night. After I got off," Cyndi said, a tentative smile on her lips, not showing any teeth.

"Business. Never know when I'm going to get a call."

"Like they leave messages for you and stuff?"

"Or call me in the car."

"Oh! You've got one of those car phones?"

"Yeah."

"They're pretty expensive, huh?"

"Business expense."

"That's what I'd like to be," she said, puffing out her chest. "A business expense."

"No you wouldn't. Kleenex is Kleenex, no matter how much it costs."

"What d'you mean?"

"When you're done with it, you throw it out."

"I know. But . . . nothing lasts forever, right?"

"Wrong."

"Oh." She tapped one shoe. Waiting for the bus. Not sure where it was going, but sure it was coming.

I lit a cigarette, not in a hurry.

"You want tuna again?"

"Ah . . . I'm not sure. Look, I have to work again tonight. Late."

"That's okay. I mean . . . maybe you could come by after . . ."

"No. It'll be real late. Way too late. But if you're getting off at six, maybe we could have dinner together. Before I go to work."

"Dinner?"

"Yeah."

"And then . . ."

"I'll take you home."

She smoothed the sides of her skirt with the palms of her hands. Bit her lip. "I'd . . . like that."

"Okay. Then just bring me a chocolate milkshake and some dry toast. I'll wait here until you get off."

"Coming up."

I ground out my smoke. Found the pay phone in the back. Called my pal John the real estate broker. He didn't have topographical maps of the area right there in his office but he sure as shooting could get me some. Have them for me by tomorrow afternoon.

I sipped the milkshake. Nibbled at the toast. Watched the traffic outside the window. The joint was near-empty. Not a hangout—it flowered at mealtimes, lay dormant in between.

It wasn't quite six when Cyndi bounced up to my table.

◊ 36

I HELD THE passenger door for her while she climbed inside, her chubby thighs flashing in the late afternoon sun. Wearing a black silk blouse over a red miniskirt, black spikes on her feet.

"I hope this is okay?"

"What?"

"This . . . outfit. I mean . . . for going out to dinner and all."

"It's fine. You look lovely."

"Thank you." Ran her hand over the seat cushion. "Leather. It even smells good. Where're we going?"

"You tell me, Cyndi—I don't know this town. Someplace nice. And quiet. Where we don't need a reservation, okay?"

"You mean *nice* nice? Like fancy?"

"Sure."

"Can we go to Ricardo's? I've never been there, but I heard it's *real* nice."

"Sure."

I followed her directions. Ricardo's was in Hammond. A small joint backed up against the lake. The lot had only a half dozen cars sitting there.

Instead of a maître d', there was a plastic sign on a stand. Please Wait to Be Seated.

A dark-haired hostess in a cocktail dress came over. Looked Cyndi up and down, glanced at me long enough to calculate the cost of everything I had on. Asked, "Two for dinner?" and led us to a table ten feet from the kitchen.

"Will this be all right?"

"How about one of those tables?" I asked, nodding my head in the direction of a long, low window.

"They're all reserved, sir."

"All?"

"I believe so." ·

"I'll call next time," I said, starting over in that direction, tapping Cyndi at her waist to come along. The hostess trailed after us, stopping at the first table at the end of the row.

"Perhaps this one?" she asked, her face set.

"Fine."

"Your waiter will be with you shortly."

I held Cyndi's chair for her. Picked a tiny box of wooden matches from the white tablecloth, cracked a flame, lit a smoke.

The waiter looked like he'd done time back when it was a credential. He must have caught the action with the hostess. Bowed to Cyndi. "Good evening, madam. Sir. My name is Charles. I'll be serving you this evening. Can I get you something to drink before dinner . . . perhaps some champagne?"

"Could I . . . ?"

I nodded, cutting her off. "Some champagne for the lady. Whatever you recommend. I'll have ginger ale over ice."

"Very good, sir."

Cyndi looked around like a kid at the circus. A kid who'd never been before. "Oh, wow! This is beautiful. And they treat you so nice. I didn't want to order champagne. I mean, I *love* it and all, but they always water it down, you know."

"Not here."

"I guess not. I mean . . . not with men serving the booze, right?"

37

SHE CHATTERED ON through her London broil. I told her why I was there. How I studied the local newspapers for a few weeks before I ever came into a town to work. She nodded, paying attention, mouth full.

The waiter cleared the plates away, doing it right, easy on the "sir," not oiling it. He knew the difference between Atlantic City respect and the kind you earn with something other than cash.

Cyndi ordered chocolate mousse for dessert. I had the lemon water ice they called sorbet.

I lit a smoke. "Seems like the hot story around here's been that sniper . . . the one shooting those kids who go parking in lovers' lane."

"Oh, they caught him. It was some kid, believe it or not. One of those crazy teenagers. God, I'm glad he wasn't running around when I was a girl, as much time as I spent in parked cars."

"They sure they got the right one?"

"Well, I think so. I mean . . . you never know, right? But ever since they busted him, there's been no more."

"Shootings?"

"Yeah."

"Why d'you think he'd do it?"

"Well . . . oh God, I just realized . . . I feel so stupid . . . I don't even know your *name*."

"Mitchell. Mitchell Sloane."

"Mitch?"

"Sure."

"Mitch, I'll tell you . . . when I used to dance, some of those men who'd come in, they just flat out *hated* women. You know what I mean? The way they'd watch you sometimes, not smiling or anything. Why would they come to a topless joint if they hated us? It doesn't make sense, I know, but it's true. Mean men. You could always tell."

"You figure someone like that?"

"Maybe. I mean . . . why would a kid hate so much he'd want to kill people just for screwing outdoors? Maybe it was one of those religious nuts. We'd get *them* in the bar sometimes too. Always trying to save us."

⚜ 38

IT WAS AFTER eight when we left the restaurant. I put the tab on American Express, tossed a trio of ten-spots on the table for Charles. "Always a pleasure to see you, madam," he said by way of goodbye to Cyndi. A man who knew how to act. He should get together with the hostess some night, teach her the facts of life.

I punched Glenda's line on the car phone, let Cyndi listen to the taped message play back through the speaker-phone.

Hit the Retrieve key. The machine's computer-chip voice said, "Hello. You have no messages. You may hang up and I will reset the unit. Or enter remote code now to change your message."

"Where shall I take you?" I asked her.

"You really have to go to work tonight?"

"If I want to pay my bills."

"Well, I left my car at work. I mean, I didn't know you'd . . ."

The Lincoln whispered past the darkened dunes near the water.

"That's where it happened. One time."

"What?"

"The killings. That's where the kids go to park. Where they *used* to go."

"They'll find another place."

"They sure will."

I pulled into the diner. "Where's your car?"

"Around the back."

It was a red Chevy Beretta, looked new. One of those Garfields plastered against the back side window. Cute.

I turned off the ignition, flicked the switch for the power windows, lit a smoke.

"I'm not sure when I'll be by again. This work I'm doing, it takes you different places, different hours."

"Well, you don't have to come *here* to see me, honey. I mean, you *can* if you want, or call me here or anything." She fumbled in her purse. "You have a pen?"

I gave her one. She wrote down her phone number and her address in a careful, round schoolgirl's hand. "Here!"

"Thanks, Cyndi."

"You know, it's funny. Blossom, she tried to talk me out of going out with you. She said you were some kind of trouble. I mean, can you imagine . . . her telling *me* something about men. Like she'd know a preacher from a pimp."

"Maybe she does."

"Not old Blossom. That girl's so straight. I told her she could go ahead and wait for Mr. Right. I was gonna have some fun while I'm still young. She said that was okay. Said you looked like Mr. Wrong to her."

"I'm just a man. Passing through."

She slid across the seat to me, one hip hard against mine, twisting her breasts against my chest, her lips so close I couldn't see her eyes.

"Well, Mr. Just Passing Through, you make sure you come and see me before you make up your mind, huh?" Kissing me hard, the backs of her fingers trailing across my fly. I pressed my hand against the back of her blouse as I kissed her. No straps. The hostess had seen it before I had.

"I will," I told her.

She kissed me again, promising.

I watched her climb into her red car and drive off.

◥ 39

I SWITCHED THE Lincoln for the Chevy and made my way to the hideout, thinking it through. Cyndi wasn't going to work. She was connected, but to the wrong side of the night. I needed somebody wired in at the other end. The sniper wouldn't be wearing a double-knit leisure suit with a white belt and gold chains. Even the topless bars would be too bright for his eyes.

When I got downstairs it looked the same. Except for a

canvas sack suspended from a beam in the ceiling by a short length of towing chain. I tapped the bag—it was stuffed with something. I looked a question at Virgil.

"Heavy bag," he said. "Best I could do. Lloyd, he's one angry young pup. I figured, let him pound on it awhile, work some of that stuff out. Like we used to do inside."

"Good idea. He know how to do it?"

"He don't have a clue. Figured maybe you'd show him a few things, give him something to work on while he's down here."

The kid was sitting on his cot, watching me in the faint light. "Would you?" he asked.

"Sure. But first, we got to talk." His face fell. "All of us talk," I said. The kid brightened up at that.

I sat down, lit a smoke. "First of all, we got to get us some breathing room. The cops still want you guys—we got to make that right."

"Roll on in?" Virgil asked. Ready for it, if that's what it had to be.

"I think so. The detective, the one who came to your house . . . the one who scammed you into waiting till his partner came up with a search warrant . . . ?"

"Sherwood, he said his name was. Don't know if it was first or last. Sherwood."

"How'd he strike you?"

Virgil gave it some thought, rolling it around in his mind. Knowing this wasn't casual conversation to kill time. Doing time teaches you the difference.

"Smart."

"Straight?"

"Yeah, I think so. There's all kindsa dope money in Gary. I heard something about him. He was up there, got in some beef with the bosses about shaking down crack houses. But the way I heard it, he was just too rough on the dealers, not grafting."

"You got a lawyer? For Lloyd?"

"Yeah. Bart Bostick. I got his name from one of the guys I play with in Chicago."

"You talk to him since you went to ground?"

"No."

I dragged on my cigarette, thinking. "I can contact him easy enough. Give him some references. We need someone to go in the middle for us. Make a come-in deal with a walk-away in front, okay? You and Lloyd surrender, they got to cut you loose even if they hold Lloyd."

"Let 'em hold me."

"It won't fly, Virgil. You're on a minor league thing and they know it. Besides, I need you out on the street. I don't know my way around out here."

"You already did your part, brother. You did what I needed you for. Lloyd, he didn't do this thing. That's enough for me. His family, we'll take it from here."

"What good is that? You know Lloyd didn't do it. Me too. So what? So he goes to jail and you all wait for him. Keep enough money on the books for him to stay in smokes? There's going to be a trial. They don't have much, but maybe they got enough. Lloyd's got no alibi and he looks good enough. Maybe not good, but good enough, you understand? They want a sniper, big time. He wouldn't be the first man to go down for something he didn't do."

"What's left?"

"Lloyd didn't do it, somebody did. There's a sniper-rapist out there."

"You could find him?"

"Remember what you called me for. I don't know who he is, Virgil, but I know what he is."

"It's not yours." The kid spoke up. "Like Uncle Virgil said, it's family. I'm family. I didn't do it. But I've been talking to Uncle Virgil. I know what it takes. I won't disgrace my people—I done enough of that already."

"Who asked you?"

"Mr. Burke." The kid's voice was steady now. Not deeper, but stronger. Growing into his lines. "I don't mean no disrespect. I know what you did for me. Like Uncle Virgil promised me—you'd find the truth . . . make it come out. My part's now . . . I'll go to trial. Stand up. Like I'm supposed to."

"Yeah. You *want* to go to jail, Lloyd? Make it right? Your uncle Virgil ever tell you how he came to do time?"

"Burke!"

"Hey, let me tell him, Virgil. You been pushing the truth like it's cocaine. You got the boy high on it."

"Whatever I did, it's long dead. It's the past—this is now."

"What you did, you didn't have choices at the time, right? The way you saw it? We got some choices now. More cards to play." I turned to face the kid. "Your uncle, he stabbed a man. A man who needed killing. The reason's not important now—what I told you is the truth. But Virgil, he did the same thing today, he'd maybe have enough sense to know he didn't *have* to go to prison. See, your uncle, he didn't want the whole truth to come out . . ."

Virgil got to his feet. Lit a smoke, watching me closely. Not trying to stop it now.

"Listen close, Lloyd. Your aunt Rebecca, she knew a man back home. A bad man, with ugliness inside him. Rebecca met Virgil. And she started her life over. The way people got a right to, okay? She came to Chicago. She and Virgil, they got together. Got married. Virgil was working, this man came around to see Rebecca. She told him to get lost. But he kept coming back. He put some pressure on her. Virgil, you know him, he's a proud man. And Rebecca, she knew how proud a man he was. She wasn't thinking of herself, just of him. So when this other guy came back with some pictures . . . pictures she thought would hurt Virgil . . . he gave her a choice . . . get back together with him or he'd go to Virgil. You understand?''

The kid nodded, laser-focused on my voice, nothing else in the room for him.

"Rebecca stabbed him. A whole bunch of times. Virgil came home in the middle of it. Nobody knows whether he finished the job or if the man was dead when he walked in the door. Rebecca told the police she did it. Virgil told them it was his work. They kept it in their family—never told the Man the real truth. Never even tried to bring it in front of a jury. And Virgil went to prison."

I tapped a cigarette filter on my thumbnail. Virgil stood against the wall.

"What could they've done?"

"Who knows? I wasn't there. Put the body in a Hefty bag, throw it in the trunk of the car, take it to the city dump. Chop it into little pieces and feed it down the drain in the bathtub. Carry him up to the roof and leave him there. Pack their clothes, dump gasoline all over the body, and leave the Arson Squad to figure it out. Whatever. It doesn't matter. You try something, it don't work, you're no worse off, see? But Virgil, all he thought about was protecting Rebecca . . . and Rebecca, all she wanted to do was take the weight on herself. They never even got their stories straight, they was so busy confessing on themselves."

"Virgil was a . . ."

"A what? A hero? A chump? Who knows . . . all we know is he was a convict."

"I . . ."

"Yeah, he's so family-crazy, this was some regular killing he thought you did, he'd probably walk down to the police, tell them he did it. Like he did before."

"I wouldn't let him."

"Take a look, kid. Look at your uncle. You think you could stop him?"

The kid looked. Saw the steel Virgil used for bone marrow. "What d'we do?"

"What we do is, we make some plans. Work the angles. It doesn't play, you can always go to jail. They're always open for business."

"Uncle Virgil . . . ?"

"Lloyd, from now on, you just call me Virgil. A man don't call another man *uncle* anything, okay?"

A smile flashed across the kid's face. Then it was gone. His face hardened, jaw tightened. Shoulders straightened. Getting ready for it. "Okay," is all he said.

▓ 40

I CALLED BART Bostick's office the next morning. His secretary got him on the line when I told her I couldn't give my name.

"This is Bostick."

"Mr. Bostick, my name is Burke. I'm from New York. You're representing a boy named Lloyd. The kid charged with those sniper killings. There's been a change of plans. I need to come in, talk to you about it. Before I do that, you need to know who I am, whether you can trust me. My lawyer's name is Davidson. He's in New York. Manhattan. And the boy's aunt, Rebecca, if you'll go by and see her . . . don't call her on the phone . . . she'll tell you too. If you can do this today, I'll come by and see you tomorrow afternoon, okay?"

"You didn't give me your lawyer's phone number."

"I figured you'd want to look it up yourself. Maybe in Martindale-Hubbell. Make some calls yourself first. Know who you're talking to."

☙ 41

IT'S ME," I told the hum on the phone line. It didn't answer. "Tell the Prof to go and see McGowan. Get a number where I can call him tomorrow night—anytime he says. And have the Prof leave a number with you too. I need to talk to him."

The hum hung up.

☙ 42

I LOOKED AT more racetrack sites until lunchtime. Found one that looked good. Stock-car track at Illiana, right on U.S. 30. In Schererville, close enough to Virgil's house so I could be in the neighborhood.

The Lake County Public Library was on the same highway. Ultra-modern, all glass. The young black woman at the reference desk showed me where to find the back issues of the *Post-Tribune* on microfiche. I scrolled through. Whenever I came across a story on the sniper killings, I pushed the button for a copy. My attaché case was stuffed by the time I left.

◗ 43

THAT NIGHT, WE started Lloyd's survival school.

Virgil taped the kid's hands from wrists to knuckles. Slapped a wide band across Lloyd's mouth.

"That's to teach you to breathe through your nose," I told him. "When you get scared, you breathe through your mouth—take in too much air. It helps you panic. That's *not* what we want, okay?"

The kid nodded, watching.

"You're going to start on this heavy bag. No jabs. That's okay for the ring, not for inside. Hooks. That's all we want. Both hands. Nothing to the head. Everything to the body. Stand close. We want a hundred punches in a row. Without stopping. You're not going to get it right away—it takes time. But a hundred punches. *Real* punches. That's what we're working for."

Virgil stood behind the heavy bag, steadying it with his hands. The kid walked over to it, drew a deep breath through his nose, fired a left hook, a right, another left. His arms dropped—he was out of breath.

I put my hands on the back of his shoulders. He was cov-

ered with sweat under the T-shirt. "Don't take a big breath
and hold it. Nice shallow breaths. In and out. You stop
breathing, you stop punching, okay?"

He nodded, weak but game.

"And stand *closer*, Lloyd. You'll always be fighting bigger guys. Get close so their arms reach over your shoulders."
Virgil left the bag, came over to stand in front of me. He was
taller. I stepped into him, face against his chest, dropping
my shoulders, hooked toward his body in slow motion. Virgil's long arms reached past me, hands slapping against my
back.

Lloyd nodded. Stepped into the heavy bag, firing hooks,
right, left, right, over and over. This time he went a good
fifteen seconds before he ran out of gas. The kid raked air
into his nose, holding his stomach.

"Much better," I told him. "But stop punching with your
arms. You're doing this . . ." I stood in front of the bag, feet
planted, launched a hook as I twisted my shoulder into the
punch. The bag popped. "That look pretty good to you?" I
asked him.

He nodded, eyes sharp on the target.

"Looks don't get it in a fight," I told him. "That was an
arm punch. Like you've been throwing. The power comes
from here." Putting my thumbs on my hip bones, fingers
spraying down to my upper thighs. Twisting my hips in slow
motion as I got off another hook. "See? Turn your hip into
the punch—what you got from the waist up isn't enough to
really *drive*, all right? Watch . . ." I double-hooked the bag
with my left hand, popped in a right, switched back to the
left. Virgil nodded approval.

Lloyd came back to the bag, stepped in, and launched a
jet-stream hook from somewhere around his ankles. Virgil
pushed the bag against him as the blow landed and Lloyd hit
the floor. He jumped to his feet and swung even harder. This

time he stayed on his feet, but he was so off-balance he couldn't throw another punch. I went back to work.

"Plant your feet. Spread 'em apart. Yeah, that's it . . . a little more. Don't punch *at* the bag, punch *through* it. Yeah! *Drive* those shots, Lloyd! Balance, balance." I kept my hands on his hips, not letting him get too far out of alignment. "Alternate the punches. Double up on the left. *Drive*, damn it! Drop down with those shots—lower. There's no below-the-belt crap where you're going. Don't be admiring your work, *drive*!"

The kid staggered forward, face green. I ripped the tape off. Vomit rushed out. Virgil wiped him off with a damp rag. Patting him on the back. "You doin' good, Lloyd. I *felt* those punches, son. Hit the showers, okay?"

The mountain man looked at me. "He was throwing up inside that tape . . . never even thought about ripping it off himself."

"He'll get it. He's got the hate, just needs some technique."

"He's one of us," Virgil said. Pride in his voice.

44

TRAINING A FIGHTER isn't all inside the ring.

"How much time we got?" Virgil asked me.

"I'm seeing the lawyer tomorrow. Tomorrow night, I'll make a call to the city. Ask this cop I know if he'll front me some references. It all comes together, it's time for Lloyd to come in.''

"We're good here till forever. Just say the word.''

When Lloyd came back inside, we started on the hard part.

⚓ 45

PRISON'S NOT LIKE jail,'' I told Lloyd. "Prison, there's nobody coming to the gate with bail money. You're down for a long time. You count the days. Some guys, they got too much time to count for themselves, so they look to take a piece of yours."

The kid nodded, focused like he'd never been in school.

"It's like the street, only . . . compressed, you got it? Everything happens close up. There's no place to go. No place to hide. So you give nothing away. Nothing. Never. Look down or look hard. Your face stays flat. You don't smile, you don't cry. And you protect your space . . . the space you carry around with you . . . the space around your body.''

"Don't take nothing from nobody,'' Virgil put in. "Nothing good, nothing bad. Inside, it's all the same. Guy offers you a smoke—no, thanks. Guy tells you the only way to get along is get down on your knees, you don't argue with him—you got to hurt him. Before he finishes the sentence. Right then.''

"The counselors . . .''

"Guards, son. Hacks, screws, cops . . . don't matter what you call them. But they ain't no *counselors* inside. What a counselor does, you tell him this booty bandit got your name on his list, he asks you maybe you want to *talk* about it. You talk about it, you end up in PC. Protective Custody. Only it ain't protected, just custody. Close custody. Like solitary."

"Okay."

My turn. "There's three ways to survive inside, Lloyd. Remember what the Prof used to say, Virgil? Cold, crazy, or connected—that's the only way to play."

"I miss that man."

"Who's the Prof?" the kid wanted to know.

"He's this little black dude," Virgil told him. "Tiny. Got the magic in him. Like some preachers got." I felt Lloyd stiffen. If Virgil noticed, he didn't show it, continuing on in the same voice. "Most of the time, he talked in rhyme." The mountain man chuckled. "Like I guess I just did. He's been jailing since they made jails. I never had much truck with black folks till I went down. Didn't hate them or anything, like some did where I'm from. Just never knew one to really talk with, understand? Anyway, the Prof, it's short for Professor. Or Prophet. He's a truth-teller. And a fearless little maniac, I'll swear that to anyone. He's the one who schooled Burke. Used to call him 'schoolboy' when Burke would act the fool."

"You?" Lloyd looked at me.

Virgil laughed. "Yeah, this hard-case was a young fool once. Had to learn. Like you learning now."

"What do I do?"

"When you get inside," I said, "look around. Pick one out. They'll all challenge you, give you those hard looks, try to back you down with their eyes. Even the weasels'll try it, not knowing you. Pick one out, like I said. Watch his eyes. You'll smell it on him. Coward. Hard in a pack, nothing by himself. Then you walk up to him, ask him if he got a problem with anything. He drops his eyes, mumbles something, you let it slide. Anything else, *any* fucking thing else, you move your left hand fast at the waist, then come overhand with the right. Aim it right at the side of his neck. And *drive* it. He goes down, don't wait for him to get up, get your foot into his ribs, quick. Don't stop until they pull you off. Don't think about it. That's what you do. What you got to do.''

"What if . . . ?"

"There's no 'if' here, kid. What if you go to solitary for a few days? What if they write something down in a report? Don't matter. When they let you back out, they'll wonder. Maybe you're crazy. That's okay. Maybe you're just a cold young man. That's okay too. And while they're thinking about it, they're gonna find out you're connected too.''

"Me?"

"Yeah. When you were in, who was the barn boss?"

"Barn boss?"

"The duke. The head man. Every joint's got one, especially the kiddie camps. The baddest guy there. Come on.''

"Oh, you mean . . . like, one of the residents."

"They got such fancy names for stuff now, don't they, brother?" Virgil's chuckle didn't reach his eyes.

"Lloyd," I said patiently, "residents, they're people who stay in hotels, okay? Now, who was the boss inside?"

"Hightower. I never knew his first name. Big black guy. One of the kids told me he was in for a homicide. In a drug deal.''

"The others, they get out of his way when he walks?"

"Oh yes."

"He only hang with blacks? Is it a racial thing?"

"I don't know. I wasn't . . ."

"That's okay. When you go back inside, you find out. This Hightower's still in charge, he got transferred, he got himself replaced by some other boy, it doesn't matter. You just let us know.''

"Okay.''

♖ 46

I CHECKED MY messages before I went back to the motel. Nothing. Virgil would keep the boy up until first light, working. I closed my eyes, asking for Belle to come back to me in the only way she ever could.

After a while, I slept.

♖ 47

I GAVE MY name to the receptionist at Bostick's. "He's been expecting you," she said, pointing down a dark carpeted corridor.

The sign on his office said Private. I knocked. Davidson opened the door.

"Mr. Bostick?" I asked. Nothing showed in my face.

Davidson laughed, turned to a short, Roman-faced, slim

man seated at a kidney-shaped white plastic desk. "Pay up," he said.

Bostick slid a hundred-dollar bill across the clean surface of the desk. Stood up, offered his hand.

I shook hands, sat down, lit a smoke. Davidson's foul cigar was burning in a deep glass ashtray.

"Bart called me. I wasn't too busy, so I thought I'd fly out, see if there was something we could put together."

I bowed my head slightly. Just enough. "Much appreciated."

"Where are we?" Bostick asked.

"Lloyd didn't do it," I told him. "We need to know how it looks for him, he comes in and surrenders. And what the Man wants with Virgil, he comes in too."

"If the kid comes in, I can work bail for him again. Take a couple-few days. The rifle they found in his room, it bounced. No connect to the murders. What they got is a kid with a porno collection, a loner who prowls around at night. Maybe a peeper," he continued, watching my face.

"I know."

"And they got a couple of kids that were out one night. Some statements our boy may have made about killing people in parked cars."

"He's a juvenile in this jurisdiction?" Davidson asked.

"Doesn't matter," Bostick replied. "Homicide's an adult offense. Here, he gets bound over for the Grand Jury no matter how old he is."

"That's good."

Bostick nodded agreement. "Yeah, a jury won't go for all this collection of crap, but a Juvenile Court judge . . . you know how they are."

I did. "You going to push it to trial?" I asked.

"It's still a crap-shoot. If this boy didn't do it, somebody did. Better to hold off, see if they make another arrest."

"They're looking?"

"I don't think so. Not most of them anyway. This one detective, Sherwood, he's got a lot on the ball. I think he knows Lloyd isn't the one. But the cops . . . they want to *close* cases, not solve them."

"Virgil?"

Bostick smiled. "We've been talking that one over. The way I see it, Virgil was out looking for Lloyd. The poor kid got scared and ran off. Virgil found him, brought him in. He should get a medal, right? I don't think they'll hold him."

"Good. You know this Detective Sherwood?"

"A bit," he said cautiously.

"Enough so you could get me a talk with him?"

"Maybe."

I dragged on my smoke. "I don't want to buy him. I want to give him whoever did this."

"You?"

"Didn't Davidson tell you? Nobody knows these freaks better than me."

"We discussed your credentials."

"I got other references."

"I'm sure you do. But . . ."

"The human who did this, he's not some lonely, scared kid who likes to look at pictures. The guy you want, he's a sex-sniper."

"A what?"

"Sex-sniper. A guy who gets sexual satisfaction from penetrating his victims at a distance. The rifle's his cock. The bullets are his sperm. Bang bang, you're fucked."

"How d'you . . . ?"

"Berkowitz . . . Son of Sam, remember? Apparently motiveless shootings. Girls alone. Or a guy and a girl together. That Zodiac freak on the Coast. That maniac in Buffalo. They're out there, and they play to a pattern."

"I never . . ."

"There was a case a lot like this one a few years back, somewhere in upstate New York."

"Is this kind of research a hobby of yours?"

"It's my work. And how I stayed alive this long."

Davidson nodded agreement, watching the Indiana lawyer. "Burke knows freaks like nobody else, Bart. In New York, even the cops admit that."

"You could find him?"

"I think so. Maybe. I know where to look."

"Where?"

"Where you can't look. That's why I may want to buy some slack from this detective, if he'll play."

"I'll ask him."

I got up to leave. "Okay. Virgil and Lloyd, they'll be ready to come in soon, maybe a few more days. I'll get word to you in front, you'll handle the surrender?"

"Sure. The bail . . ."

I opened my attaché case. "There's twenty-five K in here. Take what's left over as a front on your fee."

"You want a receipt?"

"I got one," I told him. Shook hands with Davidson and walked out.

⚜ 48

MCGOWAN ANSWERED THE phone on the first ring.

"It's me," I told him. "I'm in Indiana, just outside Gary. Working on a case. A sex-sniper, real ugly freak. My brother's cousin is a suspect. I'm looking for the real hitter. There's a detective out here, name of Sherwood. If I give him your name and number, will you go for me?''

''What's that mean?''

''Tell him what I am. What I'm not.''

''Okay, pal. He might not like what he hears.''

''I'll chance it. Out here, I'm Mitchell Sloane, okay?''

McGowan's honey-Irish voice came through the line. ''Tell him to call. I'm not in, I'll get back to him.''

''Thanks.''

He hung up.

W 49

DRIVING OVER TO the hideout that night, little tongues of flame licked at my insides. Not my old friend. Not fear. Not yet. I knew why I came to Indiana. Did what I came for. What my brother asked. I knew the Sociopath's Song by heart. Travel light and you travel fast.

But you got nothing when you get there.

I knew the man who was out there. Out there in the dark, shadow-stalking, licking his lips, directing his porno movies through a telescopic sight. Making them into snuff films.

I didn't owe it to anyone to hang around, see this thing through.

And if I owed it to myself, I didn't want to know why.

▼ 50

THE SPORTING-GOODS STORE had a good supply of boxing equipment. I ignored the rifles stacked against the far
wall, concentrating on what I needed for now.

When I got inside the hideout, I dumped the duffel bag
out on the floor. Told Virgil we'd all be going in soon.

He nodded, looking at the boxing gloves lying on the cement. "He's been beating the hell out of that heavy bag. We
gotta know the rest."

The rest. Punching bags don't punch back. If Lloyd was
going to quit, we needed to know. Now.

"Let's do it," I said.

I waved Lloyd over. "We're going to spar some now, kid.
See how those hooks of yours work when someone's trying
to block them, okay?"

Lloyd held out his hands for the gloves, head down. Hes-
itant.

"What's wrong, boy?" Virgil's voice was quiet, steady.

"What if I hurt Burke?"

Virgil's laugh had relief in it. "Hell, son, you couldn't . . ."

I stepped on his words. "You won't be able to hurt me,
Lloyd. It looks like I'm in trouble, Virgil'll pull you off quick
enough."

He nodded. I wrapped the Ace bandage over one hand.
Held out the other for Virgil. "Not too tight," I told him.

The top of the kid's head came about to my chin. I banged

114

the gloves together, rolled my shoulders, rotated my neck on its column, getting ready.

Lloyd was still watching me closely when I shot a sharp jab into his chest. He grunted, backed up, and I slid my left foot forward, hooked to his gut, chopped him down with a short right to the jaw.

The kid hit the ground, came up swinging, trying to get his face buried in my chest. I caught a double left hook on my right forearm, fired a return shot under his heart as he dropped his arm. He went down again.

He came up slower this time, face flushed. I flicked a jab in his face. It bounced off his cheek as he came forward, head lowered, butting at my chin. He dropped his left shoulder but fired with his right, catching me right at the belt line. I grabbed the back of his neck with my right glove, pulled his face into my left fist. Something squished. He hit me a half dozen hammer shots to the ribs, pushing forward, shoulders working.

Virgil pulled him off. The kid's face was bleeding, blood bubbling around his nose as he sucked in air. I sat down on the floor. Virgil raised Lloyd's hand in the air, his hard-coal voice a parody of a ring announcer. "Referee stops contest at two minutes and fifteen seconds of the first round. The fighter from New York is unable to continue. A TKO for the man from Kentucky. *Llllloyd!*"

☥ 51

LATER THAT NIGHT, we told Lloyd about the joint. "You
remember the guy we called Astro?" I asked Virgil. I felt a
laugh bubble in my chest, thinking back. "That fat dude with
the long hair in on a transfer from another *federale* joint?"

"I guess. Never spoke to him much."

"Yeah. Well, anyway, this guy Astro . . . he used to live
in this giant hippie commune. All they did was harvest grass,
drop acid, play music, and ball. Sounded good, hear him tell
it. One day one of the other hippies, Jonah, he drops about
a quart of LSD. Goes right to the moon. Sits there staring
into space, not talking, not eating. Out of it. And he stays
like that for *days*, okay? So they have a meeting, all the
hippies. What they decide to do is send someone to visit this
guy Jonah, find out how he's doing. This one chump gets
elected. Astro says the chump takes exactly the same dose as
this guy Jonah, and he goes into the same exact trance. Now
the fucking hippies got *two* guys who need a CAT scan. So,
naturally, they call another meeting. Meanwhile, the second
guy, he comes out of the nod and walks into the tent. They
all crowd around him. Ask him if he got to see Jonah. So
this other hippie, he tells them: 'Hey, I saw Jonah. He's cool
right where he is. Says to leave him alone, stop bothering
him.' "

Virgil chuckled, remembering. "Whatever happened to
Astro?"

116

"You got me, brother. He made parole and that was it. He went back to his life. But, whatever, he found his way to do the time, right? On another planet."

Virgil gave the kid a beer. Took one himself.

"This guy we're looking for . . . he's a monster, right? Like the Prof told us that one time. Remember, brother, when we were all locked down after that rumble on the yard?"

He turned to Lloyd. "We didn't have no TV in the hole. No radios, no books, nothing. So every night, the Prophet, he'd tell us stories. One night it'd be about women. He'd tell you about watching a stripper and I swear to God you could *see* the girl working, right on your cell wall. Or he'd tell us about some hustle he pulled off. Or about old-time guys, *real* cons, back when a good thief was something to be proud of. One night, he told us about the legend. That was the first time I knew what a monster was."

I closed my eyes, remembering, hearing the Prof's voice.

Myths and monsters.

❚ 52

VIRGIL'S VOICE INTERRUPTED the memories, like he was plugged into my thoughts. "Yeah, what a man he was. Sure helped me become one."

The kid's voice was tight with wonder. "How do you get that?"

"What you mean, Lloyd?"

"I mean . . . what makes a man? A real man." Questions only a kid can ask from his heart. Like knowing is all there is to it. I was thinking about how to tell the kid about Michelle, when Virgil met it straight on. "Same thing that makes a real woman, son. After the storm, all you got is the foundation."

❦ 53

SOME OF THE bounce was missing from Cyndi as she came up to take my order.

"You have a pay phone somewhere around?" I asked her.

"Maybe you need somebody to show you a phone, huh?"

I took a drag of my cigarette, waiting.

She put her palms on the table, leaned forward. "You never called me."

"No. I'm going to be pulling out soon. Finish my work. You're a fine woman, Cyndi. Not the kind a man plays with. I'm not your ticket out of here. No point throwing beautiful flower seeds on concrete."

"I never asked you for promises."

"You don't have to ask. I respect you too much not to be asking myself."

She slid into the seat across from me. "That's a sweet goodbye."

"It's not goodbye, girl. It's just . . . a girlfriend's not what I need right now. And I'm sure not what you need anyway.

There's something out there for you a lot better than whatever I am, okay?''

"You think I'll get out?"

"I know you will."

"That's what Blossom says. You know what that old girl told me the other day? She said I was smart enough, I should go to college."

"You think that's nuts?"

"I did at first. But, I don't know. I had a boyfriend once. A guy I met at the club. He was an accountant. Told me I had a real head for numbers. And he wasn't playing . . . I know when a man's playing."

"Then you know I'm not, right?"

Her smile flashed. "Right."

"Friends?"

She slid out of the booth, gave me a quick kiss on the cheek, wiggled off to give Leon the order.

Blossom walked by. Nodded gravely at me. Like I'd done the right thing. I watched the set of her shoulders, the line of her jaw. Knowing I'd seen it before, somewhere.

◊ 54

WE BROUGHT LLOYD in that Monday. Bostick met us at the police station. Introduced me as a private investigator from his office. Mitchell Sloane is a versatile man.

They charged Lloyd with bail jumping. Remanded him, set a hearing down for Wednesday.

Sherwood was there. Big man, round face, mostly skull on top. Ham hands, sausage fingers. Khaki suit, clip-on tie, walking shoes. Dumb the way a bear is slow—he wouldn't turn up the flame unless he had something to burn.

Sherwood gravely thanked Virgil for finding Lloyd. Said he did the right thing, his voice neutral, not empty. Pick what you want.

Virgil shook his hand, nodded. Watchful.

We stepped onto the sidewalk. I pulled Bostick aside. "You get what I wanted?" I asked him.

"Hightower. Jefferson James Hightower. Seventeen years old. Honcho'ed a crack posse in Gary. Allegedly shot a *chulo* from one of the Chicago Latin gangs when they tried to move on his territory. Doing real well for himself, moving up in the organization. Registry shows him owning a Nissan Maxima and a Kawasaki Ninja cycle. Only family is his mother. She lives over in the Delaney Street Projects. Visits him about three times a week."

"Thanks."

"See you in court."

▌55

VIRGIL DROVE THE Lincoln through the streets parallel to Broadway. He crossed the avenue, approaching from the Gary side. I gave him a look. "Downwind," is all he said.

Big sign dominated the wide street: MONEY TO LOAN •

NEED JACK? SEE JACK! The pawnshop was half a city block. I wondered if they sold guns, make it a one-stop shop.

The neighborhood was full of hand-painted signs for locksmiths, bottle clubs, custom car washing—no machines. Black men on the corners, watching like they watch in every city.

The Projects were a series of brick attached one-story homes. We found the number two blocks in from Harrison Street—the Maxima was parked out front.

I left Virgil in the car. Knocked on the door. A solidly built black woman answered.

"Yes, sir?" Eyes wary.

"Mrs. Hightower, my name is Sloane. I'm a private investigator. I work for Mr. Bart Bostick, the criminal defense lawyer . . ."

She nodded, waiting.

"I'm investigating a case. You know those sniper killings? Those teenagers who got killed over by the dunes, in that lovers' lane?"

"I don't know nothin' about . . ."

"Oh, I know you don't, ma'am. But I was hoping your son . . . James . . . hoping he might be of some help."

"How?"

"Well, we heard a rumor that the boy who did it might be locked up in the same jail as James. And a boy like that, you know he can't be right in the head. So I thought, James, he might have heard something . . ."

"He never said nothin' to me."

"Oh, I'm sure he wouldn't, ma'am. I'll be going down to the jail to talk with him and I just wanted to show the proper respect . . . speak to his mother first. See, you need to sign this Consent Form for me to get in"—taking what Bostick had given me out of my attaché case—"your son being a minor and all. It just says I'm working on his case. And I wanted to leave this with you"—holding up a thick white envelope where she could see it—"as a token of our re-spect."

She felt the outside of the envelope. Took the pen I gave her and signed the form.

"Please tell James I'll be by to see him," I said. Leaving the envelope in her hands.

People watched from their front stoops. Looked away when I watched them.

⫸ 56

THE NEXT MORNING, I took Main to Ninety-third, pulled in at the Lake County Juvenile Detention Center. Solid brick, cop cars parked in front. Parking lot half full. High chain link fence around the grounds, loops of razor wire across the top. They all look the same.

I showed the Consent Form to the woman on duty behind a glass wall. She asked for some ID, picked up the phone.

I read the signs while I was waiting. Visiting Hours. Rules and Regulations.

A slim, handsome black man came through a side door.

"Mr. Sloane?"

"Yes."

"You're here to see Hightower, I understand. We're full up here, so we don't have a visiting room. We usually use the cafeteria, but the boys are eating now. Visiting hours aren't until ten. But we always try to accommodate attorneys here. You're working for Mr. Bostick?"

"That's right."

"Didn't know he was handling Hightower's case. I'll have to make a couple of phone calls. Be with you in just a minute."

He left me sitting there. A careful man.

Not ten minutes later, he was back. "I'll let you use my office. You'll have complete privacy. Just open the door when you're done, give a call down the corridor."

"Thank you."

A guard brought Hightower in. I stood up, shook hands with him. He went along like he knew the play, took a seat. The guard left.

His head was elongated, forceps marks visible just past his temples, framing small eyes with a yellowish cast. They were bright and flat, like a lizard's. "Who you?"

"My name is Sloane."

"What you want?"

"I want to do something for you, Mr. Hightower. I heard you were a man who knew how to act."

"What's that mean?"

I leaned forward, lighting a smoke, leaving the pack on the desk between us. "You know how the new kids come in this joint. Scared and all? You being the top man, I guess you get to make your pick."

"Maybe."

"Now, some of these kids, you pick them to be your running buddies. And some you pick to play with, right? The weak ones."

"I ain't into that shit, man."

"Of course you're not. Anyone can see you don't play that way. But there's guys in here that do. And they don't do nothing without an okay from the Man, right?"

A quick smile. "Right."

"I wouldn't want you to make a mistake, Mr. Hightower.

A man has to know who his friends are, right? Now, I'm a private investigator. And I'm looking for somebody.''

"Who?''

"I'm looking for the freak who sniper-snuffed those kids in lovers' lane.''

"So why you here?''

"Because he may be in here too. Maybe he's here for something else. And maybe he's got a big mouth, see?''

"Yeah. Yeah, I see.''

"So you hear something, you let me know. And it's worth some cash.''

"How much cash?''

"Ten large.''

"I make that in a week on the street, man.''

"You not *on* the street, pal. You're in the jailhouse. Way I hear it, you're going to be here for quite some time. I know how things work in here. You don't want the money, say so. But let me tell you something else too. Remember what I told you about knowing who your friends are? I'm your friend. A good friend. That's what I told your mother.''

"My *mother*? Man, if you . . .''

"I paid her a visit. A nice, respectful visit. And I left her five hundred bucks for you. A token of my respect. Because I'm your friend.''

He lit one of my cigarettes, cold as a seventeen-year-old life-taker, but not cool. Letting it show. I went on in the same quiet, soft tone, eyes on his.

"I got another friend in here, Mr. Hightower. His name is Lloyd. He was here before. Just came in again yesterday. They won't let him into population until tomorrow. White kid, about your height, a little bit shorter. Slim build, black hair.''

"I know him.''

"Yeah. Any friend of mine is a friend of yours, understand? I never let anything happen to my friends. I know what to do if something does.''

"You want me to look out for this white boy?" he sneered.

I leaned forward, close to his face. Dropped my voice to a whisper. "I want you to look out for your*self*, okay? I went to see your mother—left her some cash. Anything happens to my friend, I figure maybe I made a mistake about you. Maybe you're not my friend like I thought. That happens, I'll go see your mother again.''

His eyes were unvarnished hate. I held them. Let him see the truth. Right down to the deep spot where the blood-spill starts.

⚜ 57

BOSTICK WAS RELAXED in the courtroom. Wearing one of those slouchy Italian suits over highly polished black boots. Not lazy, staying within himself. Like a good host at a party. Virgil and Rebecca were in the front row, dressed in their church clothes. I sat next to Bostick at the counsel table.

The judge was a youngish man, light brown hair carefully combed to one side, face already starting to pudge from the rewards of honest living. The ADA was the kind of guy who spends his life going through the motions and never gets good at it. The kind of guy who screws something up so many times they call him experienced.

The kind of fight you don't waste your time fixing.

A reporter from the *Post-Tribune* flipped open his pad. I

caught his eye. Whoever he was, he wasn't there to go through the motions.

"Your Honor," Bostick began, voice low and controlled. Hounds in check. "The purpose of bail is to ensure the defendant's presence at trial. The so-called evidence against my client does not aggregate to the weight of good gossip. The court knows full well that the totality of the prosecutor's case would not survive a probable-cause hearing. The crimes . . . they are horrible. Shocking to the conscience of the community. And the perpetrator surely deserves our worst condemnation. But, Your Honor, I respectfully suggest that the people of our community are ill served by illusion. The killer is not in this courtroom! As long as the press treats this case as solved, our people will sleep peacefully. But it will be the peaceful sleep of sheep who do not sense the presence of the wolf. Leads will dry up. People will not come forward and communicate with the police. If the court keeps Lloyd in jail, that time will be forever lost to him. When the killer is apprehended, all this court will be able to offer this boy is an apology. That is not the way we treat our citizens, Judge. We have been ready for the probable-cause hearing for weeks. Indeed, we are ready right at this moment. But the prosecutor's office has made no such attempt. If the police are satisfied with their investigation, let's have a trial. Let's have a trial, so my client can go home, to be with his family."

The ADA got to his feet, already exhausted. "Your Honor, the defendant *was* on bail. He jumped bail, disappeared. How can we be sure he'll show up when his trial starts?"

"He didn't jump bail," Bostick said in a mild voice. "The prosecutor knows better than that, Judge. The boy panicked. He was scared. But he never left town. All that really happened was he didn't show for an appointment with his probation officer. That was wrong, and Lloyd knows it was wrong. But remember, Your Honor, the boy's family put up his bail. And it was the boy's family who found him. And brought him right back to the police station. The only reason Lloyd is in custody right this minute is because he surrendered himself.''

The judge looked a question down from the bench. The prosecutor nodded. ''I'm going to continue bail in the same amount,'' the judge said. ''Mr. Bostick, your client understands that failure to keep one single appointment, failure to show for a single court appearance, and he's back inside. On remand, is that clear? No bail.''

''Understood, Your Honor.''

''Defendant is discharged. Same conditions of bail. Next case, please.''

The prosecutor was busy with some papers on his desk. Bostick went over to the clerk to sign Lloyd out as the kid went to stand with his family. The reporter walked by the defense table, gave me an interested glance, shrugged his shoulders when I didn't react, and went to file his story.

We came down the courthouse steps in two groups. Rebecca between Virgil and Lloyd, me next to Bostick. Detective Sherwood was leaning against the wall. He rolled his thick shoulders to push himself toward us. Virgil caught the movement, kept walking toward the car. Sherwood stepped in front of us.

''Mr. Bostick, I'd like to talk to your . . . investigator. That okay with you?''

Bostick turned to me. ''Sure,'' I said.

''Drop down to the precinct anytime,'' Sherwood said.

''Would you do me a favor first?''

''What?''

''A friend of mine, Detective McGowan. NYPD, Runaway Squad. I'll give you the number. Could you give him a call, kind of tell him what's going on out here?''

''Why would I want to do that?''

"Save you some time, okay? You want to talk to me, you want to know who you're talking to."

His eyes measured me. "Give me the number," he said.

⑴ 58

I STAYED AT Virgil's house only long enough for Lloyd to tell us he never got to use any of the stuff we taught him. He was sitting at the kitchen table, facing me and Virgil while Rebecca bustled around in the kitchen. Virginia and Junior were all over Lloyd, glad to see him—afraid he was going to go away again. Rebecca took them into the backyard to play.

"You remember that guy I told you about? Hightower? Well, as soon as I got out of that first-day isolation room they put you in, I went into the main room. Where the TV is. I was watching, like you told me. Watching their eyes. I was ready. This one black kid, I had him all picked out. Then Hightower walks in, comes right up to me. I was thinking, *damn!* I didn't want to start off with *this* boy, you know? But he comes over to me, says, 'Homeboy! When d'you raise, man?' Like we were pals forever. He sits next to me, runs down the whole place. Like which counselor . . . I mean, which *guard* you can get over on. The other guys, they see this, they don't know if Hightower's staking me out for himself or what. He puts his pack of smokes on the bench between us. I remembered what you said about not taking nothing. He leans over, whispers to me, says we got the same friends, don't worry. He had a visit. He described you, Burke. I mean, perfect. Like he knew you.''

I nodded. Hightower knew me. Better than Lloyd did.

''Anyway, later, at lunch, this other boy, big white kid, one of those skinheads, he reaches over, takes the cake right off my tray. I start across the table at him when I hear Hightower whisper, 'Chill, Lloyd. The Man!' and I see one of the guards coming down the aisle. The white boy smiles at me. Then Hightower tells him he wants to settle this later, come to the shower room after gym. Bring his shit. The white boy says this ain't Hightower's beef. Hightower says anyone messes with me, they got him to deal with. I reach over, take my cake back off the white boy's tray. Then I help myself to his piece too. Nobody says nothing. I did it right, Virgil?''

Virgil's smile was sad. ''Like you been doin' it all your life, son.''

The kids came back inside. Virginia sat down at the piano. Started pounding out the jangle-line of some country-blues song. Like her father. Junior sat next to his sister, his little hand on her shoulder. Rebecca watched over them. Virgil opened a beer for Lloyd. The kid left it untouched in front of him, knowing it was Virgil's way of telling his family Lloyd was a man now. Sacramental wine, not for drinking.

I knew it was time for me to go.

59

IT WAS LATE afternoon when I got back to the motel. Night work coming up—I lay down to rest. Slapped a cassette into the tape player Virgil lent me. "Got some of your girl on this, brother," he told me.

Judy Henske's voice charged out of the speakers, dominating the dingy room the way she overworked every club she'd ever played. Her early stuff. "Wade in the Water." Making the gospel song into a blue-tinted challenge. When they say a prizefighter hits and holds, they're talking about a dirty tactic. Like we taught Lloyd. Henske, she hits and holds those notes until they turn into beauty past what you can see with your eyes. What you feel. What she makes you feel. A channel to the root.

There was more on the tape. Bonnie Raitt. Henske's spiritual sister, like Henske was Billie Holiday's. "Give It Up." Working that slide guitar like the critics said a woman never could.

When Raitt got to singing "Guilty," I felt Belle's loss so hard I couldn't get a clean breath. I'd paid off her debts, but it didn't set me free. My soul jumped the tracks and it took a monster and a witch to save me.

It wasn't just a sex-sniper I was looking for in Indiana.

⚓ 60

I DRIFTED IN and out of sleep. Dreamed I was back in prison. The Olympics were on the TV in the rec room. 1972. The cons watched Olga Korbut twist herself into positions the *Kama Sutra* never imagined. Talking about what they'd do to her if they had her for a night. The little Russian girl was winning hearts all over the world, dancing and prancing, wiggling her teenage butt, waggling her fingers in special waves, smiling like she'd discovered purity.

The senior member of the Russian gymnastics team was a dark-haired beauty who'd been the leader for years—until right then, when Olga burst out. Lyudmila Turischeva. A proud woman, she knew it was time—time for the cubs to challenge the pack leader. When she walked out onto the mat, her shoulders were squared, chin up, eyes straight ahead. Arms moving at her sides like a soldier's. She knew she was up against it—the crowd was Olga's.

The other cons watched her hips, disappointed. I watched her eyes. She did her exercise perfectly. No flash, the fire banked. Then she turned and walked off, head high, going out with class.

A woman, not a girl.

I woke up knowing what I'd recognized in Blossom as she walked by.

⚓ 61

I DIDN'T NEED the real estate cover anymore, but I dropped by Humboldt's office just to keep the extra cards in my hand. He was out "viewing some properties." I left word that I was still around, still looking into our project.

Used the car phone to call Sherwood. Held on while they looked for him.

"This is Sloane. Did you speak to my friend?"

"Yes. Last night."

"Now a good time to come and see you?"

"A very good time."

"Okay. I'll pull up outside the station in about fifteen minutes. We'll go for a ride and talk, okay? I'm driving a . . ."

"I know your car. I'll be out front."

He hadn't seemed surprised I didn't want to sit around a police station—I guess he *had* talked to McGowan.

🖋 62

SHERWOOD CLIMBED IN the front seat, adjusting his bulk comfortably. "You show them a credit card, they'll rent you anything these days, huh?" Letting me know.

"Anyplace special you want me to drive?"

"You want to see where it happened? That last one?"

"Yeah."

"Take the left at the corner."

I followed the cop's directions until we came to a sign that said Naval Reserve Center. A couple of more blocks to the beach. A black man came over to my window, wearing a guayabera shirt, metal change-maker at his waist. "Two bucks for nonresidents," he said.

"Rest it, Rufus," Sherwood rumbled.

The change-maker looked across me to Sherwood, turned away without a word.

I pulled into the parking lot. Lake Michigan spread out before us. Only a few people on the beach, half a dozen cars in the lot.

I killed the engine, flicked the power window switch, lit a smoke. Waited.

"This is it," he said. "Victims were parked just about there"—pointing at the corner of the lot closest to the dunes. "We figure he took a position somewhere up around there"—pointing again. "No use trying that trajectory stuff—too many bullets."

"Kids still park here at night?"

"Yeah, they do. But over on the other side. Where there's no cover."

"Wouldn't need much at nighttime."

"No," he agreed, sadly.

I scanned the scene. A thousand places to shoot from, stationary, unsuspecting targets who couldn't shoot back, the cover of night. Surprise. A human-hunter's paradise.

"McGowan, that's your friend?" Sherwood asked.

"My friend. Not my brother, not my partner, okay? We've done some things together over the years."

"Want to know what he said about you?"

"Up to you."

"He said you got felony arrests for everything from hijacking to attempted murder."

"Not everything."

"Okay, he was clear about that. No rapes, no sex cases."

"No narcotics, no kids."

"Right."

"So now you know."

"He said you may have been a firearms dealer at one time. There's an FBI file on you for that. You took a federal fall for interstate transport, but it was only a couple of handguns. That's where you met your man Virgil, right?"

I nodded. That was back when the state joints were using the *federales* as a dumping ground, transferring cons all over the country. Bus therapy, they called it. They moved the Prof for preaching—race war is more to prison authorities' taste than brotherhood. I never did find out why Virgil came down as well.

"And a CIA file too—still open. Suspected mercenary."

"I was in Biafra," I said, watching him closely, "not Rhodesia."

"He told me. Said you cleaned up a real mess for them awhile back."

I dragged on my smoke.

"He said you make a living working the edge of the line. Finding missing kids, stinging kiddie-porn dealers, roughing off pimps."

"Any of those on your protected list?"

"No."

"So?"

"So you're a criminal. Not just an ex-con like your pal Virgil. A working criminal."

"McGowan tell you I know anything about freaks?"

"He said you know more than anyone he's ever met."

"You think Lloyd did the snipings?"

"Do you?"

"I know he didn't."

"Which means . . .?"

"Which means someone else did."

"Maybe."

"You got 'Exceptional Clearance' in this state?" I asked, challenging him. Sometimes the cops arrest a guy who didn't do the crime and mark it closed. Sometimes they know who did it but they can't make an arrest. Then they call it "Exceptional Clearance." The same tag they use when a baby-raper turns out to hold some political markers.

I flashed back on standing next to an old black woman in a cemetery. Watched as they put the little casket in the ground. Her grandson. Tortured to death. Scanning the crowd. Hoping the freak would want one last look at his work. The kid's mother was in jail. Crack. The old woman was bent over slightly at the waist from a hundred years of cleaning other people's houses. Her eyes were clear and hard. She'd offered me the money she'd put aside for the boy's college fund to find the killer. "The money was for Alexander, and the Lord knows he doesn't need it now."

Dirt rattled on the coffin. Her hand tightened on mine, holding herself rigid. "If God was going to make life so filthy, seems like he didn't have to make us dirty when we die."

My file was open.

Sherwood met my eyes. "Not for homicides. Not on my beat. I asked around, got the word about you. Do the same before you make your charges."

"I got it. I figured you hadn't closed the books on this one . . . that you're still looking. That's true, I want you to know I'm looking too. I don't want to step on your trail, give you the wrong idea."

"McGowan told me, some of the people you look for, they might not get found."

I tossed my cigarette out the window.

"Not around here," he said. Making it clear.

I nodded. "Will you show me what you got?" I asked him.

"The forensics?"

"Everything."

"Why not? It's not much."

"You got a profile?"

"Profile? One of those FBI things? Tell me the killer probably had an unhappy childhood or something? No, thanks."

"I got one."

"Where?"

"In here." I tapped the side of my head. "You've got this guy pegged as a loner, right?"

He nodded.

"He's alone inside himself. Where only freaks like him can go. But he may reach out, understand? Find people he can relate to."

"Like who?"

"Gun freaks. Survivalists. Like that. You got Nazis around here?"

"Like in the Klan?"

"Yeah."

"Sure."

"There'll be a connection. These freaks, they're all quasi-cops in their heads. Like to play soldier. Wear the clothes. Handle the toys."

"Quasi-cops?"

"You got cop buffs here, right? Got police scanners in the houses, join the auxiliary force, work as security guards . . . you know?"

"Yeah. We always look through that file when we got filth—a hooker killing. Or a kid raped."

"If this freak's looking for a group, that's where he'll look."

"Okay."

"You got a friend in the postal service?"

"What if I did?"

"Then I'd write out this list of magazines. And you'd ask your friend who gets them delivered."

He gazed out his window for a minute. Down into the ravine where they found the bodies. "Write out the list," he said.

It only took me a minute. Then I started the engine, backed out.

As we drove along Lake Street, Sherwood turned to me. "You carrying?"

"No."

I pulled over outside the precinct house at Broadway and Thirteenth to let him out. The big man nodded like he'd made up his mind about something. "Burke, that's your name, right? Burke, you're not the only one looking for this guy."

"I know."

"I don't mean me. Someone else came around, asking questions. Spoke to me."

"Who?"

"We're not there yet, you and me."

He closed the door with a snap of his wrist as he exited the car.

ῷ 63

THE NEXT MORNING, I picked up Virgil and Lloyd. Dropped Virgil off at the plant, said we'd pick him up at lunchtime.

Lloyd and I drove around for a few hours. I had him show me the high school, the woods, the dunes, lovers' lane. Questioned him about every kid he knew, trying to listen with *his* mind. Straining to hear the music, pick out the false notes.

If Lloyd had run across the sniper, he hadn't seen the shadow.

ῷ 64

I PULLED THE Lincoln into the diner parking lot. Walked in, Virgil and Lloyd close behind me. Virgil was back to himself, the worry-lines off his eyes. Like he was in the joint—

not asking questions, waiting and ready. Virgil slid in first, right across from me, leaving Lloyd on the corner.

Cyndi flounced up to the booth. "Hi, Mitch! These your friends?"

"My brother Virgil, and his nephew Lloyd."

"Pleased to meet you. Mitch, if Virgil is your brother . . . and Lloyd is his nephew, what's that make him to you?"

"Close enough," I said. Virgil laughed.

I had tuna. Virgil had burgers, fries, and a beer. Lloyd ordered exactly what Virgil did.

The jukebox came on. Jim Reeves. "He'll Have to Go."

A voice from a booth behind us. "Hey, get your ass over here! We ain't got all day."

Blossom walked past us, order pad in her hand. I turned. Her booth was full of greasy humans in biker-drag. Big fat slob on the end, wearing a denim jacket with the sleeves cut out over a T-shirt. Weaselly little guy in the middle. Two drones on the end.

I couldn't hear what they said. Blossom came past us again, two bright red dots on her cheeks.

Bonnie Tyler on the juke. "It's a Heartbreak."

Cyndi came back with the food. Leaned over. "See those slobs in the back booth? I told Blossom to watch out for them. Offered to take the table for her. Those boys are trouble."

Virgil peered over. "They don't look like trouble to me," he said.

Blossom came by, a tray in each hand.

I chewed the tuna slowly, thinking about my target.

A crash from the booth behind us. "Get your hands off me!" Blossom. I turned. The fat one had his hand under Blossom's skirt, laughing as she pounded at his face, warding her off easily with one hand.

Lloyd was out of the booth like he'd kicked in an afterburner. "Let her go!" Voice cracking and squeaky. Fatso flung Blossom aside with one hand, stood up just as Lloyd charged into him, face against the bigger man's chest, hands pumping like pistons on nitromethane. I whirled out of the booth, feeling Virgil on my back.

The fat man backed up under Lloyd's attack, grunting at the body-shots. The kid was holding his own until the fat man grabbed the boy's ears, butted him sharply in the face. Lloyd fell back, blood spurting. I grabbed a table with both hands, spun on my right foot, tilted my body parallel to the floor and shot my left boot into Fatso's ribs. He doubled over as I knife-edged my hand and chopped into his neck. Lloyd piled on, pounding with both hands.

The two guys on the other end started out of the booth just as Virgil slapped the nearest one with an open palm. It sounded like a rifle shot. Virgil flicked his hand. Bloody glass from the ashtray fell out.

The weasel-face in the middle got to his feet, back arched against the wall. His hand went to his pocket. Click of a switchblade. Smile twisting on his face. "Maybe you like to play with knives," he snarled, crouching and coming forward.

I backed off, giving him room, shrugging out of my jacket to wrap it around my hand.

"Try playing with this, boy!" Blossom's voice. A meat cleaver in her hand, face darkened with blood. Trying to push her way past me to get to the knife-man.

"That's all! Back up!" Leon. A double-barreled twelve-gauge in his hand.

The fat man got to his feet, breathing hard, one hand on his neck. "This ain't your beef, man," he said to Leon.

Leon held the shotgun steady. Said the most damning words in our language. "You ain't from around here. Get out. And don't come back."

They filed past us. Muttering threats they'd never make good on.

You ain't from around here. I'd heard that all my life. It was the first time I'd heard them shot at someone else.

We sat back down. Blossom and Cyndi cleaned up the mess. Leon sat by his cash register, watching. Cyndi switched over to him, gave him a big kiss. "You're a hero, Leon!" He turned red. Kept his eyes front.

Blossom brought some ice wrapped in a dish towel, held it against Lloyd's face. "You're quite a man," she said, her voice husky. The kid's chest swelled. She bent forward, kissed his forehead. Said "Thank you" in that same voice. And walked away.

Virgil looked over at Lloyd, chuckled, "Son, don't even be *thinking* about it."

"What?"

"One time, I was about your age, I saw this girl get slapped by her boyfriend on the street. I went over, told him to cut it out. We fought. He damn near beat me to death before they broke it up. Then one of my kin broke *him* up. Well, that girl gave me a kiss like you just got and I spent the rest of that summer looking for girls to rescue. There's easier ways, son."

He looked over at me. "But the boy sure as hell can hit, can't he, brother? Wasn't for that head butt, I figure Lloyd would've whipped him straight up."

"No question about it."

Jack Scott on the jukebox. "My True Love."

Blossom came back with a little penlight. Tenderly lifted the dish towel from Lloyd's face. He didn't make a sound. She could have done brain surgery on the kid without anesthetic.

She shined the light into his eyes, asked him some questions. Checking for a concussion. She hadn't been a waitress all her life. "You're going to need a few stitches," she said.

"It's okay."

"You get the stitches now. When the girls ask you where

you got the scar, you tell them come around here and ask for Blossom. I'll tell them what a man you are.''

The kid's face was a neon rainbow.

▒ 65

I SPENT THE next day in the library. Closing off the corners. Looking.

On the way back to the motel, the car phone purred. Sherwood.

I left his office with a thick manila envelope.

When I spread the papers out on the motel bed, I found a list of twenty-nine names. Red check-marks next to five of them. Photocopies of rap sheets, FBI investigative reports, reports from local detectives. The five were all members of something called the Sons of Liberty. Three were suspects in vandalizing a synagogue, never formally charged. All on the subscription list for racial hate sheets, mercenary magazines. And mail-order video-porn.

If the sniper wanted to join a club, he'd have to crawl under the right rock.

◊ 66

THE CAR PHONE went off the next morning. My pal the real estate broker? I picked it up.

"Yes?"

"Mr. Sloane?"

"Yes."

"This is Blossom. At the diner?"

"I'm here." Nothing in my voice. In my mind: how did she get the number?

"I need to talk with you. Can you come by this afternoon? After closing? I get off at four."

Not at six, like Cyndi? "Okay," is all I said.

"Come around to the back. You . . ."

"I know where it is."

◊ 67

I HAD THE whole rest of the day to think about it. Eight hours. A day to a citizen, a lifetime to a convict. I was born sad—I don't remember another time. Sadness was never my friend, never coming into me like those electric fear-jolts when I needed them. It was just always there. Ground-fog on my spirit. I'd go deep into myself, the only safe place I knew in the places where I grew up. Dropping so far down nobody could see me. But the sadness would float on gray tendrils too soft to tear, finding its way between the cracks. I'd feel its misty wet weight settle on me. I could never chase it, so I lived in it. Surviving.

There was something fine about being where I was. Not in Indiana. With my brother. In a place where I wasn't a stranger, an outsider. New York was a rancid underbelly turned on its back—the maggots at home, not running from a sun that would never shine. A city of ambulatory psychopaths, choking on ethno-insanity. Unsafe even for predators.

A city that taught me whatever ugliness prison left out.

You want to make obscene calls, you go where the phone book's the thickest.

⩗ 68

SHE WAS STANDING just to the side of the back entrance when I pulled up to the diner. Wearing her white uniform, a canvas sack that looked like a horse's feedbag slung over one shoulder by a thick strap. I wheeled the car around so the passenger door was parallel to the steps. She climbed in without a word. Reached up and snapped her seat belt into place.

Tilted her chin toward the highway. I pulled out into the light afternoon traffic.

"You know how to get to Hammond?"

She didn't seem surprised when I turned left at the first light. I let the Lincoln find its rhythm inside the knots of cars, not pushing her. A pickup truck rolled past on our left, two high school girls in the back in shorts and T-shirts, their legs draped over the side, giggling girls' secrets.

Blossom sat straight-backed in her seat, knees together primly under the white skirt. A faint trace of lilac perfume mingled with cooking smells.

"You mind if we wait until we get to my house?"

"It's your play."

She nodded, calm inside herself. Her face straight ahead, eyes sweeping the interior of the Lincoln, the big car as anonymous as a motel room. If she was looking for clues, it was a dead tie at zero.

Something about the way she sat in the big car. With me, but by herself.

Just outside Hammond, we drove up on a freestanding drugstore, as big as some supermarkets. "Can you pull up there for a minute? I need a couple of things."

I nosed the Lincoln into the mostly empty parking lot, figuring to stay in the car and wait for her. A car engine roared on my left, freezing Blossom to her seat. Screech of tires. An orange Camaro was leading a black Ford and a blue Nova in a tight circle, pebbles and dirt flying off the blacktop. The Camaro pulled out of the circle, looped back and shot toward the center, bisecting the other two cars. It looked like aerial maneuvers on the ground, the cars peeling off to dive-bomb the center.

The cars fanned out and we both saw it at the same time. A seagull, one wing extended, dragging on the ground, awkward on its webbed feet. Trapped—beak hanging open, its orange eyes watching the cars.

I saw a little boy, tears swelling his eyes, his face red from the last slap, backing away from his bunk. Three bigger boys moving in on him. Laughing, taking their time.

I was inside the gull's mind. Knowing what he knew. Waiting for humans to hurt him. Wanting only to get one good rip in with that beak before they took him down.

Something crackled in my chest. My hand shot inside my jacket. Found only my pounding heart. I jammed the Lincoln into low, stomped the gas and stormed between the gull and the prancing cars. When I hit the apex I jammed the brakes, flinging the Lincoln's rear end around, blocking off the gull.

I jumped out, hands empty, too much inside the gull to care. Sun bounced off the windshields of the other cars—I couldn't see the drivers.

The Camaro revved its engine, its nose aimed at where I stood. I heard the Lincoln's door slam behind me. I didn't look back. Spread my legs. Shook my hands at the wrists, breathing through my nose, watching the car doors. If they came out together, I knew what I had to do. Drop the closest one, jump in the car he left behind. And see how the others liked being chased.

Rubber fought with pavement as all three cars shot out of the lot, leaving me standing there. I watched, expecting them to regroup and come back at me. Taillights winked as they hit the brakes at the end of the lot, but they pulled onto the highway. I turned back to the Lincoln. Blossom was bent at the waist over the Lincoln's fender, her hands inside the big canvas purse.

The gull hadn't moved. I dropped into a squat, started toward him.

"Wait!" Blossom's voice. She came up behind me, handed me a pair of thick leather gloves. "Use these. That boy's got a beak like a razor."

I slipped on the gloves, wondering how she knew what I had to do.

I moved in again. Duck-walking. One slow step at a time. Feeling the blacktop through the soles of my shoes. Talking softly to the gull.

"It's okay, pal. The punks took off. We faced them down. You're a hell of a gull. Boss bull of the flock you'll be when we get you fixed up. Everything's okay now. Easy . . . easy, boy."

He let me get to about ten feet away, flapped his good wing, and faked a run to his right. I was already moving to my right when the beak lashed out at me. I moved just out of his way, talking to him. He centered himself, watched. I let him have my eyes, willing him to feel the calm. "We're not all alike," my mind called to him.

My legs were starting to cramp when he moved. Toward me. Dragging the broken wing, eyes stabbing into mine. He was out of gas. Coming to trust or to die. I held out a gloved hand. He took it in his beak, experimentally. I felt the pressure, didn't move. Rubbed the back of his neck. His head bowed, eyes blinked. I reached back for the good wing, pinning it to his body as he flapped the broken one, shrieked his battle cry, and ripped at my gloved hand. I pinned the beak closed, stepped over and smothered the bad wing, holding him close, crooning to him.

Blossom. She snapped open a roll of Ace bandage. Left it on the ground as she manipulated the gull's bad wing, carefully folding it against his body. I got what she was doing, held him as she wound the bandage around his body. He had most of the leather glove ripped open when Blossom slipped a heavy rubber band around his beak.

"Hold him—I'll be right back," she said.

She came trotting out of the drugstore with a carton. It said Pampers on the sides. "Give him to me." I handed her the gull. She cradled it against her. "Take off your shirt—he needs a bed inside the box before we close him up."

I dropped my jacket to the pavement, unbuttoned my shirt,

piled it into a soft cushion on the bottom of the box. Blossom slowly lowered the gull inside, closed the top, leaving him in peaceful darkness.

She held the box on her lap as I drove. Told me to turn on McCook Avenue, off 173rd. "The gray house, the one with the shingles . . . see it?"

I pulled into the pebbled driveway, up to a closed single-car garage. Followed Blossom around to the back door.

She put the box on the kitchen table. Left me standing there. Came back with a leather satchel. Filled a copper-bottomed pot with water and put it on to boil.

"Let's take a look at him," she said, opening the top of the box. I lifted the gull out, carried him to the counter next to the sink. Sound of metal being tossed into the pot. Blossom deftly made a circle of white surgical tape, fastened cotton balls on the inside, and slipped the soft hood over the bird's beak to cover his eyes. She poured off the boiling water. I glanced in the sink. Gleaming surgical tools: scalpel, scissors, probes.

"I'm going to cut the bandage loose on his bad side. Hold the other wing in place—I need to spread him out, see what the damage is."

The broken wing covered a good piece of the counter. Blossom talked to the gull as she worked, hands and eyes one perfect unit. "Take it easy, boy. We'll have you chasing girl gulls in a short piece. Let me take a look, now. Don't fuss."

More probing. "Here it is. A clean break. I can set it after I cut away these little fragments. There!"

She wrapped the wings together again, the tip of her tongue peeking out between her lips as she concentrated. "There's some old birdcage in the basement. Big enough for a parrot or something. In the left corner off the stairs."

I found the cage. The handle came almost to my chest. I

carried it upstairs. "Put it out on the back porch—we'll have to hose it down."

I did that while Blossom shredded newspapers for the flooring. She handed me a pair of pliers. "Take out all that other stuff—give him some room."

I removed the perches until the cage was an empty shell. The door wasn't big enough for the gull—I pried the bars apart to make room. Blossom gently lowered him inside. He made no move to fight. Watched us.

"There's some salmon in the cupboard. Open a can for him while I get him some cover."

I opened a can, dumped the salmon inside the cage. Filled the empty can with water and put that inside too. Blossom came back with an army blanket. Cut it into strips with the surgical scissors and draped it over the top of the cage.

"Have yourself a nice rest, boy," she said. "In a couple of weeks, you'll be back to work."

⫴ 69

I SAT AT the kitchen table. Blossom stood next to me. "Let's have a look at that hand."

Blood across the knuckles, one finger sliced cleanly. "Wash it off in the sink. Cold water, no soap. Make sure the blood runs clean."

She dried off the hand, spraying some stinging stuff across the open cut, put a butterfly bandage in place. "Won't even leave a scar," she said.

"You were a nurse once?"

Her turquoise eyes searched my face, a smile rippling across her wide mouth. "No. No more than you're a real estate speculator. Be right back."

◗ 70

WHEN I HEARD the rush of the shower, I knew she'd be awhile. I cracked a wooden match into fire, lit a smoke. No ashtray on the kitchen table. I went looking. Four small clay pots on the windowsill, clogged with thick greenery. Looked like parsley. A twig planted in each one, standing tall and clean above the growth. Looked closer. Thick-bodied black-and-white-striped caterpillars, one in each pot.

I opened the dishwasher. No ashtrays, but I found a drinking glass. Opened the tap, poured a half inch of water inside. It'd do.

Blossom came back inside, wearing a tightly belted pink terry-cloth robe, a towel wrapped around her head.

"You want some coffee?"

"No, thanks."

"A beer?"

"No."

She busied herself with making coffee, pouring ground beans into a filter. The beans came from a plain white bag, no brand name. Somebody had handwritten Kenya AA on the side.

A motorcycle snarled in the street. Mother calling her kids inside for dinner. Dogs barked conversationally. Safe sounds.

She sat across from me, cradling her heavy white coffee mug in both hands, unselfconsciously plucking at the opening of her robe. At home, unhurried.

Maybe I couldn't mend a broken wing, but I could outwait a stone. Tossed my cigarette into the water glass and settled down into myself.

"You're not curious?"

"About what?"

"About why I asked you to come and talk to me. About what I said about you not being a real estate speculator."

"Curious enough to take the ride."

"But . . ."

"I can't play a hand until it's dealt."

She tapped long fingernails on the tabletop. "I've been here six weeks. Summer's almost over. Then I'll have to go."

I watched her. Laugh-lines around her wide mouth. Trace of crow's-feet next to her eyes. Harder lines. Her skin was as clean and clear and glowing as a young girl's, but she was older than I first thought. Even at ease, her back was straight, shoulders squared.

"I'm not a nurse. Never was. I'm a doctor. Just finished school. I start my internship in late September. Back home. In West Virginia. Pediatrics."

I lit another smoke.

"You're not surprised or . . ."

"Or I was raised in places where you don't show much on your face."

"Yes. I saw that the first time you came in the diner."

"And ex-cons don't put together real estate deals?"

"That's not how I know. How I knew. I wasn't sure why you were here until I saw you with that boy. Lloyd. That's his name, isn't it? The boy they thought did those killings?"

"They were wrong."

"I know. His name was in the papers. People only remember killers, never who they killed."

I dragged deep on my cigarette. Her face was contrasts: huge eyes, a tiny nose, that broad slash of a mouth. So different from the way she looked in the diner. I locked on her eyes, my voice gentle, like reading a menu I wasn't trying to sell. "Merrilee Marshall, Tommy Deacon, Rose Joanne Lynch, George Borden."

Two fingers stroked her cheek. "Why?"

"There's a dead sheep in the meadow. All cut to pieces. Wolves make different marks than mountain lions. And humans, they make their own marks."

"Sherwood told me. Told me you were looking for the sniper."

"He questioned you? The people at the diner?"

"No. Rose is . . . was my sister. My baby sister. There's three of us. Mama said we were her garden. Violet, me, and Rose. She was seventeen years old. Came up here to spend the summer with some of our kin before she started college. Just to have some fun, see someplace new. When we heard she was killed, we thought they had the killer. But then . . . things changed. Couldn't be sure. So I came up here myself. To look around. The way my mother would have wanted."

"Why the waitress job?"

"I just followed the pipeline. The migrant pipeline. My people have been coming out of the hills into the steel mills forever. I didn't want to work in an office, didn't have much time. The diner was the first job I saw open, close to the ground."

I thought about how the diner was at the nerve center of everything that had happened, a checkpoint in the human traffic pattern. Wondered about accidents, coincidence. "But Sherwood, he knows?" I asked her.

"He knows Rose was my sister. He knows how blood

runs, that man. He said he'd keep me in the picture, tell me what's going on.''

"He think Lloyd did it?''

"No. I don't think he ever did. After the boy first got arrested, he told me it would be a tough case to make. But then he got scared.''

"Scared?''

"That I'd fix it myself. Make it right if the jury wouldn't.'' Shrugging like that was ridiculous. "Anyway, I think he told me about you to kind of settle me down. He said you were a private investigator.''

I nodded.

She smiled.

I imitated her shrug, watching close.

"But you're in it?'' she asked, a trace of metal in her voice.

"I'm in it.''

"And you can find him?''

"I don't know. I don't know where to look. That's where my brother comes in. But I know who I'm looking for.''

She regarded me steadily, her eyes doing a diagnosis she never learned in medical school.

"I believe you do.''

⚑ 71

WE TALKED AS soft darkness filled Blossom's kitchen, night filtering in slow, not dropping like a New York curtain.

"You want something to eat?"

I looked at my watch. "Can't. I have to meet some people. Get to work."

"It'll only take me a minute to get dressed."

"These people . . . I can't bring a guest, you understand?"

She leaned forward, elbows on the kitchen table. Her robe billowed open. My eyes never left her face.

"I understand. Be sure you do. I told you some things, but there's a lot you don't know. About me. Ways I could help. Places I could go."

"I'm not cutting you out. Whoever this guy is, he comes out at night. Before I go where he is, I have to do some day work."

"I'll give Leon notice."

"Why don't you just walk out? You don't need the money, right?"

"That's not the way I was raised. I'll give him notice. Then we'll go around together, you and me."

◊ 72

I PULLED INTO Virgil's block, feeling the eyes. A safe neighborhood, if you were a neighbor.

The house was built in Indiana working-class style—the back door opened into the kitchen. Virginia came to the door when I knocked—I saw Rebecca fussing over the stove over her shoulder.

"Hello," the child said gravely.

"Hello, Virginia. Is your mother at home?"

She looked at me the way women have been looking at me for years. Stepped aside to let me in.

"You want some supper, Burke?" Rebecca asked, not turning around.

"If it's not too much trouble."

"Already cooked. You like chicken and dumplings?"

"Sure."

"Coming up. Virginia, go tell Daddy his brother is here."

Virginia ignored her, rummaging in the refrigerator.

"What did I tell you?" Rebecca asked, her voice sharp.

"Daddy will want a beer anyway."

"Is that right, Miss Know-It-All?"

"Oh, Mama. You *know* Daddy likes it when I bring him a beer."

"Daddy'd like it just as much you brought him a nice glass of apple juice."

The kid giggled, pulled a can of Pabst from the shelf, expertly poured it into a tall glass, creating a perfect head. Marched off to the living room.

Rebecca put a plate of steaming food in front of me. Glass of ginger ale. "Virgil said you don't drink . . ."

"It's true. Thank you. Your daughter is beautiful."

"That's her mother's blood," Virgil said, coming into the kitchen, a beer in one hand. His son at his side. Looked like the boy grew another couple of inches since I saw him last. Sat down across from me.

"Where's Lloyd?" I asked him.

"Out in the garage. I set up a heavy bag for him. The boy's turning into King Kong."

"He rescue any more waitresses lately?"

"Not that I know of."

Junior stood at his father's shoulder, eyes wide. Watching the stranger.

"Was he always such a big boy?"

"Nine pounds and change at birth. The baby doctor we take him to, he's the team physician for the junior high over to Hobart. Said we ought to move there before Junior turns ten. Says we got a natural-born linebacker here."

"Looks like it to me too. You want him to play ball?"

Virgil lit a smoke, blew a puff at the ceiling. Talking to me with words meant for his son. "He wants to play ball, that's okay with me. But he don't *have* to. Back home, there wasn't but two ways—the mines or the mills. Football, basketball . . . that was a way out for some. You know the other ways. But my son, he's not gonna need that. He wants to play ball, his old man'll come out, watch him crack some heads. He wants to be an actor, I'll watch him up on the stage. Don't matter. Whatever he does, we'll be proud of him. Right, Reba?"

Rebecca walked over, kissed the boy on the top of his head. "Of course."

The kid squirmed, turned red. His father gave him a look, telling him it was just one of those things he'd have to put up with. Virginia watched both of them intently.

Virgil saw her watching. Laughed. "Virginia, your little boy's growing up, huh, darlin'?"

The girl frowned. "Oh, Daddy!"

Virgil turned to me. "Virginia, she about raised Junior when he was a baby. Couldn't do enough for him. Used to dress him up, take him for walks in the stroller. The boy's getting his growth now. He don't want to mind his sister like he used to."

Virginia stalked off into the living room, stopping only to plant a kiss on top of the little boy's head just like her mother had done.

Tinkle of piano keys. Warming up. Then the concert started. "Twinkle, Twinkle, Little Star" was her opening selection.

"Who taught her to play?"

"She just picked it up somehow. Used to sit next to me on the bench when I was playing. One day, she just started hitting those keys."

"Virgil, you're not fooling nobody," Rebecca said. "You notice how his chest just went out about a foot, Burke? Virgil used to play the piano for that child when I was still carrying her. Music was the first thing she heard in this world."

I ate my chicken and dumplings, sipped my ginger ale, listened to their love. Wondered what it would be like . . . me.

Then I remembered why I was there. Visiting Day.

◗ 73

LATER THAT NIGHT, I stood in the yard with Virgil. The house quiet and dark behind us.

"You know that waitress? The blonde one Lloyd jumped in to protect?"

"Yeah."

"She's kin of one of the little girls who got killed. Came up here looking for the shooter."

"She think Lloyd's the one?"

"No. Says even Sherwood never thought so."

"Sure acted like he did."

"He's a cop. That's the way they play. The good ones, they don't let their instincts get in the way."

"How come you know about this woman?"

"She told me."

Virgil grunted, waiting.

"I need a gun," I told him.

"Figured you might."

"You got some?"

"Not what you want. Some of 'em even registered."

I gave him a look.

"Reba, she ain't no ex-con. All nice and legal. Where we come from, people're raised on guns. No big thing. Ain't a house in this neighborhood you won't find at least a deer rifle, shotgun, something like that."

"The shooter, it all goes right, he won't even see me coming, but . . ."

"I got it, brother. I'm not much for that psychology crap you was always studying in the joint, but I know two things for sure about this boy. He's one sick puppy. And he's got him some serious firepower."

I worked it around in my head. When I was hijacking, I had guns stashed all over the country. In safe-deposit boxes. Paid ten years' rent in advance. That's when I lived in hotels, went South for the winter. Before I had a home. It wasn't worth going back.

"I need a pistol," I told Virgil. "A cold one. I use it, I'm gonna lose it."

"Tomorrow night, I'm playing with my band. Over in Chicago. You come along, okay? Your kind of music." He dragged on his smoke. "Reba's coming with me tomorrow. Virginia can take care of Junior. You come along. I'll make a phone call. After my set, we'll step out to the back, meet a man. Get you what you want, okay?"

"Can I bring a date?" I asked him.

74

WE PICKED UP Blossom at her house, paid the tolls through Hammond, and took the Skyway into Chicago. Virgil directed me past Rush Street until I found a parking place right around the corner from his club.

It was a big joint for a blues bar, but not enough seating capacity for the high-dollar acts. Still, Chicago's a blues town and sometimes you get lucky—Virgil said he caught Buddy Guy and Junior Wells there once and they weren't even on the bill.

Virgil went out back to get ready. Rebecca, Blossom, and I found a little round table near the back. The waitress was wearing a black body-stocking with an apron tied in front.

"There's about a half hour before the next set. You all want something to eat?"

I ordered a roast beef sandwich and ginger ale. Blossom asked for a plate of sliced red cabbage, radishes, carrots, and two hard-boiled eggs. The waitress gave her a strange look. "Anything to drink?"

"You have bottled water?"

"We don't even have bottled beer."

"Just a glass of seltzer, then."

Rebecca had a hamburger and a glass of red wine.

The waitress was just clearing the table when they started to set up on the little stage. I watched the musicians, wondering what this was going to be. A strange collection. Tall man with a gospel singer's face was hooking up an electric fiddle, like Sugarcane Harris used to play. Steel guitar, Virgil at his piano, drums. A rail-thin black man who looked old enough to be a runaway slave sat on a stool cradling a slide guitar on his lap. Fresh-faced chubby kid wearing dark glasses stood to the far side, a cartridge belt of harmonicas around his waist. It took the front man awhile to make it to the microphone. He had a chest big enough to play solitaire on, a head the size of a basketball, thick long hair swept back from his forehead in crashing waves. He was standing on metal crutches, the kind that angle about halfway up. A massive upper body on useless legs.

They never announced the name of the band. The electric-fiddle player cranked up a low floating scream. The drummer laid down a hard sharp track underneath as the harp player barked his way in, waiting for the piano man to travel along the high keys. The chesty guy on crutches took them through a gambler's version of "Mary Lou." Like the way Ronnie Hawkins used to do it, but with the harp man doing the backup voices. He gave us "Suzy Q" and a nasty twist on "Change in the Weather." I couldn't put any name to it but the blues. Virgil's piano was a magic thing—sweet water flowing over crystal rocks, breaking and falling, spooling out a ribbon of purity across the bottom, climbing again. He and the fiddle player laid down a carpet of neon smoke, the slide guitar man lancing through, long fingers high up on the neck, counterpointing the harp, bending unreal notes between them like playing jump-rope with metallic strands. The steel guitar cried to itself.

Rebecca's voice: "My Virgil can *play*, can't he?"

Blossom: "You couldn't get closer to the Lord in church."

Then the band went into its own stuff. Telling the truth. Nightclub women and working girls, cocaine and do-without pain. Hell's hounds, jailhouse-bound. Dice players and pimps. Cheating wives and gunfights. Don't mind dying. Hard times and hard people.

The baby spot hit the players as they each took a solo, the singer saying each man's name for the crowd as they played.

They finished the last number. The slide guitar worked the bass notes, with only Virgil's piano helping him along. The man on crutches talked to us.

"Men, you ever have a good woman? I mean a *gooood* woman . . . the kind of woman who'll stand up when she has to and stand by while you do time? You know what I mean. A woman who can give that good love, that real love? Answer me if I'm telling the truth!"

They answered him. Tapped their whiskey glasses together, yelled "That's right!" up at the stage, groaned their encouragement.

"And you threw her away, didn't you? You let her go. You gave up a used Cadillac for a new Ford, you know what I'm saying?"

They knew.

"You ever want just *one* more chance? Well, listen to me now." The electric fiddle worked under the harp this time, the chubby kid welding the notes into new shapes. The man on crutches came through the music like a fist punching through a door, his cobalt voice nailing the crowd.

> *I've done you wrong*
> *So many times*
> *Treated you cruel*
> *Played with your mind*
> *I know you're leaving*
> *And I'll miss your loving touch*
> *But won't you listen just one more time?*
>
> *Woman, don't you owe me that much?*
> *I drank and I gambled*

But you always let me come home
Yes, I drank and I gambled
But you always let me come home
You always forgave me
Till you heard that little girl on the phone

A woman in the crowd screamed something up at the stage. The singer bowed in her direction and went back to work.

I lost my job, even went to jail
And you always stayed by my side
When I lost my job, and I went to jail
You always stood up, right by my side
But you saw me with that other woman
You swore your love had died

First you said you'd kill her
And then you changed your mind
Yeah, you said you'd take her young life
But then you changed your mind
You threw my clothes in the street
And told me to stay with my own kind

He hit us with verse after verse, telling his story. Telling the truth. When he got to the end of the road, he had us with him.

I need you for my woman
I need you for my wife
You know I need you, woman
Lord knows I need my wife
But if you won't send an answer
I guess I don't need my life

He finished the set with a razor-wire version of "She's Nineteen Years Old." In case there were any tourists in the audience.

The crowd wouldn't let him off the stage. A woman in an electric-blue dress stood up, holding a beer glass in one hand, shouted something at him I couldn't hear.

The bandleader's voice came back at her through the mike. "Maybe I can't run the hundred-yard dash, darlin', but I'm still a sixty-minute man."

He owned the crowd. "One more," he said. And meant it. The drummer switched to brushes. Virgil intro'ed off the bass keys. A piano doesn't have special notes inside it like a guitar, but Virgil played them special. The slide guitar stayed low with him.

"God Bless the Child."

The band held the fort as the singer slowly moved himself off the stage. Then it went dark.

◊ 75

A TAP ON my shoulder. Virgil. I got up, followed him through the darkness to the bar. "Wait here. I'll be back for you in a minute."

I ordered a whiskey from the bartender, left it sitting on the counter. A white man was making noise at the end of the bar, drunk, whining to his friends.

"Why can't I sing the blues?" he demanded. "Because I'm white?"

A factory man's dark voice answered his call. " 'Cause you can't sing, sucker!"

Virgil took me into a back room. The massive blues shouter was sitting in an armchair big enough for a meeting. "Doc, I want you to meet my brother. Burke," Virgil said, bringing me over.

He held out his hand. I took it, felt a palm leathered from years of holding crutches. "You're the best I ever heard," I told him.

"Thank you, brother."

The harp man was talking on the phone, intensely. The slide-guitar man was smoking a joint. Nobody else around. Virgil moved his head a couple of inches. I followed him to another door.

Inside, an old chrome-and-Formica kitchen table. Four chairs. One of them occupied by a featureless man in a white shirt, balding, bifocals perched on top of his head.

"Arnold, this is my brother. The guy I told you about."

"How ya doin'?" he piped up, in a thin voice younger than his face.

I sat down. Lit a smoke. Bowed my head slightly to greet him. Waiting.

"Virgil said you needed some stuff?"

"A pistol."

"A pistol? What's that supposed to mean, pistol? I got more kinds of pistols than you've had birthdays. Give me the specs. Or give me the job, I'll pick one out for you."

"Revolver. No more than three-inch. Thirty-eight or .357. Blue. Something decent, a Colt or a Smith. Ice-cold."

"You want this for . . . ?"

"Protection. Protection I can carry around with me."

"Look, man, you're talking Stone Age stuff. Take a look at this little piece of perfection." He opened one of the suitcases on the floor next to him. Came out with a dull gray automatic. "This here's a Glock, ever hear of it? Designed by an Austrian. The guy's a genius, not a gunsmith. Started with a blank piece of paper. Plastic undercarriage, metal frame. Takes nine-millimeter ammo. *Any* nine-millimeter, see?'' He held up a bullet, black-tipped. ''You know what this is?''

''Uzi.''

''Right you are, my friend. You put high-pressure sub-machine slugs like this in a regular semi-auto, you blow it up in your hand. But not the Glock. Holds sixteen rounds, fast as you can pull them off.''

''Automatics jam.''

''Bullshit. *Some* automatics jam. I do all the work myself. Custom. You got my personal guarantee.''

I didn't waste time explaining to him how I'd have trouble getting my money back if his toy jammed. ''I'm not going to be in a gunfight,'' I told him.

His eyes shifted but his expression didn't change. ''Okay, I understand. I recommend you take the Glock, plus this Wilson suppressor I just happen to have machined for it. Instead of the Uzi ammo, we switch to subsonics. Makes a little pop, that's all. Never draw a crowd.''

''I appreciate it, but I got to use what I'm familiar with, okay? You got any revolvers in that case?''

''Three-inch max?''

''Yeah.''

He rummaged around. ''How about this? Ruger Speed-Six. I modified the trigger pull myself. It's so smooth you won't feel it go home even in double-action.''

I took the piece from him. Black rubber handgrips, blue steel. Looked new.

''This been around?''

''Virgil, you tell your brother *anything* about me or what? The *pieces* of this weapon, they've been around, you understand what I'm saying to you? This little unit has been hand-assembled from a wide range of similar units. Made it myself, from parts. You finish with this one, you *mail* it to the ATF, they won't be able to do nothing with it.''

''How much?''

''A piece like this, new, maybe four hundred retail.''

''But you don't sell retail.''

''Sure, I sell retail. I got me an FFL and everything. But over the counter, you know, there's a lot of paperwork. Besides, I got a lot of custom labor in this piece, like I told you.''

''So?''

''Seven-fifty. And I'll throw in a box of Plus P, hundred and fifty-eight grain. That's about all you want to load in this baby.''

I dragged on my cigarette. Some dealers like the bargaining part. This guy wasn't that kind—all you could do was wait him out.

''Or maybe you'd rather have an assortment. I got a few hand-loaded thirty-eights here. Mercury tips, hollow points, full metal jacket . . .''

''Got some wad cutters?''

''You got to be *very* close for those.''

''I understand.''

''We got a deal?''

I ground out my smoke. ''Tell you what. Why don't we make it an even grand. For the pistol, some ammo, and some advice.''

''I like it.''

I handed over the money in hundreds. He eye-counted it, passed me the pistol, sorted through his collection of shells, filled a box.

I lit another smoke. ''You hear anything about those sniper killings over in Indiana? The Lovers' Lane Killer, the papers call him?''

''Yeah.'' Waiting.

''Let's say, just for a minute, that we know something

about the guy who did it, all right? Let's say he's a Rambo freak. Lives at home, don't get out much. Likes to play dress-up in camo gear, that kind of thing. He's *not* military, not a cop. Not a merc either. Probably no training, no contacts, okay?''

"I'm with you."

"So he's probably buying mail-order. He wouldn't have the cash for a really quality piece. What would he have?''

Arnold's face flickered, computing. "Got to be one of those 'assault rifles,' '' he sneered. "Which is just about anything with a Kalashnikov action. The caliber isn't the problem. Damn near *has* to be .223. Could be Russian, Chinese, even Brazilian. Everybody makes a knockoff of the original. But your guy, he'd want the *look*, okay?''

"The look?''

"Like high-tech, man. Dark and evil. I figure him for a Mini-14 with all the goodies. Black plastic stock, flash suppressor, maybe even a bipod on the front for prone-position fire. Maybe an AR-15 but . . . I like the Mini. You can get 'em anywhere, real cheap.''

"Through the mail?''

"Hell, yes. Buy all the camo gear he wants too, boots to hats. Underwear, he wants it. The Mini, it'll take anything from twenty rounds up. Up to a hundred, he wants to go with a drum.''

"Silencer?''

"Now *that's* a different game, man. You can buy books on how to make them, but a good one, one that'd work, he'd have to know somebody. That .223 stuff, it pulls a high harmonic. Like a crack, you know? Not a boom.''

"Arnold, let me ask you one more question, okay? You sell a rig like the one we're talking about here in the last few months?''

"Oh, man. I don't sell junk.''

"But if some guy had only so much cash . . . ?"

"Guy like you're asking about, he wouldn't know where to find me."

⚱76

WHEN WE CAME back to the table, Blossom and Rebecca had their heads together, whispering. We sat down. The waitress brought Virgil a bottle of beer, looking a question at me. I shook my head no.

Virgil looked at his watch. "We need to pull out of here in a few minutes. There's another band coming on—we don't want to walk out in the middle of their set. Wouldn't look right."

Blossom rested her fingertips lightly on my forearm as we walked to the car.

Just before we crossed into Indiana, Rebecca spoke from the back seat. "Want to visit with us a bit, have some coffee?"

"Blossom has to work early tomorrow morning," I told her.

The blonde woman's voice was sweet and soft. "I'm a big girl now. I can get myself up in the morning."

Virgil laughed. "You as smooth as ever, Burke."

I caught his eyes in the mirror. The Prof was right—once a Hoosier, always a Hoosier.

Blossom curled in her seat, looking out the window.

77

A LIGHT SHONE in the kitchen as we walked up the path to the back door. Lloyd was seated at the table, a book propped in front of him. Line of fresh stitches across the bridge of his nose. Saw Blossom. Blushed. Kind of ducked his head, mumbled something that sounded like "Hi."

She gave him a dazzling smile I didn't know she had. "You watching the kids?"

"Sure. They're in bed, fast asleep. I figured . . . maybe I'd better wait up till you all got back."

Virgil nodded his approval.

"Any calls?" Rebecca asked.

"Just your friend Bette. Said she'd see you tomorrow."

"Okay, honey. Thanks. You want some coffee—we're all having some."

"If it won't . . ."

He didn't take his eyes off Blossom all the while we sat and talked. About nothing. Soft stuff. Virginia was getting to the age where she cared about the clothes she wore. Junior was starting first grade as soon as summer ended. Lloyd had cut the lawn without being asked.

The pistol felt heavy in my coat pocket. If I was back in New York, I wouldn't have noticed the weight.

⚊ 78

IT WAS ALMOST one in the morning when I brought Blossom back to her house. I walked her to the door. Stood outside while she put the lights on. Lit a smoke.

She came back onto the front porch. The gull watched us from his cage, waiting his time. "When do we start?" she asked me.

"Start?"

"Looking."

"I've already started. I'll fill you in tomorrow night."

"I told you . . . there's things I could do. With you. On this."

"If it's still running when you quit your job, then we'll see."

"No night work for me on this job?"

"Maybe. Not yet."

"See you tomorrow night."

I turned to go.

"Burke . . ."

"What?"

"Don't be mad at Virgil. I knew your name wasn't Mitchell Sloane."

"How?"

"Sherwood."

"The man opened right up to you, didn't he?"

"Some men do."

I tossed my cigarette away.

"Come here," she said. Gentle.

She stood on her toes, kissed me lightly on the cheek. "Thanks. I loved hearing your brother play."

"See you tomorrow."

"Okay."

◊ 79

I STOPPED AT a pay phone. Dumped in handfuls of quarters. Called the junkyard. When the phone was picked up, I said, "Tell the Prof to find Vincenzo at the library tomorrow. Bring him over to Mama's. Have him wait between eight and nine. I'll call."

The phone went down.

◊ 80

THE NEXT MORNING, I started to look. The way it works, you draw a blank page in your mind. Fill in everything you know. See what's left. If there's too much left, too

much white space, you make some guesses. Test them
out.

I had plenty of white space. I slapped the black tiles down,
moving them around. Not enough. I switched the tiles, part
of my mind seeing the pattern they made.

Pattern.

I played with it.

⚓ 81

LUNCHTIME, I WENT to the diner. Cyndi was happy to see
me. Told me about a new guy she was dating. He worked at
the plant. "But he's going to college at night. Says he doesn't
want his kids working in the mill."

"He's got kids?"

"No." She giggled. "The kids he's *gonna* have."

I saw the police cruiser roll up. Ford Crown Vic, cream-
colored, dark brown fenders. Two cops got out. Came inside,
stopped at the counter. Talked to Leon.

On the jukebox: Maxine Brown. "It's All in My Mind."

Blossom came up to my table, her canvas bag slung over
one shoulder. She leaned over. "Give it to me."

"What?"

"What you picked up last night. Hurry!"

I slid the pistol into her bag. Went back to my tuna on rye.
Shadow fell across my plate. Cops. Big heavy one, potbelly
looming over his gun belt. Smaller one, narrow all the way
up through his eyes.

"How you doing?" the big one asked.

"Just fine, Officer."

"That's good," his partner said.

"Anything I can do for you?"

"Could tell us what you're doing around here."

"Working for Bart Bostick. The lawyer."

"We know who he is. Heard about your little arrangement with him."

"So?"

"So Sherwood don't run the department. Captain does, you understand?"

"Sure."

"Good. This work you're doing for Counselor Bostick . . . it wouldn't involve carrying concealed weapons, would it?"

"Nope."

"Mind if we take a look? With your consent, of course."

"Look where? For what?"

"In your car. Maybe in your jacket. For a gun."

"And if I don't consent?"

"Then we just . . ." the smaller one said. The other guy jumped on his lines. "Then we just ask a judge for a search warrant. You understand, we got laws here. About ex-cons carrying firearms."

"You gonna do this every day?"

"This isn't a roust, friend. You're clean now, we figure you're working clean, okay?"

I handed him the car keys. "If the phone rings, take a message, will you?"

The smaller cop's face got tight. "Think I'll just stay here. Keep you company."

"I got a better idea. How about if I go outside to the car with you. Let you take your look. Look at me too, you want."

The big cop nodded.

We went outside. They took a look, patted me down.

Carefully. Got back into their cruiser. The big one said "Have a nice day" through the window.

"Same to you," I told him.

⚰ 82

BACK INSIDE. WHEN Blossom came back around, the canvas bag was gone.

"How'd you know?" I asked her.

"One day, when I was leaving the precinct, one of those cops came up to me. Sort of implied Sherwood and I had been trading something besides information."

"He knew why you were there?"

"No. Guess he asked Sherwood and got blown off. A real philosopher. Had a lot to say about niggers and white girls who didn't know where they belonged."

"Revis?" Remembering the name on the smaller one's badge.

"Yes, that's him."

"Thanks."

"We're partners, right?"

I felt those turquoise eyes on me. It didn't feel like she was talking a fifty-fifty split.

"I'll give it back to you later. Tonight. Today's my last day. I gave Leon notice—he said he had a dozen other girls with applications in, no problem."

"Want me to wait, give you a ride home after work?"

"No, I have to hang around. Cyndi's boyfriend's coming in. She wants me to meet him."

"Check him out? See if he's right for her?"

"You think I can't?"

I nodded a disclaimer. Thinking how good she was at watching people.

〰 83

I DROVE BACK over to Virgil's. Picked up Lloyd. Had him take me to where he and the other boys had been prowling when he'd opened his puppy mouth and brought all the trouble down. Went over the ground, getting nothing. I don't know what I expected to find—it wasn't a job for a scientist.

The rest of the time, I drove around, learning the streets. Lloyd at my side, filling in the blanks when I asked him where we were.

⚓ 84

CALLED BOSTICK. "YOU entitled to discovery even if Lloyd's not indicted?"

"No. He's got to be charged with something first. What d'you need?"

"Anything the killer might have left at the crime scenes. Blood, hair, shell casings."

"I can probably get that. Anything else?"

"He would've left something. I'll think about it, get back to you. On the meter, okay?"

"You're covered. Your man Davidson's handling a federal matter for me over in New York. We'll work it out."

⚓ 85

I DUMPED QUARTERS into the pay phone. Dialed Mama's number, expecting the Prof.

"Gardens."

"It's me, Mama. The Prof around?"

"Everybody around. Everybody here except you."

"I'll be back soon."

"Max ask . . . when?"

"Soon. I told you."

"Any trouble?"

"No trouble."

I heard the phone being put down on the counter.

"Read me a poem, 'home."

"Prof, you bring Vincenzo?"

"I got him, bro'. Go easy. My man gets real strange when he's off his range."

I knew what the Prof meant. Vincenzo lived in the Public Library. Main branch on Forty-second Street. Every day he showed up to do his "research." A tall, gentle-looking man, walking his own road. Carries a knapsack full of notebooks with writing only he can read. Lives on another plane from us. Vincenzo, he's one of the few guys who wouldn't know where to buy cocaine in the city. But he could tell you the precise spot in Colombia where the soil composition and annual rainfall would yield the best coca crop. If it was on paper, he could find it.

"Hello?"

"Vincenzo, my friend. You know who this is?"

"Yes."

"Can you do a research job for me?"

"I'm very busy with my own work. Did you know . . . ?"

"Listen, Vincenzo, I know how important your work is. But this is kind of an emergency. And you're the only one with the ability to do it."

Silence.

"Okay?"

"What do you need?"

"I need anything you can find me on sex-snipers. Like Son of Sam. Or Zodiac, on the Coast. And there was a case in New York, within the last few years. Lovers' lane sniper. *Anything*, Vincenzo. Anything you can find. Okay?''

"I don't do analysis—I just find facts.''

"That's what I need, pal. Facts. The Prof'll take care of you, any costs involved.''

"I can give it one research day, that's all. Then I have to get back to my work.''

"Okay. So I'll call you tomorrow night.''

"You can't call me. There's no phones . . .''

"I'll call you *there*, Vincenzo. Right where you are now. The Prof will bring you back again, pick you up at your office tomorrow at closing time. Okay?''

"All right.''

The Prof came back on the line. "You find your thrill in the hills yet, man?''

"Still looking. Thanks for t.c.b. on Vincenzo. Can you bring him back tomorrow night? Same time?''

"I say what I mean, I mean what I say, and those who don't listen, they'd better pray.''

⚜ 86

ALMOST TEN WHEN I tapped on Blossom's door. Wearing a T-shirt that reached almost to her knees, feet bare. Her hair was tied in a loose knot on top of her head. I followed her back to the kitchen.

There was a black plastic ashtray on the kitchen table. I lit a smoke while she brewed coffee. One of the caterpillars had formed a cocoon. "What kind are they?" I asked.

"Black swallowtails. Beautiful big things. Long-distance fliers."

"How come you do that . . . raise butterflies?"

"When I was a kid, I used to try and catch them. The way kittens do. Not to be vicious, just chasing them because they're so pretty. My mother explained it to me. If you love something, you don't crush it. You can't hug a butterfly. She got me some caterpillars. Monarchs, they were. I remember, they only lived on milkweed. I learned patience, watching them eat, get fat, spin their cocoons. When the butterfly comes out, it's never so lovely as it is then. They come out wet. That's when they're most vulnerable. Until the powder dries on their wings and they can take to the sky. You hold them right on your fingers. They trust you then. Let them flap their wings until they're ready. Then you raise your hand and they fly away. I bring the cocoons into the hospital. On the children's ward. It's so good for them to see something get better. Fly away."

"I tried something like that once."

"Butterflies?"

"No. One foster home I was in. Out on Long Island. The old lady who ran the place, she had these rose bushes that she loved. Her pride and joy. All different kinds. That summer, we had this attack of Japanese beetles. What they do is eat rose bushes. Mrs. Jensen, she sprayed and sprayed. Tried everything. But the beetles kept on coming. It was breaking her heart."

She brought her cup to the kitchen table, holding it in two hands, watching.

"I was just a kid. Tried picking off the beetles, one at a time. But it didn't do any good—they just kept coming. So I went to the library. Looked up Japanese beetles. I found out they had what you call a natural enemy. Praying mantis. You ever see one?''

She nodded.

"Anyway, the praying mantis, it makes a cocoon. Like your caterpillars, but much bigger. Heavy strands like fiber, light brownish color. About half the size of a golf ball. I found some in a field near her house. Spent days collecting them. Put each one in a mason jar. I figured, one giant praying mantis would come out of each one. I'd hatch them, put them on the rose bushes. Have them stand guard.''

"What happened?''

"When the first one hatched, it wasn't one praying mantis, it was like *thousands* of them. Little tiny things. So small you could hardly see them. Then I was stuck. See, I knew that birds would eat the little ones. But if I left them in the jar where they'd be safe, they'd starve to death. So I poured the whole jar over the rose bushes. When each one hatched, I did the same.''

"Did it work?''

"Oh yeah. I poured out so many of the little suckers that the birds couldn't deal with them all. We had wall-to-wall praying mantises. They whacked every Japanese beetle for miles. When they get their growth, they're huge. Those front paws, hell, you could really feel them when they grabbed. So Mrs. Jensen's rose bushes were safe. But you couldn't go outside without getting dive-bombed by the praying mantises. They were all over the place. On the bushes. In the trees. In the house. All over the cars. The neighbors wanted to murder me.''

"Sounds like you went overboard.'' She chuckled.

"Mrs. Jensen, she stood up for me. Said I meant well. I was only a little boy.''

"She sounds like a fine woman.''

"She was.''

"Did she raise you?''

"No. I was only there for the summer. The State raised me."

"Are your parents dead?"

"I don't know. Never met them."

"Oh."

"You can get that sappy look off your face. You don't miss what you never had."

"You don't know my looks. You don't know what they mean. And folks *do* miss what they never have. They do it all the time. Now tell me what you found out."

₩ 87

LATER, I WAS on the couch in her living room. Blossom was curled up at the other end.

"Why are you in this?" she asked.

"Virgil's my brother."

"I understand that. But you came to help Lloyd, right? I know he's been arrested and all, but nobody thinks he did it. Why don't you go back home?"

"I could never explain it to you. The guy who did this, I know him. Not his name. I was raised with humans like him. I know why he does it."

"You want to stop him before he does it again?"

"I'm no hero. That's not it. I told you, I can't explain it."

She slid closer on the couch, voice quiet. "Cyndi tell you what I told her? About you?"

"To stay away from me?"

"Yes. She tell you why?"

"Not exactly."

"You're a trouble-man, Mr. Burke."

"What's that?"

"There's men who walk on the edge because they like the way it feels under their feet. Risk-takers."

"That's not me."

"Yes. Yes, it is. You've got the mark. Clear as a signpost. It's got nothing to do with bravery. But wherever you go, there's trouble. Trouble for somebody."

"You don't know me."

"And you don't know the sniper?"

I dragged on my smoke to have something to do. Thought it through. "I won't be around here long."

She stood up. Held out her hand to me. "You'll be around here till it gets light anyway."

⍙ 88

IN HER BEDROOM, she pulled the T-shirt over her head and stepped into my chest, tilting her face up. Her lips were full and rich. Swollen. I kissed her softly, my hands trailing down her back. Her skin had a fine sheen of powder and sweat. Her arms came up, linked around my neck. She leaned back, one bare foot on my shoe. Her breasts were small, round perfect things, tiny nipples dark against the milky flesh.

Blossom pushed my jacket off my shoulders, opened the buttons on my shirt with a pickpocket's touch. She sat on the bed while I pulled off the rest of my clothes. Held out her hand again. Pushed me onto my back on the bed. Got to her feet. Hooked thumbs in the waistband of her powder-blue panties and pulled them down to her thighs. Bent at the waist as she stepped out of them. Came onto the bed again, her face in my neck. I gazed down the line of her back. Her ankles were slim, calf muscles standing out strong. A woman who spent a lot of time on her feet. Her buttocks swelled from a tiny waist. I patted her, feeling the firm flesh bounce back against me.

"It's a handful, huh?"

"Bigger than I would've thought."

"I had to learn how to walk to keep it down. Boys used to follow me home from school."

"I would have, I saw all this in motion."

She slid one leg over mine, trailing wetness. Kissed me deep, tongue curling up against the back of my top teeth. Her hand found me. "You left something in your clothes," she whispered. "Go get it."

"What?"

She propped herself up on her elbows, regarding me with those searchlight eyes. "Don't tell me . . ."

"What?"

"Why do you carry that pistol, trouble-man?"

"For protection."

"Yeah. You wouldn't leave home without it. That the only kind of protection you can think of?"

"Oh."

"Yeah. Oh. You have any or not?"

"Not."

Her little fist thumped me lightly on the chest. "Nice work, boy. You get lucky enough to come along when I'm having an estrogen-fit, then you blow it."

"Speaking of which . . ."

"Forget it. What year do you think this is? I didn't go to

medical school to have some strange man playing with my life. I don't know where you've been."

"I . . ."

"Don't even tell me. A stiff cock's got no conscience."

"Your mother tell you that?"

"Matter of fact, she did. Best time to ask a man for a favor is just before he comes."

"When's the best time for a woman?"

"Just after." A gentle twist to her mouth, playing with a smile.

I cupped my hands behind my head. Looked at the ceiling. "How long do these estrogen-fits of yours last?"

Her full smile bloomed in the darkness. "Not long enough for you to find a drugstore, you dope. You know *anything* about women?"

"Not much."

A faint coppery smell came off her body. She nuzzled against my neck. Whispered, "Wait here." Like I was going anywhere. I watched her walk out of the bedroom. She didn't bother to keep it down. Cyndi could have taken lessons.

I closed my eyes. Felt her hand on me. Slick and wet. A long fingernail trailed down my shaft. Electricity ran from my spine to the back of my neck.

"You found something?" I asked her.

"Like what?"

"I don't know. A diaphragm, foam . . . something." Not saying anything about the vasectomy I'd had years ago . . . like I'd told her too much, somehow.

"Feel this," she said, guiding my fingertips to her upper arm. Five tiny little lines, fan-shaped under the skin.

"What is it?" I asked her.

"Progestin. Best birth-control chemical there is. Each implant is a time-release bar. The whole thing's good for about five years. Unless you weigh more than a hundred and fifty-four pounds. You think I'm a good risk?'' Patting her butt, smiling.

"You're well on the safe side."

"You're not exactly a silver-tongued devil, are you, boy? Anyway, this version's called Norplant. It just got FDA approval—I was one of the volunteers they tested it on. No ugly side effects like the Pill.''

"So why . . . ?"

"I know how to keep from having babies. Know what to do if that doesn't work too. You never heard about Safe Sex?"

"Sure." I didn't tell her where I first heard about it. From a child molester. Safe for him.

He thought.

Her hand stroked. I opened my eyes a slit. White fluffy bath towel lying on the bed.

"That isn't going to work," I told her. "I haven't gotten off like that since I was a kid."

"Shhh, baby. Close your eyes. I'll tell you a story."

She whispered all I'd missed out on, coming to her house without protection. Whispered and stroked and teased and played and chuckled.

Then she spread the towel over me, curled up against me, and we slept together.

◊ 89

I WOKE UP to the sound of the shower. Wrapped the towel around me, went into the kitchen, lit a smoke. Heard the bathroom door open. Found Blossom seated at her dressing table, working some cream into her face. She nodded her head at the bathroom, concentrating.

The place was full of steam, mirror fogged. I took a shower with the liquid soap she left there in a clear push-top bottle. Washed my hair with shampoo I found in a black squeeze tube. Put on last night's clothes.

Blossom was still in the bedroom, still fussing with her face when I came back.

"I don't want you to take this the wrong way," she said, "but I can be saying this only once. I'm not mad at you. There's nothing wrong. But I *can't* talk to people in the morning when I first get up. I need to be with myself. It's okay if you stay, do what you want. There's food inside. But don't talk to me till I talk to you, okay?"

"Okay."

She was letting me see pieces of her—the ones she wanted held up to the light. No more today. I walked out. It was still before rush hour—it only took me twenty minutes to get back to the motel, even with stopping at a drugstore.

90

I SEPARATED OUT my dry cleaning, stuffed underwear and socks into the laundry bag Rebecca had given me. Showered again, shaved, changed my clothes. Time to work.

Called Sherwood from the car. "Want to meet me someplace?"

"Okay. You know your way around?"

"I can find you."

"The Police Community Relations Outpost. It's on Twenty-fifth, just off Broadway. In about an hour."

"I was hoping for a little more privacy."

His laugh was a bass rumble.

₩ 91

I TURNED THE Lincoln onto Broadway, motored past the Y&W Drive-In Theatre. Glanced at the marquee: first-run flicks, no slasher-porn. Still in Merrillville. I crossed the line into Gary at Fifty-third. The stores got closer together, muscling each other for sidewalk room. Package joints, tire stores, BBQ, brick-fronted bars, shoeshine, barbershops. An abandoned gas station. Pizza parlors, law offices, auto body shops. A dozen different dumps with "Lounge" after some name. XXX video stores. Signs: Go-Go Dancers Wanted. Burlesque. Poolroom. Ladies Welcome. Exotic Dancers. Hand-painted, red letters: LIVE GIRLS.

I thought of the Ghost Van.

I crossed into Glen Park, where even the billboards turned Afro. Fast food, ribs and chicken. Sex shops, private booths, a quarter a play. Storefront churches. Check cashing. Pawnshops. Bible Book Center. Tattoo parlor. A closed-front store advertising Swingers' Supplies and Marital Aids.

They probably got the last word right.

At Twenty-sixth a sign: Welcome to Gary. Sherwood's home ground.

I hung a left on Twenty-fifth. The Police Community Relations sign hung limply from a bombed-out ruin, rusted metal gates padlocked across its face. A black unmarked Ford parked in front, conspicuous as a pigeon among peacocks in that neighborhood. The front seat nearly filled with one body.

I pulled in behind him, killed the ignition. He maneuvered his bulk out of the car, light on his feet. Came around to the passenger side. I hit the switch and he climbed in.

"Let's take your ride. Leave this thing on the street around here, it won't be around when you get back."

"Where to?"

"Straight ahead. Past the high school. Over by the Delaney Projects. You know where they are, right?"

I didn't say anything. But Hightower's mother must have.

Sherwood pointed to the curb with a cigar-sized finger and I pulled over.

"You wanted to talk?"

I lit a smoke. "Remember that postal stuff we talked about? There's a few possibilities in there, but I can't be sure. They're for real, I don't want to just roll up on them at their houses, right?"

He didn't even nod, watching close.

"You must have crews around here. I've been checking, asking around." Remembering something Virgil had told me. "That little town, Lake Station, wasn't it once called East Gary?"

"Yep. Sure was."

"And the people there, they wanted a different name. Not be associated with Gary in people's minds."

"That don't make them Nazis."

"Didn't say it did. But you got a Klan in Indiana, at least south of here you do. And what *they* do is recruit, right? I don't mean hold rallies and stuff. They ask around, see who's interested. They may not call themselves by any special name, but there's no shortage of hate groups around here.''

"Black *and* white."

"Sure. I'm not a sociologist. The guy I'm looking for, he's white."

"Random killings. Sniper fire. What's white about that?"

"Nothing by itself. But this isn't about race. That's not the key. The Zebra killings in Frisco, that was race war."

"You know about that?"

I dragged on my smoke, letting him have my eyes. "Death Angels. With little dark wings drawn on their photographs. Take Five. Carry devil's heads to Mecca. Extra points for kids. The cops never got all of them. The BLA, that was color too. But the color they were hunting was blue. That white guy in Buffalo. He shot random, but only blacks. The shrinks are working on a new word for it: Afrophobia.''

His smile was bitter ice. "Yeah, they always know what to call a lynching."

"My man won't be a Nazi. He's alone. Inside himself. But he may have tried. Flirted with the edges. Likes the costumes. So what I need, I need to know where I could maybe find some of these freaks."

"You gonna sign up?"

"I don't do undercover work. Takes too long. It's not them I'm after."

"So how d'you talk to them?"

"I'll offer to sell them some guns."

"Those boys are suspicious. Paranoid. They'll think you're the Man."

"Not if they run my prints. These guys always have friends on the force."

"Could be . . . I heard rumors on my own job."

"Officer Revis maybe?"

His eyes glinted. "You do get around, don't you? Where d'you hear that?"

"Same place you heard I'd been to the Projects before."

Sherwood fired a smoke of his own. Looked as thin as a chiba joystick in his thick fingers. "There's a truckers' motel out on the Interstate, right across from the power plant. You know it?"

"I can find it."

"Yeah. Like you said before. Anyway, there's a bar just down the road. Freestanding, big parking lot. Sign out front says they have fashion shows there."

"Fashion shows?"

"You'll see. Look for a white Chevy Blazer, little Confederate flag on the antenna. White Power bumper sticker." He pulled out a notebook, wrote something, tore out the page, handed it to me. "License number. David Matson is the owner. In his forties, about six one, about half bald, always wears some kind of cap, even indoors. He's the head of the local chapter."

"Of . . ."

"Of whatever they call themselves this week. But it don't matter, Matson'll be the boss."

"Thanks."

I dropped him back at his cruiser. He turned to me, getting out of the car. "You said this wasn't about race. What is it about?"

"Sex."

"People get those mixed up around here, my friend."

After he left, I called Blossom from the car.

"You want some company?"

"I want yours."

₩ 92

LUNCH WAS A salad, all red and green.

"You'd rather have meat, wouldn't you?"

"I guess."

"This is better for you."

"I'm sure"—wondering when it was coming.

"You take vitamins?"

"Ginseng."

"That's not a vitamin, it's an herb. You're going to smoke, you should take nine, ten thousand milligrams of Vitamin C a day. And fifty thousand IU of beta-carotene."

"IU?" I asked, pretending like I was listening.

"International Units."

"Okay."

"Okay what?"

"Okay, boss."

Her laugh was throaty. "You never had a boss in your life."

"I've had cottage leaders, counselors, directors, superintendents, wardens . . . you name it."

"No employers?"

"No."

"Didn't think so."

"You think you know me, girl? You talked to Sherwood, maybe got a look at my rap sheet. Watched me around the diner. Drove around in my car . . ."

"Held you in my hands."

"That too. Think you know me?"

"Yes."

"Why am I here? Right now."

"You want to see if I'm still having an estrogen-fit."

I locked her eyes, voice serious, just the edge of a chill. The same voice that's backed up punks all through the underground. "I'm here because I got work to do . . . *we* got work to do. The cops think they got a pattern to the killings, but there might be more. Random shootings. *Not* deaths. Shootings. Maybe this freak dipped it, got it wet before he plunged in. We could get it out of the newspapers, but it might take weeks of work, go back a couple of years. So what we need is a reporter. Every paper's got at least one real one. Some hungry guy, wants to know what's going on. That's why he's in the journalism racket, to *know* things. We find one, get his nose open. Make him a deal. Tell him why we're looking, get him to go through the clips. Attempted murders, shootings. Drive-bys would be the best. Or snipershooting into some woman's window. See? Give us a few more pieces."

"I . . ."

"I'm not finished, Blossom. This pattern thing, it could lead to nothing. I don't know where the flower is, but I know the root. Like a preacher knows the devil. But where I have to look, it'll take a scam. And a doctor, now she'd be just perfect for it." I lit a smoke, pushing my salad plate away. "Now you understand what I came here for?"

She got up, walked around behind my chair, put her hands on my shoulders, her lips against my ear. "I'll carry your gun in my purse, in case you get stopped again. Besides, you probably got no room in your pocket, all those rubbers you brought with you."

〰 93

IT TOOK ALMOST an hour for her to come out of the bedroom. I looked up from the newspaper. Blinked.

Blossom in a teal-blue silk sheath cut an inch or two above
the knee, thin black belt at the waist, black spike heels with
ankle straps, tiny black-faced watch on her wrist. A pair of
black gloves in her hand.

"Like it?" she said, twirling a full spin, looking at me
over one shoulder. Showing me another side of her, promising more. Her lemon-blonde hair was swept off her face,
done up in a thick French braid. A touch of soft blue eyeliner,
lips glossy and full. Seamed stockings caught the afternoon
sunlight.

"You're a doctor . . . I look dead to you?"

She let me hear a grown-up girl's giggle, smoothed the
sheath over her hips. "I'm lucky I can still get into this one."

"How come . . . I mean, why'd you . . . ?"

"You said something about getting a man's nose open, last
I heard."

〰94

BLOSSOM CROSSED HER lovely legs, arched her back. Reached for the car phone, punched in a number. I told her we'd start with the reporter who'd done the feature story on the family of one of the dead kids. She got him on the line.

"Mr. Slater, my name is Blossom Lynch. I wonder if I could talk to you about one of the stories you wrote . . . about those lovers' lane murders?"

. . .

"I've got a special interest. A personal interest."

. . .

"Well, I'm on my way to Gary right now. Could I just stop in, maybe take a few minutes of your time?"

. . .

"Thank you so much."

She sat back in her seat. "He'll be a good reporter."

"How could you tell from that?"

"He knew I was a beauty even over the phone. And don't be asking me how I could tell *that*."

𝕍 95

WE CROSSED THE railroad tracks on Broadway, stopped in front of the *Post-Tribune*. Blossom gave her name to the guard at the desk. We took seats, Blossom frowning as I lit a smoke.

Slater came into the waiting room. Took one look at Blossom and thanked God for sending him to journalism school. A medium-built youngish man with an honest, open face, shirt coming out of his suit pants, needed a haircut.

"Miss Lynch?" he said, walking over.

"Doctor Lynch," I told him, getting up before she did.

The same reporter who'd been in the courtroom when Lloyd was bailed out. He must have recognized me, but he didn't miss a beat. "And you're . . ."

"Sloane. Mitchell Sloane. Private investigator."

"Come on with me," he said, moving his arm for Blossom to step in front of him. He was young, not stupid.

We took seats in the conference room. Slater took out a reporter's notepad. I lit another smoke.

"What Mr. Sloane told you is true, Mr. Slater. I'm a doctor. But that's not why I'm here. One of the girls who was killed, Rose, she was my sister. It seems the police don't have a viable suspect, just this young kid they arrested. So I retained Mr. Sloane to help me look into the situation. He had some ideas he wanted to check out, and I thought we'd come to you about one of them."

"Which one?"

My cue. "Maybe this sniper worked up to what he eventually did. Maybe he tried out the weapon on some other people first. Not killing, just shooting at them. Or maybe he tried a different gun. But, I figure, maybe there's been some other shootings in the past few months, maybe back a year or so. Unsolved shootings."

"This is Gary, Indiana, friend. You think every time somebody fires a shot on the street it makes the papers?"

"If somebody's hit they would. Hell, they even do that in Detroit."

"Okay. Why come to me?"

Blossom leaned forward, flashed a smile, promised more. "This isn't a job for a thug, Mr. Slater." Excluding me from the conversation. "It's a job for an investigative reporter. You help us look, you'll be the first one to know if it works out."

"What if I look and there's nothing?"

"I'm going to look other places. Maybe you will too . . . and we can compare notes, maybe come up with something that will help."

"How can I reach you?"

Blossom gave him her phone number. I smoked my cigarette. They talked some more. I tuned them out.

I followed behind them as Slater walked Blossom to the car.

96

"WHAT'S THE SCAM?" she asked on the drive back.

"Scam?"

"The one you said I'd be needed for."

"It's too early for it. Have to wait. See if Slater comes up with anything. And there's a man I have to see."

"What can I do now?"

"You got a car of your own?"

"Sure."

"We could use some detailed street maps. And I need you to learn how the Child Abuse Registry works out here. Where they keep the central records, what the access level of authority is. Especially if the records are on computer storage."

"Why?"

"Just do it, okay?"

"You mad at me?"

"No."

"Then what?"

"I listened to you when you knew what you were talking about. Like about the vitamins, right? I know about this."

"Didn't I do well with the reporter?"

"You did great."

"Then . . . okay. Where're we going?"

"I'm looking for somebody."

She sat in silence while I rolled down the Interstate past

the motel Sherwood told me about. Cars in the lot. No Chevy Blazers.

I stopped the car outside Blossom's house.

"You're not coming in?"

"I got work to do."

"When will you be finished?"

"Maybe eleven."

"Toss a pebble against my window," she said. "You know where it is."

⚜ 97

ARE YOU GOING to live with us?" Virginia asked me at dinner that night. Flat out, the way a kid asks. Wanting to know, not playing with it.

"Child, where did you put your manners?"

"She don't mean nothing, Reba. You like folks to live with us, don't you, honey?"

"Not everybody, Daddy. Just my family. That's how I got my Lloyd, when he came to live with us."

Lloyd sat up straighter in his chair.

⚓ 98

WE WENT RIDING that night. Looking. It was just after eight when I pulled into a gas station. Virgil filled the tank while I reached out for Vincenzo. The Prof put him on the phone.

"The kind of person you want is a piquerist," he told me.

"A what?"

"Piquerist." He spelled it for me. Explained how the word came from the French, meaning to penetrate. I didn't interrupt him—Vincenzo flies down the track when he's got a full head of steam, but he derails easily.

"That sounds right to me," I told him.

"It wasn't in the DSM-III, not even in the latest revised edition. It's a pathological condition: it means the realization of sexual satisfaction from penetrating a victim by sniper activity. Or stab wounds, or even bites. And I found that case you wanted. *People* v. *Drake*. The defendant went to the city dump late at night. He fired nineteen rounds from a semi-automatic rifle into a car parked there. Two people were killed. He said that he didn't know anybody was in the car—he was just taking target practice. When the police examined the bodies, they found the female victim had bite marks on her and a bruised rectum. The female was dead before the bite marks were inflicted. Do you want the citation?"

I knew better than to say no.

"The official designation is 129 A.D.2d 966, Appellate Division, Fourth Department, decided April 3, 1987."

"Perfect job, Vincenzo. Can I ask you some questions about the case?"

"I have a copy with me."

"Okay. Was the shooter wearing camo gear?"

"Camo gear? It says . . . he was dressed in battle fatigues."

"Yeah, right. The weapon, do you have any specifics?"

"It says .22 caliber semi-automatic rifle, plus a high-powered 5.69-millimeter rifle and two large hunting knives. That's all."

"Just one more, Vincenzo. It was a psychiatrist who said this guy was a . . . piquerist, right?"

"Yes."

"Did he testify for the defense or the prosecution?"

"For the prosecution. The defendant said the whole thing was an accident. He was just practicing."

"You're the world's best researcher, Vincenzo."

"Thank you. I have a lot of notes, should I . . . ?"

"Hang on to them for me, okay? Let me speak to the Prof."

"I'll bet a dime my man was on time."

"Right on time. I'm in the picture now."

"They got freaks everywhere, bro'. You should know."

⚡ 99

BACK IN THE car, dark all around. Moving slow. Watching. I told Virgil about the call.

"Sounds like our man."

"Yeah. Sounds like the way Bundy worked. I knew it, just didn't know what to call it."

"Man like that, he wouldn't stop?"

"Not stop for good. He could hold up for a while. Until the pressure starts to pop his valves."

"Think he'd have a record?"

"No. Maybe some juvenile thing we couldn't find out about. It's a young man's crime."

We did a long, slow figure eight around the area. Merrillville, Glen Park, Miller, Gary, Lake Station. I didn't know the way in yet, working on the different ways out.

"Virgil, I got something from Sherwood. You ever hear of a guy named Matson?"

"No."

"One of those Nazi types. Got some little group. You know: white power, save the race, kill the Commies and the niggers."

"Yeah."

"If our boy ever tried to link up, that's the place he'd go. Where he could wear his gear, carry his weapons, be part of something. I figure, maybe I'll try and talk to this Matson. Tell him I'm selling guns. Maybe he saw this freak."

"Those boys're not wrapped too tight."

"I know. I don't have an address for him. Just a place he hangs out. On the Interstate, a strip joint."

The windshield reflected Virgil's face, Cherokee cast to his features. "There's a number you can call at the mill. Pay phone. Anyone answering, you just tell them to get me. I can be anywhere around here in maybe fifteen minutes."

₩ 100

IT WAS WELL past eleven when I tossed a handful of pebbles and dirt in a gentle arc against Blossom's bedroom window. A light blinked on. I went around to the back door, an airline bag in my hand. She was wearing the terry-cloth robe, her face puffy with sleep.

She grabbed the sleeve of my jacket, turned around, and went back to her room, tugging me behind her.

❦ 101

IT WAS AFTER three in the morning when I felt her hands on my shoulders.

"Why are you sitting out here by yourself, baby?"

"I wanted to smoke a cigarette. Figured you didn't want the smell in your bedroom."

"Come on back with me. Bring your damn cigarettes."

❦ 102

THE PHONE RANG in her bedroom. She didn't stir. Voice of an answering machine picking up. Man's voice. A hard man. "Nobody's available to talk to you right now. Leave a message and one of us will get back to you."

The machine beeped. Hang-up tone.

"Working at the diner, you meet all kinds of folks. It's not hard to get a phone number. They call, hear that voice, they figure I'm not living alone. It wouldn't bother anyone with a real message for me."

"Who made the tape for you?"

"An old friend."

"You know a lot of tricks for a country girl."

She propped herself on one elbow, eyes luminous. Leaned across my chest, found the cigarettes. Stuck one in her mouth, snapped a match alive, took a drag. Handed it to me.

"My mother ran a bawdy house. That's what they called them then. I was raised with working girls. My mother was one herself, before she went into management. You know West Virginia?"

"A little bit. I worked the riverfront once. Both sides. Steubenville in Ohio, Weirton in West Virginia."

"That's the spot. Mama started with a little crib on Water Street, back in the sixties."

I remembered. Only place I'd ever been where you could buy moonshine and heroin on the same block. Made Detroit look like Disneyland.

The red tip of the cigarette pulled highlights from her hair, flowing loose around her shoulders.

"My mother got left with a baby. Pregnant prostitute, you heard all the jokes. That was my sister Violet. She made it by herself, did what she knew how to do."

"You were never . . ."

Blossom laughed. "I never went to church. Mama wasn't enough of a hypocrite for that. And the kids at school, they knew. I learned how to fight real young. But turn a trick? She would've taken the skin right off my backside. Same for the other girls . . . the girls in the house, I mean. Some were silly, some were mean. But most, they were real sweet and loving to me, like family. I used to have to take four baths a day, scrub off all that perfume and powder they'd put on me when I was a little girl."

Two girls. How many faces? I turned to her. "And you went to medical school . . ."

"Yes."

"Those houses were rough joints. How'd your mother keep things quiet?"

"She always had a boyfriend. And we had a manager. House man. He wasn't for the girls, Mama did that. He'd work the door, handle things. She had the same one, J.B., long as I can remember. Boyfriends, they'd come and go, but J.B. was always there."

"Never got busted?"

"Oh, sure. Once in a while. It was never much of anything. Pay a fine, pay the sheriff, Mama said it was all the same. It was a sweet house. Blue light. No rough stuff. You could gamble downstairs, but it was no house game. Just the boys playing cards among themselves. No dice, no wheels. You give a man a card table, some good whiskey, let him smoke his cigars, have some pretty girls walk around in high heels and fishnet stockings, serve the drinks, light their smokes, they'll stay all night. Mama used to tell them, you set aside enough cash to spend an hour upstairs, and you go home a winner, no matter what."

"She knows how it works."

"She died five years ago. When I was almost twenty-four. Lung cancer."

"That's why you went to medical school?"

"Partly. Funny, I was always the one Mama worried about the most. Violet was wild, but she settled right down. And Rose, she was quiet. Everybody's pet. I spoiled her rotten my ownself."

"Why'd she worry about you?"

"Mama used to say, a girl who's got a taste for a trouble-man once, she keeps it forever."

"And you did?"

"Chandler Wells. God. Used to be I could just write his name in my school notebook and get trembly right above the tops of my nylons thinking about him. He was a wild boy. Not bad, not evil like some. But wild. He ran 'shine just for the kick of it. Gambled away all the money he made. Folks said he'd be a stock-car champion, he could ever settle down long enough, get him a good ride at the track. He even tried it a couple of times. Told me it wasn't much of a thrill going round in circles.''

"What happened to him?''

She wasn't listening. Her long nails absently scratching my chest. Back there, then.

"Mama ran him off a dozen times. She couldn't get mad at him, not real mad. He'd come around to the back. And the girls, they'd help me sneak out, be with him. One time, the troopers chased us. Just for speeding, but Chandler, he wanted to play. He had this old Mercury he put back together from a stock car and there wasn't a car in the county could catch him when he was flying. The troopers had the road blocked off at one end. They used to leave just enough space between the cars to let one through. *Just* enough. Like a challenge: that opening looked like a slit when you were going fast enough. They played it square: you got through, they wouldn't chase you anymore that night. But if you didn't, they'd call the meat wagon. Chandler was smoking down this old dirt road when we saw it. 'You want me to stop?' he asked me. 'Go on through, honey,' I told him. Holding on. 'I love you, Blossom.' It was the first time he said that to me. Like he did then. We shot through the roadblock like it was a mile wide. Weeks after that, folks would come to see Chandler's Mercury . . . there was paint streaks down both sides from where he passed so close. When he finally brought me home that night, Mama grabbed a strap, chased me all around the place. The girls had to sit on her, hold her down, she was so mad. Later, when she was calm, she sat me down. Told me what Chandler was. A trouble-man. She said some men are rogues and ramblers, and some women are just drawn to them. After a while, the good ones, they settle down. But a trouble-man, he never gets quiet.''

"Chandler never got quiet?"

"Got real quiet. Dead quiet." A tear tracked her face. "He got into an argument with another boy in one of the riverfront joints. Chandler asked him to step outside. The other boy had a knife. Chandler didn't. He was twenty-two. I was still in high school then. Thought I'd never stop crying."

I lit another smoke. "Some people, they never get to find their love."

"You ever love a woman, Burke?"

"Two."

"Where are they?"

"One's dead. One's gone."

"The girl who's gone . . . why'd she go?"

I dragged on the smoke. "The woman who died, Belle, it was my fault. It didn't have to be. I used to think all the time about the woman who's gone, Flood. Why she left. Now, maybe I know. Maybe she knew what you know. Didn't know what to call it, but she knew."

"Trouble-man," she whispered, coming to me.

▽ 103

LIGHT WAS BREAKING across the bedroom window. Blossom lying on top of me, wetness still holding us together below the waist. "Trouble-man," she said. "Troubled man, you are. What did you go to prison for?"

I looked into the center of her eyes—the way you do with a parole officer. "For something I didn't do."

"And what was that—what was it you didn't do?"

"Get away," I told her.

Her body trembled against me, giggling. "You want a cigarette?" she asked.

"Yeah."

She lit one for me, supporting herself on her elbows, holding it to my mouth.

"Cigarettes are an addiction."

"Bullshit."

"You could stop any time you wanted?"

"Sure."

"I know how to do a lot of tricks I never actually did myself. Listening to the girls. You want to see?"

"Un-huh."

"Close your eyes."

I put my cigarette in the ashtray, felt her eyelashes flutter on my cheek. "That's a butterfly kiss. You ever have one before?"

"No."

"You like it?"

"Do it some more."

"Keep your eyes closed." A wet slab sliding across my face. I opened my eyes. Blossom was licking her lips, smiling. Licked me again. "That was a cow kiss."

"Ugh! Save that one for the farmers."

"I told you, baby"—her voice play-sexy—"I never tried these tricks before." Her voice turned quiet, little-girl serious. "You could really stop smoking?" Raising herself higher on her elbows, rolling her shoulders so the tips of her breasts brushed my chest.

"That's what I said."

"Why don't you?"

"Why should I?"

"I'll make you a deal, trouble-man. The best deal you ever had in your hard life. You stop smoking for one week. Seven days. You do that, I'll do whatever you want. For one night. Whatever you want to do, whatever you want me to do. Show you some of those tricks I never got to try." Her eyes were wide, mocking. "What d'you say?"

I put the cigarette in my mouth, took a long, deep drag. Ground it out.

▼ 104

BLOSSOM WAS ALL in black and white the next morning. White wool jacket over a black silk blouse, white pleated skirt, plain black pumps. Black pillbox hat, white gloves. She'd worked the makeup expertly around her eyes so she looked older.

"You going to need your car today?"

"Sure."

"Not *a* car, *your* car. You could take mine. I figure, the Lincoln, it'd make a better impression if anyone's looking."

"Where?"

"At the hospital. I'm up here for the summer, visiting my relatives. Thinking about doing a paper on medical responses to child abuse emergencies. So I figured, I'd stop by the hospital, make some friends. Get some questions answered. Your questions."

I handed her the keys.

"Is it hard?" she asked, pulling on her gloves.

"You mean still?"

"I mean giving up smoking, you dope," she said over her shoulder, walking out.

❦ 105

I WAS IN the back in the prison yard, walking the perimeter with my eyes, checking the gun towers. The Prof materialized next to me. Like he'd always been there. He didn't have to ask what I was doing.

"First place to look is inside your head, schoolboy. Over the wall don't get it all."

I took out a smoke. Fired a match. Remembered. Blew out the match. Started to look for the sniper. Inside my head.

I've known a few. A nameless Irishman working in Biafra—a big, unsmiling man who got his training on the rooftops of Belfast under the blanket of blood-smog. A desert-burned Israeli, part of a hunter-killer team meeting at the Mole's junkyard. El Cañonero. The FBI said he was a terrorist. And Wesley. Terror itself.

Faceless men, with interchangeable eyes.

Even in wartime, they stood apart from the soldiers.

Wesley once told me, you don't shoot people, you shoot targets.

But the freak who stalked the lovers' lanes—he hunted humans.

⚘ 106

I TRIED THE Interstate joint. No sign of the Blazer. When I swung past Blossom's house, the Lincoln was out front.

She was sitting at the kitchen table, still in her black-and-white outfit, a bound sheaf of computer printouts in front of her, drinking her coffee.

I stepped behind her, put my hand on her shoulder. She reached up, brought it to her face. Sniffed deeply. "You're not smoking," she said, not looking up. Kissed my hand, put it back on her shoulder.

"What'd you get?"

"This is a sample," she said, all business. "They gave it to me. For my research." Accenting the last word, sneering at someone being naive. Maybe not them. "Here's the way it works, Burke. There's an 800 number. State-wide. Where you call if you have a case of suspected child abuse. Everyone calls the same number: social workers, ER nurses, school-teachers, next-door neighbors. The call goes to Indianapolis, where they keep the Central Registry. Then the call gets dispatched back out to a local agency. That agency sends someone out to investigate. Then they make a report: it's real or it's not. Either way, the report goes back to Indianapolis. Every report's in their computer."

"How long do they keep the records?"

"Near as I could tell, they never get rid of them. They have records go back a couple of generations anyway. But the computer, it only has data for about the past fifteen, twenty years.''

"They break it down by county?"

"Yes. This is Lake County. All the records for the region are in the DPW Building.''

"On the computer too?"

"Yes. But all the computer has is the information that's on this form,'' she said, pushing a dull green piece of paper across to me. It looked like a police pedigree: name, age, date of birth, address, check-places for type of suspected abuse or neglect.

I scanned the paper. I'd seen it before. They all use the same form. ''You actually see the computer?''

"The central data-bank's not there. But there's terminals all over the place.''

"On-line access? Twenty-four hours a day?"

She nodded.

"They segregate the local data?"

Blossom nodded again, watching closely now.

"Okay.''

"Okay what?"

"Just okay. See you later tonight?''

"I'll be here.''

"Blossom . . .''

"What?"

"Give me my pistol.''

〰 107

THE RAIN STARTED about ten. The building was dark, lights burning on the third floor. Rebecca was at the wheel, me next to her in the front seat, Virgil in the back. They both smoked in silence, waiting for me.

B&E. Back to myself, back to crime. Started to think like myself then. Working with what I knew. Knowing when a woman spreads her legs, it's not the same thing as opening up. Blossom was compartmentalized, and I hadn't looked inside all the boxes.

It was eleven before the lights went off. Almost midnight when we heard the back door open, close. A dark-colored compact came down the driveway, braked, took off slowly to the left.

"Cleaning lady," I said. "She must work six to midnight."

We gave it another two hours. A police cruiser went by in the darkness. Didn't stop. No foot patrols.

"Nothing anybody'd want in there," Virgil said.

My birth certificate told how right he was.

❦ 108

THE RAIN WAS pounding harder as I drove back to Hammond. A light flicked on as I turned off the engine. Blossom was in her robe in the kitchen, no sleep-signs on her face.

"You want something to eat?"

"No, thanks."

"Have just some dry toast. You don't want to take this stuff on an empty stomach."

"What stuff?"

"What's it look like to you?" Moving her shoulder to indicate the kitchen table.

"It looks like three fat gray coffins and a red dot," I told her, sitting down.

"The big ones are Vitamin C. The red one's the beta-carotene."

"You bought this stuff?"

"This afternoon. While you were out prowling around."

"Thanks."

"It was the least I could do. You've been a good boy."

My eyes went up to her face, voice soft, wanting her to understand. "I'm not a boy."

She brought the toast over to the table, a glass of cold water in her other hand. Put them down. Smoothed her robe over her hips and sat on my lap, primly, one hand on the back of my neck for balance.

"All men are boys. Different kinds of boys. You're a bad boy."

"Blossom . . ."

"A bad boy. Not a mean one. Eat your toast. Take your vitamins."

I ate slowly, feeling her warm, solid weight on me. Only her feet and a piece of her calves showed under the hem of the robe. Dark nylon stocking on one leg, the other bare.

I swallowed the last vitamin. She bounced sweetly in my lap. "Let's go see," she said.

❦ 109

LATER. THE RAIN slapped the house. Blossom's cheek against my chest, blonde hair trailing halfway down her back. Legs slightly parted, one sheathed in the dark stocking, the other bare.

"Tell me about him," she asked, a tiny tremor in her voice.

I didn't answer her, translating inside my head, putting it in a package.

"You know what DNA is?"

"Yes."

"One thing you'll always find around any lovers' lane, discarded condoms. The cops didn't collect them from the murder scene. They'd done that, maybe they'd have his fingerprints."

"You mean . . ."

"Yeah. He's not a mass murderer, he's a serial killer."

"What's the difference?"

"A mass murderer, he straps down, walks out the door to do his work. Hunting for humans. He's not coming back. Like that maniac who strolled into McDonald's, turned it into a splatter film. Those kind, they *walk*, understand? When they hear the music, they march. Like a Geiger counter. The ticks start to run close together, it's a hum in their head. They pull the trigger, make it stop. Leave a lot of bodies around."

"Like that girl who killed all those schoolkids? Just outside of Chicago?"

"Just like her. She had to do her work. Her work was done, she was too. That's why so many of them kill themselves. Right after their work is done. Not because they can't face going to jail. It's just . . . over. The humming stops. What they need is a lot of humans in the same place. Doesn't matter which ones."

"The one who killed my sister . . ."

"That's not him. He's the other side of the moon. The human-hunters, they kill to stop the humming in the head. This guy, he looks for it. Only way he can get it is to kill. Then it starts. He wants to hear it again. That special song. The one only he hears. So he goes again."

"So he wouldn't kill himself?"

"Never."

"It was just . . . random, wasn't it, Burke? You don't think he was tracking anyone in particular . . . like my sister?"

"No. He's no man-stalker. I think he looked a long time before he did this. Started slow. They have trigger-signals. It's different for every one. Like a message, only for them. I talked to a guy once. Slasher-rapist. He told me, the women, they asked him to do it. Sent him a message. Not every woman, just some."

"What was the message . . . his message?"

"He said, if he could see the panty-line under their skirts, that was it."

"God."

"If there's a God, someone needs to sue him for malpractice."

She shuddered against me.

⚑ 110

JUST BEFORE LIGHT. "Burke, do you know what his signal is?"

"I think so. Some of it anyway. It's his way of having sex. The only way that works for him. He knows he's a beast. A lonely beast, the only one of his species. He can't find a mate. He sees the mating act, sees sex. It's like they're laughing at him. Waving it in his face. When he started shooting, the first time, maybe it was rage. Like he was being mocked. Then one time, he fired, saw someone go down. And he got off. Came. Released. He went over the line then—now it's the only place where it can happen for him. He wouldn't go back if he could."

She shifted her weight against me, listening with her whole body. "One thing Mama always said—the most dangerous thing a working girl could do was laugh at a trick."

"She knew, your mother. This guy, I think he's rooted. Close to home. His base. He doesn't live in a furnished room, out of the back of an old car. Most serial killers, they're drivers. Nomads. Cover a lot of territory. Not this one. He's hit at least twice. Close by, each time. We'll check those news clips, maybe we'll know more. One thing I know already—he's not a team. He's more alone than anyone in the world.''

''You sound like you feel sorry for him.''

''I'm trying to feel him, Blossom. Be him, in my mind. Get close. It's the only way.''

''You can do that?''

''Yeah.''

''How can you be sure?'' She felt the chill from me. ''I'm just playing devil's advocate,'' defensive sound in her voice.

I remembered something the Prof told me once. ''The devil don't need advocates, Blossom. I know because they taught me. We're all branches from the same root.''

''All men . . . all people?''

''No. Not all.'' I closed my eyes. Saw a sturdy little boy, big eyes almost hidden under a thick thatch of hair. Standing in the corner of Lily's office, face a mottled patch of red and white pain. Holding the arm of a teddy bear doll in one tiny fist, the stuffing coming out the end. The battered doll lying in the corner where he'd thrown it. ''I *hate* Teddy!'' he cried. ''I told him what they did. I asked him to make it stop. He was my friend. And he *wouldn't*. He wouldn't make it stop.'' Lily held him on her lap, telling him it wasn't Teddy's fault. Teddy did his best. Teddy loved him. And so did she. He was safe now. The child cried against her chest, still clutching Teddy's ripped-out arm. Lily looked over at me. Her Madonna's face was composed, watching me. I caught the fire-dots in her reflective eyes. Then I went out to do Teddy's work.

''It's a Zen exercise,'' I told Blossom. ''Dark Zen. You have to cross over the line to where he is, you want to find him. I can do that.''

She nestled against me, half asleep. Murmured something that sounded like agreement.

I didn't tell her the rest—getting over the line is the easy part.

⬙ 111

I WATCHED BLOSSOM dress in the morning. Not talking, not moving. Sweet smells, soft motions. Round-top little chair at her dressing table, padded seat like a piano stool. Blossom in her slip, walking to it, humming to herself. Her shoulders moved in line with the stool, knees bent as she swung her hips onto it. Hips moving a microsecond slower than the rest of her, after-image of the rounded swelling touching down.

"You can talk to me now, trouble-man."

I watched her in the mirror, blonde head bent forward, working on her nails. Said nothing.

"You miss your cigarettes?" she asked.

I didn't tell her. How you give up cigarettes every time they lock you up. How guys throw the *Miranda* decision out the window when the cop offers his pack in a friendly gesture. How you don't borrow anything inside the walls. Sooner or later, you make your own connections. Stopping isn't quitting.

"Come over here. Give me a kiss, tell me I look nice."

I got off the bed. Blossom slipped a wine-red light wool dress over her shoulders, cinched it with a wide black belt. She held out her hands to me. Clear lacquer on her nails except for the index finger. That was the same red as her dress.

I took her hand. "How come?" I asked her.

"Remember last night? When I was sitting on your lap, feeding you your vitamins? Remember when you noticed I only had one stocking on?"

"Yeah."

"Remember how bad you wanted to see? Remember how I looked, lying on the bed, one dark stocking?"

I did.

She put one hand on my shoulder, steadied herself as she slipped a spike heel on her foot. "I'm going to see the reporter this morning."

⍋ 112

I HIT PAY dirt just past noon. Car phone conversations aren't private—I found a booth a short piece away. Called Virgil.

"He's here. Everything set?"

"I'll be there, ten, fifteen minutes."

𝕎 113

VIRGIL AND I walked in together. No cover, no minimum. The bouncer stood in the corner. A heavy-duty piece of work. No bodybuilder poses on this one—hard, rubbery muscles under a thick layer of fat, no bridge to his nose, scar tissue for eyebrows.

We found a table in the corner. Women in lingerie and high heels walked the runway. You bid high enough, you got to buy the cheesy crap right off their bodies, grope around handing it to them. Some stuff never goes out of fashion.

Watching the room, we ordered shots and beers. Virgil drank mine. It took another round before I spotted Matson. Alone at a table right across from the bouncer. I got up, walked over, beer in my hand. He looked up as we approached, hands where he could see them. In case he learned anything from his magazine collection.

The bouncer watched us, indifferent.

We sat down across from him. No bracket, leaving him room to move. My back to the door, Virgil with a clear sight-line over my shoulder.

His eyes were squinty under the bill of his red Budweiser tractor cap.

"Buy you a beer?" I asked him.

"I know you?"

"Burke," I said, holding out my hand. He waited a heartbeat, shook it. "My partner, Virgil."

"What can I do for you boys?"

"I heard you were the man to see around here. If you were interested in certain things."

"What things?" he asked, leaning back in his chair. Liking this.

"Doesn't matter. I'm not looking to buy, I'm looking to sell."

"Sell what?"

"Ordnance."

"We got all the guns we need."

"I'm sure you do. But the way I heard it, you could always use some special stuff."

"Like you said, I don't know you."

I took a metal Sucrets box out of my pocket. Opened it to show him it was empty. Handed him a fresh white handkerchief.

"What's this?"

"Wipe it down. Get it clean as you want. Then I'll leave you a print, okay? You take the box with you. Check it out. See I'm what I say I am, maybe we can do business. I can give you some references too, you want them."

He pursed his lips. Dragged on his cigarette. Took the metal box, wiped it down. Watched as I carefully rolled my thumbprint onto its surface. Wrapped it in the handkerchief, stowed it away in the pocket of his jacket.

"Say I was interested . . ."

"I'm a full-auto specialist. Anything you want. Even got some long-range stuff. Hand-held, shoulder-operated. Disposable."

"Where could I find you?"

"Right here. Say, in three days? Around this time?"

He nodded. Big man, considering his big deals carefully. The bouncer watched. I could feel the sneer.

⚘ 114

I DROPPED VIRGIL a quarter mile down the road. Rebecca was parked in her cousin's Chevy a few feet away. Paid no attention to us.

I wheeled the Lincoln around, went back the way I came. The Blazer was still in the parking lot. A white Dodge sedan waited by the side of the road, Lloyd hunched over the wheel, eating a hero sandwich.

⚘ 115

I PICKED UP some more clothes at the motel. Called Bostick, Glenda. Nothing new. Asked Bostick if I could pick up a few things from him.

Blossom got back around eight. Put a leather portfolio down on the couch, slipped off her shoes. "Let me take a shower, then I'll make you some dinner."

"We could go out."

"I already ate."

✌ 116

LATER THAT EVENING, the kitchen table covered with press clips. "What'd he do?" I asked Blossom. "Pull every file in the morgue?"

"He's a nice boy."

"You tell him that?"

Her smile was wicked. "I just thanked him. Politely. The way I was raised. You're my only boy."

I sorted the clips, speed-reading, Blossom at my shoulder. "What are we looking for?"

"First, we throw out what we're not. These, so far." Tapping a stack of body-count dispatches from the front lines they call city streets. Shootings where the gunman was apprehended at the scene. Shootings in the course of another crime. Where the victims were only male. Gang fights. Bars, nightclubs, bowling alleys . . . all discards.

I kept working. On instinct now. Tossed out anything except white females. Anything outside the past eighteen months—two birth cycles. The thick stack was down to a few clips.

White female, age twenty-four. Reported shot fired at her while she waited at a bus stop at midnight. Police investigated. Nothing more.

White female, age thirty-one. Shot fired into her bathroom window while she was taking a shower after she got home from the night shift. Separated from her husband, history of domestic violence. He was under a court Order of Protection. Working his job at the plant when the shot was fired. Questioned and released.

White female, age seventeen. Girl Scout leader. Shot in the arm while leading a troop of girls through the woods in the late afternoon, learning about nature.

Human nature.

▽ 117

I HAD THE contact-address for two of the shootings. The woman whose bathroom window was shattered was listed in the phone book I'd gotten from Bostick's office. I tacked the street maps up on Blossom's kitchen wall.

"You got a Magic Marker?"

"No."

"A crayon, anything?"

She brought me a tube of red lipstick. I dabbed a tiny blood-dot at each address. Stood back to look.

"A triangle," Blossom whispered.

"Doesn't mean anything. Three dots, you're more likely than not to get a triangle."

"Oh."

"It's okay. Look at the dates. The first one was the bus stop, back in the late fall. The Girl Scout, that was in December. Then the woman in her own house, that was the spring. The lovers' lane killings, they were all this summer."

"Why is that important?"

"I don't know if it's important. If they're all his work, it is. See it building . . . ? The first shot, like an experiment. The woman standing there, all bundled up against the cold. Probably only could tell she was a woman by her coat. Then the Girl Scout. All covered up too. But a lot of girls around. Little girls. He may have just stumbled on them. Felt the rage. See, here? The bullet they took out of her? A .22 Long Rifle. A plinker's gun. Not a sniper's. Then the woman in her bathroom. Her naked image against the pebbled glass. Maybe he passed there before. Saw her. Watched. Got the signal and came back. The paper doesn't say what kind of bullet they recovered."

"Burke?"

"What?"

"You're scaring me. Your voice. Like you're . . . him. Like you see what he saw."

⚘ 118

BLOSSOM'S PHONE RANG at one in the morning. The caller hung up before the answering machine could kick in. Rang again. Same thing.

Again.

I got up, started to dress in the clothes I'd brought with me.

"Where're you going, baby?"

"I'm not going anywhere. I've been right here, right next to you. All night. Never got out of that bed."

"I'm coming with you."

"No you're not."

"Burke . . ."

"Shut up, little girl. Close your eyes. I'll be back before you open them."

⚔ 119

THE CHEVY PULLED up outside Blossom's, headlights off. I climbed in next to Virgil. Saw Lloyd in the back seat.

"What's he doing here?"

"Caught me sneaking out."

"He knows?"

"You know how we are, brother. One of us got something on his plate, we all got it. Sometimes it ain't gravy."

"Lloyd," I told the boy, "you wait in the car. You wait until we come out, understand? A cop comes by, you *stay* there. You don't panic, don't run. Worst that happens, they'll take you in. Got it?"

"I got it," he said, voice steady. Streetlights picked up the slash of honor across the bridge of his nose.

"Any luck with the Nazi?" I asked Virgil.

"Reba tracked him right to his house. Lives over in Lake Station. Little nothing of a house, he got. Chain link fence, chest high. Got him a dog, though. Big German shepherd, Reba said. Saw him in the yard."

"Let's see if he wants to talk first."

⚜ 120

THE BUILDING WAS dark. Virgil pulled around the back into a narrow alley, climbed out with me. Lloyd slid behind the wheel. Virgil opened the trunk, shouldered the duffel bag.

The lock on the back door was a dead bolt. I couldn't see alarm wires anywhere. I felt crude, clumsy. Wished for the Mole.

"Only one way," I whispered to Virgil. "I'm going to smash a window. Then we wait."

If he was disappointed in his master-criminal brother from New York, it didn't reach his face. He nodded okay, walked back toward the car. I found a good-sized chunk of concrete block. Walked over to a ground-floor window and tossed it through.

Nothing.

Back in the car, I told Lloyd to drive slowly across the street, turn off the engine, and wait.

We gave it half an hour, Lloyd fidgeting behind the wheel, Virgil smoking. Watching.

Still nothing.

"I didn't hear a sound when I broke the glass. If there was a silent alarm, the rollers would have been on the scene long ago. Let's do it."

◊ 121

I REACHED MY gloved hands inside the window frame through the broken glass, found the latch. Shoved it open. Virgil followed me inside.

The third floor had several computer terminals scattered about. Virgil hooked army blankets over the windows. I used my pencil beam, turned it on one of the terminals. The screen flickered into life.

I took a deep breath. If the machine asked for a password, I was finished.

No.

I followed the prompts, remembering what Blossom had been shown. Found the index for Reported Cases by Year. Figured my target for somewhere between fifteen and thirty years old just to play it safe. Typed 1960—and pressed the Return key.

The screen said Select Sub-Index. I scrolled the cursor down. Stopped at Indicated. Hit the Return again.

A new menu: Outcomes.

I selected: Petition Filed.

New menu. Selected: Adjudicated.

I entered, scanned the new list of choices. Found the one I wanted: Family Reunified—Closed.

I typed quickly through the next series of screens. Used the Sort key. Race = White. Sex = Male. Family Composition = One Child.

Entered. Screen Message: Data Prior to 1972 Not Downloaded. See Central File.

I tapped the Return key again to bypass the message. Hit the Print key.

Nothing.

Hit it again.

Nothing.

Selected Printer Menu. Blinking Message: Printer Is Not Connected.

I turned to see if Virgil was watching. His back was to me, facing the door.

I hit the On switch for the printer. Watched the lights blink as it warmed up. The screen asked me for printer speed. I selected the fastest.

"Gonna make some noise now," I warned Virgil.

He nodded, not moving from his post.

The Print key rattled the machine into life. I went to the window, looked down. The Chevy was still there. Alone.

I stood next to Virgil. "You think he's in there?" the mountain man asked.

"Maybe. Wherever he is, he's not far."

"You sure, now?"

I shrugged. Feeling it more than knowing it, not sure why.

The printer ran on like a machine gun in the darkness, spitting chewed-up lives onto paper.

◊ 122

VIRGIL PUSHED LLOYD over, took the wheel. I climbed into the back seat, holding a bundle of fan-folded paper as thick as the phone book.

◊ 123

THE BACK DOOR was unlocked. I found my way inside. Blossom was in bed, lying on her side, facing the bedroom door.

"You okay?" she asked, wide awake.

"Sure."

I took off the dark prowler's clothes, put everything I'd worn into a pillowcase, tied it closed.

Blossom didn't ask any questions. Patted the bed. Opened her arms.

₩ 124

YOU WANT SOMETHING to eat? Take a break from that?''

I rolled my neck to loosen the cramping feeling. I was in the easy chair in Blossom's living room. The fan-folded stack of printout was on the coffee table next to me, a yellow legal pad to my right. ''What time is it?''

''It's almost one in the afternoon, honey. You've been at it for hours.''

I stood up. Followed her docilely into the kitchen. Ate a sandwich I couldn't taste.

''There's so many of them, Blossom. Even narrowing it down, taking the big guesses, there's so many.''

She was barefoot, in a pair of pink shorts, a T-shirt with balloons on the front. Looked sixteen. ''Tell me,'' she said.

''Two questions, right? Who he is, where he is. I can find who he is, I could get lucky. Point right to where he is. So I played with it. Patterns, like I told you. So I could see him in my mind.''

''What d'you see?''

''He's shooting women. The boys who died, they were just in the line of fire. White women, I figure a white shooter.''

''Just like that?''

''There's things I can't explain to you. It's not a black man's crime, sex-sniping.''

''Like white women don't throw lye?''

"Don't be cute, girl. This isn't a job for the ACLU. There's a way you just know things. Your mother, she knew men, right?"

"She did."

"Could she explain everything to you . . . *how* she knew? There's something way past the red-light district, Blossom. A million miles underground. A white-light district maybe. The white light of the video cameras where they make kids perform for freaks."

"You've been there?"

"Yeah. And now, that's where I hunt."

"I'm sorry. Just tell me, okay. I'll keep my big mouth shut."

"Something happened to this kid. Something so ugly the social workers don't have a name for it. Maybe nobody ever found out about it, but I'm betting they did. Maybe through the back door. Maybe he was torturing little animals and a teacher caught him. Maybe a fire-setter. The way I dope it out, somebody caught wise, but they missed the boat. Missed the reasons. And they took him away for a while. Fixed him up. Gave his parents some counseling. And then they sent him home. Where he still is. Those files, they don't get you inside a kid's head. Or his heart. But I feel like this kid's *rooted*, you know. Like he never went far. Like he's been out there, brewing. Stewing in freakish juices."

"You're giving me the creeps."

"Something you don't know. Virgil brought me out here not to save Lloyd. To find out the truth. Whatever the truth was, he was going to stand up to it. The reason I know Lloyd didn't do it, it has nothing to do with what the cops know. The reason he didn't do it, he's not the person who *could* do it."

"Burke . . . if he's in there . . . if you're so sure he's in there . . . why do you look so depressed?"

"There's so many . . . so many. I can't bring it down too

tight. I could miss him if I do. These reports are full of busted-up babies. Burned, beaten, crippled. Sexually abused. And every one of these files, they sent the kid home again. Everything all right again.''

''And you're sad because you're not sure he's in there.''

''I'm sad because . . . of what else is. All the success stories.''

''You sound so evil when you say that. Like there's a chill in here.''

''How should I sound?''

''I hate him too, honey. He killed my sister. But that boy . . . he has to be so . . . sick.''

It felt like I was being baited. Goaded into something. ''You think he needs a psychiatrist?'' I asked her.

''Don't you?''

''No.''

◊ 125

IT WAS TEN o'clock that night before I finished. Counted the files I had set aside. Almost two hundred. I closed my eyes. Went down inside. Where only the devil knew my secrets.

Called his name.

Wesley. The monster who signed his suicide note with a threat—*I don't know where I'm going, but they better not send anyone after me*.

''Where is he?'' I asked the monster.

"Out there."

"Can I find him?"

"He can find you," the monster said, in his dead-machine voice. "Fire works."

I knew. He wasn't talking about the Fourth of July.

⋓ 126

A HAND ON my chest. Foggy voice. A strangled scream. Blossom's face inches from mine, the pink glow gone dark. My fingers locked around her throat. The soft flesh turned to acid—I whipped my hand away.

Later, on the couch, her head in my lap. Cold water dripping onto my thighs from the ice pack she was holding against her throat.

"I never saw anything move so fast. It was like a steel vise . . ." Her voice was raw, raspy.

"Don't talk."

"Burke . . ."

"I'm sorry. I was somewhere else. Didn't know it was you."

"It's okay. I thought you were asleep. I just wanted you to come to bed."

"Close your eyes, Blossom. Go to sleep."

She found my hand, separated the fingers like she was counting them. Put my thumb in her mouth, curled onto her side, closed her eyes.

I felt the cold go through me, reaching where the ice pack couldn't touch.

◊ 127

VIRGIL AND I spotted the Blazer in the parking lot. Matson was sitting in his spot. Two guys with him. Looked like he did: mean-eyed, blotchy-faced, chinless. The Master Race.

We sat down.

The fashion show went on behind us.

Matson leaned forward. "You got yourself quite a background, friend."

"Satisfied?"

"Yeah. What was it like?"

"What was what like?"

"Africa. I thought of doing that kind of work myself. Merc stuff. Pay's good?"

"Good enough."

"Must be heaven. Killin' niggers and gettin' paid for it too."

One of his boys laughed. I swiveled my head slowly, catching his eyes. Weasel. He stopped laughing, waiting for his cue, not knowing the script.

"You go by Mitchell Sloane?" Matson asked. So he wrote down the Lincoln's license number. Or Revis was more helpful to him than just running my prints.

"I go by a lot of things."

"Yeah. Yeah, I understand. Where'd you hear I was in the market for some hardware?"

"Around. I heard you were a serious man. Had serious business."

He nodded sagely, basking in the praise. "That's the truth. Lots of groups like ours around, but we're the real thing. Everybody knows that. It ain't just the niggers, you know. Maybe it ain't as bad as Jew York yet around here, but we're workin' on it. Got homos in the government, Jew-bastard IRS on our necks, no room for a white man to breathe anymore."

"That's what I sell. Breathing room."

"I got you. You know, a nigger once came in here. Right in the fuckin' door. Like he owned the place. Lickin' his ape lips at the girls. Now that don't happen no more. The word's out. We've been growing. Slow but steady. Have to be real careful, who you let in."

"Yeah, the feds are everywhere."

"Undesirables too. You hear about Patterson's crew, down in Crown Point? They had a guy in there, ranking member and all. Turned out he was a Jew. Patterson's a fuckin' fool—he shouldn't be in a leadership position in the movement."

"How's he supposed to know who's a Jew?"

"There's ways. We got our eye on them. On some of them. Send 'em a message one of these days."

Virgil watched, bored.

The Nazi's voice droned on.

White Noise.

I cut in at an angle, merging with his rap. Talked his talk. Guns and blood. Freedom for the Race. I let him bargain me into a half dozen Uzis, five grand for the package.

"You use these, the cops'll think it was some nigger dope dealers, right?"

"Yeah!"

"COD."

"Deal. I'll meet you right here on . . ."

"I look stupid to you, I'm gonna ride around with a truck-ful of a life sentence?"

"The cops won't bother this place."

"It's not the locals I'm worried about."

"So where, then?"

"Chicago. I got a warehouse in Uptown. You drive in, drive out."

His eyes went crafty with the chance to impress his punks. "No way, partner. Not across a state line."

I pretended to give it some thought. "Okay. It'll take me a few days to get the pieces together from my source. Give me a number, I'll call you. We'll make the exchange on the road. Wherever you say."

"I'll give you our Hot Line. When you call, you get our message. The Race Word. There ain't no beep, but it's an answering machine. When you hear a voice saying 'White Power!' that's the sign-off. Just leave your message after that, I'll get back to you."

"Good enough."

The bouncer's eyes tracked me and Virgil out the door.

⚓ 128

I HANDED BLOSSOM the pistol. "You better hang on to this, find a safe place for it." Thinking of Revis.

"Okay, boss."

"Be careful with it—it's loaded."

She popped the cylinder, pointed the barrel at the ceiling as the cartridges dropped into her palm. "I know about guns. From the Army. M-16, M-60, grenades . . . we even practiced with LAWs."

"You were in the Army?"

"Don't look so surprised, baby. They paid for medical school. It was a good deal. And Mama didn't leave us a fortune. Violet and I agreed, we'd save the money for Rose. Pay her way through school."

I held her against me until she stopped trembling.

⫟129

LATER, THE PHONE rang. Answering machine picked up. Virgil's voice: "He went to the same place. Alone."

⫟130

TWO HUNDRED NAMES. For the first time, I missed New York. If I was home, if I could tap into my machinery, call in some markers, work the angles, make some trades . . . I could narrow them down. Find out which of the kids had later died, gone to prison, been institutionalized, moved away. But out here . . . I was working in the dark.

I needed a match.

⚘ 131

CALLED BOSTICK. "CAN you check some real estate for me?"

"If it's local, sure. Take about an hour."

I gave him Matson's address.

⚘ 132

IN VIRGIL'S BACKYARD, night falling.

"She checked the place again?"

"Yep. Reba says he lives alone, looks like."

"The house is in his name. Nobody else on the mortgage. He could have a girlfriend living there. Or maybe one of his Nazi pals. We'll play whatever's there."

"He's got that dog, though."

"It's a long shot. We can't wait for him to be somewhere

else. Have to go in while he's there, brace him, take a look. He's gonna guess who we are, tell his pal the cop.''

Virgil shrugged. ''Kids go to bed early. I'll be up, watching TV with Reba. Lloyd too.''

''He's dirty anyway. Can't see him going to court. And I'll have a message for him, he does that. Let me do the talking, it comes to that.''

''Okay.''

''We'll leave Lloyd in the car, like last time.''

Virgil nodded. I caught a look on his face. ''What's wrong?'' I asked him.

He dragged on his smoke. ''I don't hold with killing dogs, brother.''

''Matson, he's an amateur. Probably thinks the way to make a good watchdog is to starve him. I'll take care of it.''

▲ 133

''I NEED TO knock out a dog.''

Blossom didn't change expression. ''What kind of dog? How fast?''

''A shepherd. Figure, eighty, ninety pounds. He needs to go down pretty quick, stay down for at least a half hour.''

''Can you use a needle?''

''No. Unless you got a tranquilizer gun lying around.''

''Let me look.''

She came back with a black medical bag. Opened it on the countertop, started stacking little vials and bottles in a row. I leaned over her shoulder to watch. Opened a bottle, spilled out some tiny round orange pills. Cupped a handful. Stared down at them. SKF T76 in black letters.

"You know what those are?" she asked.

"Yeah. Thorazine. Fifty milligrams."

"How come . . . ?"

"When I was a kid . . . before I learned to keep inside myself . . . they used to give it to me."

"You were in a psychiatric hospital?"

I didn't like the sound of my own laugh. "I was in what they called a training school."

"You still remember . . . ?"

I nodded, remembering it all, saying nothing. It was always dark in there. The gym was fear, the shower room was terror. Nothing clean, nothing private, nothing safe. Some kids ran. They brought them back. Some found another way to go—a swan dive to the concrete, a belt tied around a light fixture. Viciousness was worshiped, icy violence was God. When the rage-dam broke inside me, I didn't know when to stop. Stabbing inmates was okay, but not fighting a guard. So they went to the Thorazine. Chemical handcuffs. They didn't work the same on everyone. This one boy in there with me, the stuff worked on him like an anabolic steroid—he raged against the chemicals inside his body so his life was an isometric exercise. It got so he could crush a man's life with his hands. And that's what he did. Me, all I wanted was to learn to ride the storm.

The prisons were full of men they trained in those training schools. By the time I went down, I was ready.

Blossom was quiet, pawing through her supplies. Then: "Here it is." Holding up a stainless-steel needle, encased in plastic.

"Here's what?"

"Secobarbital sodium. Like Seconal, you know what that is?"

"Sleeping pills."

"Like that, but this is damn near an anesthetic dose. It's in Tubex. One-shot needles, preloaded. Just inject them right into whatever the dog's going to eat."

"Is that enough?"

"There's a grain and a half in each cartridge. I've got four here. Enough for a whole kennel."

"How long would it take to work?"

"Depends. It has to go through the GI tract. He laps it right up, runs around some to get his blood pumping, maybe five, ten minutes."

"Okay. You got any chopped liver around?"

"Chopped liver?"

"Like you get in a deli. Never mind. I'll be back in a little while."

▥ 134

TWO MORE DAYS of working with the clips, trying to match an address for any of the "Family Reunified—Closed" cases with something close to one of the shootings.

Nothing.

ꙡ 135

TWO A.M., AT the end of Matson's block. Lloyd at the wheel, Virgil and I in the back seat, me on the passenger's side.

"Tell me again," I said to the kid.

"I drove by last night. Like you said. The dog didn't do nothing. So I got out of the car, walked up to the fence. He started barking like all holy hell, snapping at me. I get in, drive away. Wait ten minutes. On my watch. I drive back, he's quiet again. Simmered right down."

"Okay. Put it in gear, cruise by slow. You see anyone, see another car, just keep on going."

Virgil gave him a couple of hard pats on the shoulder and the Chevy rolled forward.

No lights on in the house. The dog's sleek shape loomed in the shadowed front yard. Lloyd slowed to a stop. I got out, the softball-sized glob of hamburger with its chopped-liver core in my gloved hand. The dog hit the fence, snarling. I slapped the meat against the chain link with an open palm, feeling his frenzied gnawing against my glove as I stuffed it through. The dog grunted his rage, clawing at the fence.

I backed away, jumped in the car. No lights went on in the neighboring houses—they'd probably heard all this before.

⚜ 136

WE GAVE IT fifteen minutes. The dog was lying in the front yard. He didn't stir as we approached. Virgil worked the bolt cutters and the padlocked chain gave way. We were inside. I watched the dog with my pistol. He didn't watch back.

The Nazi had a lock on his back door even I could open. Door chain lasted one snip of the bolt cutters.

We reached inside our navy watch caps, pulled down the panty-hose masks, adjusted our eyes to the gloom. No carpet on the floor, but our rubber-soled shoes didn't send a warning.

Downstairs: a kitchen, dirty dishes in the sink; a living room with a console TV, staircase.

No basement.

Up the stairs, linoleum runner down the middle. Bathroom at the top, door standing open. Another room with file cabinets, desk, telephone with an answering machine next to it.

He was sleeping on his side in the other room, snoring softly. We stepped inside, Virgil across from his face, covering him with my pistol. I took the heavy gym sock filled with hard-packed sand from my jacket pocket, wrapped my fist around the knotted end, swung it back and forth for balance, nodded to Virgil.

Virgil prodded Matson in the chest with the pistol. The Nazi stirred, said "Wha . . ." and propped himself on one elbow just as I slammed the sock into the top of his head. I spun back for another shot, but he was down.

I handed Virgil the sock, pulled out my flashlight, and went into his office.

It didn't take long. There wasn't much. Stacks of magazines. Guns and girls. Loose piles of hate sheets on cheap newsprint: swastikas, drawings of blacks, Negroid features exaggerated to make them apelike, Christian crosses and devil-lyrics to racist songs. Three rifles on wood pegs stood ready on the wall.

The file cabinets were mostly empty. Except for some personnel folders he must have brought home from his job. One for each freak. Writing on the front in thick black Magic Marker. One folder had two stars. I popped a green plastic garbage bag from my jacket, snapped it open, threw in the files.

One look around before I left. Nothing else worth taking. I found his Magic Marker. Picked a clean piece of wall. Wrote: We Know Where You Live.

I threw the bag over my shoulder, checked on Virgil. He was still holding the gun on Matson's body.

We went past the dog, closed the gate gently. Stepped into the Chevy and Lloyd motored away.

Virgil looked back over his shoulder. "I hope that dog's gonna be all right," he said.

ψ 137

IT WAS ON the news in the morning. He hit again. Just on the other side of the dunes. Three couples were parked, a little past midnight. Shots zipped out of the night, puncturing the last car in the row. The girl was dead, the boy wounded, on the critical list.

Nothing about Matson.

ψ 138

I CALLED SHERWOOD from the Lincoln. Met him in the Illiana Raceway parking lot. The place was quiet—they only run on Saturdays. If he was wasted from working all night, he didn't show it.

"We're going to shut him down, put him in a box," the big detective said.

"You want to talk to Lloyd? About the shootings last night?" I asked the big man, watching his face.

"No. He's got an alibi for last night, doesn't he?"

I met his eyes. "Probably does. How you gonna shut this freak down?"

"We close the parks. Should of done it before, after the first ones. Have squad cars cruise the lovers' lanes, all the parking spots. Chase the kids away. No parking after dark, period. Stupid fucking kids, you think we wouldn't need to be telling them."

"Hormones."

"Yeah. I ain't *that* old. But they don't get it, these kids. You ever been in combat?"

"Yeah."

"You think about sex while you were getting shot at?"

"Okay, I get it."

"We got nothing else to do. We must of rousted every ex-con with a sex sheet in the county. Blank. I'm beginning to think, maybe your idea wasn't so fucked up."

I raised my eyebrows.

"Some gun-freak degenerate motherfucker. One of those Nazi-boys. You know, I'd *like* it to be one of them."

"Me too."

He lit a cigarette. "Notice you haven't been smoking, last couple of times."

"You don't miss much."

"I'm missing something here. Someone."

"I got an idea. Maybe not much of one. Something. You can really shut the parking places down?"

"Oh yeah. Cold fucking turkey."

"I got to take a look at something. I'll call you soon."

▼ 139

I WANTED TO look at Matson's files, but I'd bolted out of Blossom's house as soon as I'd heard the news. One stop to make first.

The phone picked up in the junkyard.

"Mole," I said, "I need a shark cage."

▼ 140

MATSON WAS ONE selective Nazi. His files showed nine "actives," seventeen "affiliates," three "candidates," and thirty-four "rejects."

I looked closer. The "actives" were listed by "MOS." Rifleman, Communications, Infiltration. Every military occupation except Intelligence. Between the arcane symbols and the lavish praise for the "warriors," a collection of life's losers lurked, waiting for their flabby Armageddon.

The "affiliates" were members of other groups who occasionally came to meetings or corresponded. About half lived in southern Illinois or Indiana, the others were scattered throughout the country.

"Candidates" turned out to be humans who Matson thought had potential. One human's credential was a news clipping saying he had been arrested for spray-painting filth on a synagogue.

And the "rejects" were a clump of former "candidates" whose hostility wasn't exclusively confined to blacks. One was rejected after he fractured the jaw of one of Matson's boys in a bar. In his black Magic Marker, Matson neatly printed Unsuitable for Service across the file. Most of his other reject-reasons weren't so sweetly phrased: Jew! Suspected Homosexual. Suspected Government Agent.

I went through them again. Carefully.

Nothing. Nothing. Nothing.

Blossom came into the kitchen, face glowing from her shower. Dark purplish band across her throat. My fingerprints drew my eyes.

"It's okay, baby. I'll be pretty as a prom queen in a few days." Her voice was a sugar-edged rasp.

"Yeah."

"*Yeah!* Just stop it, okay? I know what happened, why it happened."

"Blossom . . ."

"You want a cigarette?"

"What?"

"Your time's up. A week, like we agreed. And you been *such* a good boy too. Not one drag, huh?"

"How would you know?"

"I can smell it. All over you. On your hands, in your hair. You've got nice thick hair for such an old man."

"It won't be a week until tonight."

"That's okay. You're off the hook. I lost. I know you could do it now. For as long as you wanted."

"I wish I could do this."

She fumbled in her purse, brought out a fresh pack of smokes. My brand. Slit the cellophane with a fingernail, struck a match, got it going. She walked over, pushed her shoulder against me, sat in my lap, her legs dangling over the sides like a kid on a boat. Held the cigarette to my lips. "Maybe this'll help you think."

⚜ 141

BLOSSOM WOKE ME with a quick tap on my chest, standing her distance. "Supper's ready, honey."

I couldn't taste the food.

⚜ 142

LATER THAT NIGHT.

"Blossom, can you make a list of all the names from the child abuse stuff? Just the names and dates of birth?"

"Sure."

I went back to the Nazi files, grinding at the paper with my eyes.

Blossom's list was printed in a clean, sharp hand, slightly slanted to the right.

"Can I read you some names, you check to see if any of them are on your list?"

"I should have alphabetized them."

"It's okay, it's short."

I lit a smoke. Too old to be playing long shots. Too black&white for this movie.

Quiet time passed. Name after name. Blank. No match. Rustle of Blossom's papers.

"Luther Swain."

"Burke, I swear I . . . yes!"

"Give it to me . . . not the damn list, Blossom, where's the printout?"

"Keep your pants on, boy. I'll get it."

Luther Swain. Only child of Nathaniel and Margaret Swain. Born February 29, 1968. Removed from his home by Social Services, November 4, 1976. Department alerted because child had not attended school, parents had not responded to letters. No home telephone. Whip marks from an electrical cord, cigarette burns, severe eye damage from being kept in a dark basement for several months. Father committed to Logansport, the State Hospital for the Criminally Insane. Child kept in state institution, released to foster care, returned to institution. Finally: Released to mother, August 9, 1979. Family Reunified—Case Closed.

Blossom on her knees, surrounded by a floorful of paper. Watching me.

The Nazi file. Swain, Luther. Answered one of their ads, requested further information. Sent to a PO box in Gary. Called. Matson and two others met him. "Applicant was evasive about personal details. Suspected homosexual. Rejected."

"Is it him?"

"I don't know. He's as close as we got so far. Let's go through the other names, see if there's another match."

No.

◊143

MIDNIGHT.

"The only address on the Social Services files is more than ten years old. Even the PO box, that's a couple of years dead. No phone listed. Tomorrow, I'll take a look."

"Me too."

"No."

"Burke!"

"Do what I tell you, Blossom."

She leaned over the couch, pearly breasts a soft spill against my face, whispered, "I will. Right now. Like I promised. Let's go to bed. Then you can tell me what to do."

Sure.

₩ 144

IN THE BEDROOM. I was lying on my back, two pillows behind my head, smoking. Blossom stood to my left, standing straight as a soldier, thin straps of the blue negligee on her shoulders.

Smiling, her eyes wicked.

"What d'you say, boss?"

"Take that off."

She pulled the straps down. A cloud of wispy blue drifted to her feet.

"Come here." Grinding out the cigarette.

I took her hand, pulled her down to me, kissed her softly. I rolled her onto her back, my face against the dark hollow of her throat. My lips touched a tiny jewel of a nipple. I curled against her, found my place, closed my eyes. She made comfort-sounds against my ear as I drifted away.

⚘ 145

IT WAS LATE morning when I left. Stopped at the motel. Showered, shaved, put on a dark gray pinstripe suit. Studied the street maps again for a few minutes.

At the center of an intricate web, cross-connected by blood and honor. Virgil, Reba, Lloyd. Virginia and Junior. Blossom and her sister. So much. And, somewhere, a maniac with an axe in his hands, his eye on the hard knots lashing my people together. Me, spinning between the loves. A visitor, welcomed for the gun in my hand.

I passed the Marquette Park Lagoon, turned into a series of dirt roads, watching for the street signs. Past a pizzeria, grocery store, bait shop.

The Lincoln nosed its way into the slough. Termite-haven wood houses with rickety steps up the outside, cloudy plastic sheets covering broken windows. Grungy soot-colored cars dotted the yards. A pickup truck with monster tires, suspension jacked up, Kentucky plates. Satellite dish next to one shack. Barefoot, disinterested children watched.

The sun slanted through the murk—the barren ground defied photosynthesis.

The address was three houses down from where two pieces of barbed-wire-topped fence didn't quite meet. I parked the car, got out. Next door, a thick-bodied beast who looked like he'd been kicked out of a junkyard for antisocial behavior rumbled a greeting, baleful eyes tracking me.

I climbed the steps, knocked. TV sounds from inside. I hit it again.

A scrawny woman opened the door. Pasty skin, lank hair, dull grayish teeth. Somewhere between nineteen and dead.

"What is it?"

"Mrs. Swain?"

"No, I ain't her."

"Well, it's her I need to see. Is she around?"

"*Ain't* no Mrs. Swain, mister. Not around here."

"Look, it's important that I speak to her. Real important."

"Cain't help you none."

"You sure?" Holding some bills in one hand.

"Mister, Lord knows I'd like some of that money you showin', but I ain't never heard of no Swain people."

"You lived here long?"

Sparkless eyes held mine. "Three years. Three fucking years."

"Did you buy the house then?"

"Buy?" Her laugh was bile-laced mucus. "We *rent*, mister. Man comes once a month, get his money."

"What's his name?"

"The Man," she said, closing the door in my face.

⍦ 146

SUPPOSE I TOLD you there was this kid. Abused kid, really tortured. Burned, locked in a basement for months. Social

Services takes him away. His old man goes down to Logansport. Years later, they send him home to his mother. This same kid, he tries to join up with Matson's Nazis. They turn him down, or he spooks, not sure which. You knew about this kid, would you be interested in talking to him? About the killings?"

"I might," Sherwood said. "Should I be?"

"I think so."

"You haven't said enough to get a search warrant."

"If I had his address, maybe I could say enough, a couple of days from now."

"Which means you don't."

"Right."

"Just a name."

"His name, parents' names, date of birth, last known address."

"Which you tried and drew a blank?"

"Yeah."

"Give it to me."

〰147

I SHARKED AROUND, looking. Blossom at my side, not talking. Knowing I was listening to someone else.

We passed under railroad tracks, past a stone dam. Huge swastika on quarry rocks. Satan Rules!

Kids.

Two more dead days slipped by until the monster led me

there. Through the gate of the Paul Douglas Nature Center. Two teardrop-shaped blobs of blacktop joined by a narrow connecting loop like a drooping barbell. Neatly marked parking lines painted in white, slotted between mercury vapor lights suspended high on metal posts. I slid the Lincoln into a space. The park entrance was to my left, past a wooden footbridge. To my right, over Blossom's shoulder, I could see an eight-foot chain link fence, woods behind it.

"Stay here," I told her. "Just stay in the car."

I found a foothold, pulled myself to the top of the fence, dropped down to the other side. Climbed a rise through some underbrush until I got to the top. Abandoned railroad tracks that hadn't seen a train for years, rusting in disgust, connectors broken loose. The other side of the tracks was a copse, black even in daylight. A deep drop-off behind the copse, leading to the streets below. I worked my way down, followed along the edge of the drop-off, feeling my way.

I was at the lakefront in ten minutes. White dunes in the distance. Dunes where the killer had roosted.

I climbed back, emerging out of the copse. Lay down prone on the tracks.

A clear view of the Lincoln. I could see Blossom stretching her slim arms in the front seat. It felt like watching a woman in a window.

Killing ground. Sloping to a perfect pitch for the sniper's song.

I closed my eyes, feeling the sun on my face, darkness at my back. Sucked clean air through my nose, down deep past my stomach. Expanded my chest on the exhale, centering.

Felt for the sniper in my mind. Listened to the child. "I hurt," he said.

Once a child's cry for help. Now a killer's boast.

"He'll be here." Wesley's voice.

◊ 148

I WORKED THE ground. No shell casings, no condoms. Not even a beer can. The spot was virgin, waiting for a rapist. I absently pulled some long green reeds from the earth. Climbed into the car, tossed them on the front seat between us.

On the way out, I checked the sign. The Nature Center closed each night at six.

◊ 149

YOU OKAY?''

"That's his spot, Blossom. It's perfect."

She fingered the green stalks. "You know what these are?"

"No."

"This is a scouring rush. Horsetails, we call them. Prospectors used to use them. You crack them open, like this, see? They're hollow. The story is, you could see tiny flecks of gold, where it was leached up out of the ground if there was any underneath.''

I wondered if they leached blood.

⚓ 150

THE NEXT MORNING, the Lincoln circled the Nature Center in tightening loops, pawing the ground before it moved in.

"When are you going to try it?" Blossom.

I lit a cigarette with the dashboard lighter. "I have to get a call first. There's something I need.''

The car phone rang. But it was Sherwood, not the Mole.

I let Blossom ride along to the meet with me. Let the cop know what I knew.

Most of it.

⚓ 151

THE UNMARKED CAR was positioned at the gate to the beach. I pulled in alongside, got out. Blossom followed. Sherwood fell into step with us.

"Good news and bad news. This Luther Swain, he could be the guy. But he's gone. That address you had, it was the last one on record."

"What about his mother?"

Sherwood pulled out a thick slab of a notebook. "According to DPW records, she left about five years ago. The locals terminated her Welfare grant. The kid stayed on in the house until 1986, when he turned eighteen. They offered him some services: outpatient counseling, group therapy. Even said they'd hook him up with SSI Disability. But one day he just up and disappeared."

"You run them on SSI national?"

"Yeah. Zip. If they were getting checks from the government, we'd have located 'em."

"Tax records? Military? Passport?"

"Blank." His look was measured, just short of offended. "We know how to do it, pal, chase the paper. There's no trail. The kid don't even have a driver's license."

"Fuck." Me.

"Detective, did you by any chance pull this boy's medical records?" Blossom.

"Yes, ma'am. They're in the car." His tired eyes tracked her. "If you're thinking the blood banks, it won't fly. He's got type O."

"No, I was thinking . . . maybe it's not so strange he doesn't have most kinds of ID, but you'd think, a young man, he'd have a driver's license."

"So?"

"Burke, remember that report you read to me? Something about severe damage to his eyes? Maybe that's why he can't get a driver's license."

"I don't know anything about any reports," I said, the words evenly spaced, like rocks dropping into a pond.

"Me neither," said Sherwood. "We had this report of an attempted break-in at the DPW Building, but I figure it had to be some kids playing a prank. Real rookie move, toss a rock through the glass. Not the kind you'd expect from any big-time New York heist-man.''

Blossom's face flushed.

Back at Sherwood's car, we found the records. Blossom translated the big words. ''He'll always have trouble with his vision, especially in daylight.''

''He couldn't get a driver's license?'' Sherwood.

''Not hardly.''

''They got no test for buying a gun,'' the big man said.

▨ 152

I TOLD HIM about the Nature Center. We went by to take a look. I showed him what I'd seen. He nodded.

''Wait here.''

I saw him talking to a uniformed park ranger. He walked back slow.

''He says they drop the gate every night. Padlock it. Wood gate. Anyone could get through it. Nobody does. Says the kids never park here. They patrol about twice a night. If they'd see someone, they'd chase 'em off. Maybe bust 'em for trespassing, if they were smoking dope.''

''He'll work with you?''

''On this? Sure. We shut down the parking spots, like I told you. This one won't get patrols.''

''How about if a car was going to park in here. Every night. Would he look the other way? Stay down?''

His eyes were someplace else. "What d'you have in mind?"

"Drawing his fire."

He walked a few feet away, back to me. I let him have his silence, waiting.

Sherwood turned to face me. "You're crazy. Crazy as he is. If this boy's the one you want, he's certifiable. Got him a Get Out of Jail Free card behind his past record. Hell, he was on medication right up to the time he cut loose and disappeared."

"I'm not crazy. I'm waiting for a car. Special car. You'll see. It should be able to handle anything he can throw."

"And what's my piece?"

"You got to be in position before dark. Nice and early. I'll park right where the Lincoln is right now. You can work anywhere from the left."

He scanned the terrain. "I was in 'Nam," he said. Absently, under his breath. "Infantry. It looks like that. I could deploy a dozen men in there. Spotlights, the whole works."

I moved close to him, my voice pitched low. "It has to be a deal, Sherwood. A square deal, both sides. You work from the *left*, okay? Nothing to the right of that point . . . see, where the tracks make that kind of peak?"

"Who's gonna be on the right?"

"Someone for me. I'm not gonna testify in court, okay? This works, he throws down on me, opens up, I'm out of here. Turn the key and go. Just make sure you fire across, not down."

"What else?"

"Just your own people. You post this on the bulletin board, Officer Revis takes a look, I could have trouble. The way this is, you and your team, you're staking out the place. On a hunch. You be as surprised as anyone else, a car pulls in."

"You want me to risk my badge?"

"Up to you. All I want, you either stay out of here or come in the way I said. Either way."

"When you gonna start?"

"I'll let you know."

◊ 153

AT VIRGIL'S HOUSE that night.

"What've you got that you're sure of?"

He brought down an old lever-action .30-30 carbine, the stock burnished with generations of hand-rubbed oil. "This Winchester was my daddy's. He taught me to use it. Before this all started, I was teaching Lloyd. We was going deer hunting, this winter, him and me."

"There's no paper on this?"

"No. I got me an old thirty-ought-six too. The one I was gonna have Lloyd use."

I lit a smoke.

"You started up again?"

I ignored him. "Lloyd, you sure you want to do this? This isn't some bar fight now."

"Yessir."

" 'Cause of all the trouble this guy caused you?"

The boy's fists were clenched, voice vibrating, working for control. "Not him. The other one. The one who . . ."

"I know," I told him.

〰154

BLOSSOM WAS IN the kitchen with Rebecca, Virginia mo-
nopolizing the conversation, Junior sitting quiet.

I thought about all Virgil had. Watching him polish the
cut-down barrels of a twelve-gauge with emery paper.

"You could walk away from this," I told him.

"Why didn't you?"

I didn't answer him.

Wesley knew.

"He knows I'm coming," I told my brother.

The mountain man jacked a shell into the chamber of his
carbine. It made a sharp, clean sound in the living room. His
face was set in lines of bone.

"The bear can't leave the woods just 'cause he knows it's
hunting season."

ᚠ 155

LATE THAT NIGHT, in bed.

"Do you know why they do it?"

"They?"

"Perverts, freaks, degenerates . . . whatever you want to
call them." Her face was soft, little-girl questions in her
eyes. But I felt the long muscles tense in her thigh, testing.
Pushing the buttons, watching the screen.

"What'd your mother call them?" Testing back.

"If they liked to play dress-up, harmless stuff like that
. . . she called them customers. Clients. Somebody wanted
to really whale on a woman, really hurt her, he'd know better
than to come to my mother's house."

I lit a smoke, buying time. "One way you can tell a
country's gone real evil . . . when the doctors are working
the torture chambers. Telling the sadists how much a prisoner
can take before he checks out completely. You know what a
snuff film is?"

"I heard of them. Just rumors."

"They're no rumors. And they didn't start a couple of
years ago. A guy I met in Africa told me the Shah of Iran
had video cameras in his torture chambers. Idi Amin too.
Why do you think Hitler's freaks kept the cameras rolling?
There's always been people who get off on pain. Other people's pain. And people who like to watch."

"Everybody has that in them?"

"No. Hell, no. But some do. And we keep breeding them. Monsters."

"Not criminals?"

"Past criminals. I'm a criminal, Blossom. My buddy Pablo, he's a doctor too. A psychiatrist. I asked him once, what I was. He said I'm a *contrabandista*. An outlaw, you understand?"

She sat up, hands clasping her knees. "Not like them. And not like us either, huh?"

I thought of Virgil, his family. Who's "us" anymore?

"Right on the borderline," I told her.

⚓ 156

THE NEXT AFTERNOON, on my way to Virgil's, the car phone made its noise.

"What?"

"Place your bets, I'm on the set."

"Prof?"

"No, fool, it's Jesse Jackson."

"Is the thing ready?"

"Have no fear, your ride is here."

"Here?"

"Time to jump, chump. Boston Street, northbound from Thirty-ninth. Cruise it slow, lights down low. When the honeybees swarm, you found the farm. Ask for Cherry."

ᚖ 157

VIRGIL SAT NEXT to me in the Lincoln, Lloyd in the back seat.

"He's really here?"

"Must be. Said to take Boston Street, northbound from Thirty-ninth."

"Boston Street? There's no Boston Street anywhere around here."

"He said to see a hooker. Cherry."

"He's holed up in Cal City maybe?"

"On the stroll, Virgil. A street girl. Where'd they be, close by?"

"Off Broadway, I guess." He dragged on his cigarette, thinking. "Ah, he has to mean Massachusetts Street. Over in Glen Park. Make a left up there."

The sun didn't reach all the way to street level on Massachusetts. Three-story frame houses leaned against each other for comfort. A slow-moving line of cars worked its way up the block. I drifted over to the curb. A flock of girls descended: spandex pants, tube tops, high heels. Working.

I pushed the power window switch, letting them know I was the man to talk to. Ebony woman with long straight hair, lipstick slashed carelessly across her mouth, leaned into the car, unbound breasts slopping against the windowsill. Up close, the hair was a wig.

"I don't do triples, honey. Your friends want to wait their

turn, or I can ask a couple of my girlfriends along? Whatever you say, anyway you want to do it.''

"I'm looking for Cherry. Wasn't that her that just went by? Girl in a red leather coat?''

"Yeah, catch Cherry wearing somethin' that'd cover her ass. Fat chance, get it?'' She blew smoke airily at the night ceiling. "Cherry? Cherry ain't nothin', man. Whatever you heard 'bout her, you can double up for me.''

They all sing the same sad song.

"How much is the ride?'' I asked her.

"How far you want to drive, honey? Around the world?'' And they all use the same lyrics.

"Short time,'' I said, looking for the quickest way in.

"Twenty-five.''

"Bring Cherry to the car, I'll give you twenty.''

"I don't see no cash.''

"I don't see no Cherry.''

They came back together. Cherry was shorter, stockier. Her wig was blonde.

"Hi, honey! You lookin' for me?''

"If you're Cherry.''

"That's me, baby. You heard about me, huh?''

"I'm looking for a friend. Your friend. He'd of told you I was coming.''

"Oh yeah. He's right . . .''

"Tell me his name.''

"You mean the Prophet, don't ya? *Yeah!* An ugly white man would come to set me free . . . Wow! Just like he said.''

I handed the other girl a pair of tens. She moved into the line of whores working the other cars. Cherry got into the back seat. Virgil took one whiff, pushed his own window down. Lloyd sat across from her, watching like he'd seen E.T. up close.

Cherry told me where to drive. One block up, a right turn into an alley. ROOMS, the wooden sign said, hanging lopsided over a door to a house that looked older than greed. I followed her inside, Lloyd behind me, Virgil last. Up a flight of stairs. We were the only whites in the joint. We watched their hands, looking for the truth.

Voices from an open door at the end of the hall. A pimp's sandpaper voice on top.

"I don't give a fuck who you say you is or what you say you want, you midget motherfucker. You don't come in here and work no girls. This is my place. Now you get your black ass outta here or I cut a piece of it off!"

We stepped inside. Burly thug with a shaved head, dressed all in white leather right down to his cowboy boots. Holding a straight razor in his hand.

The Prof was seated in a ragged armchair, wrapped in a khaki raincoat tenting around his tiny body. As calm as a man watching a movie—one he'd seen before. The pimp stepped aside as we entered, dropping into a slight crouch.

"Hey, schoolboy," the Prof greeted me. "You got a pistol with you?"

"Sure," I told him, taking it out.

"Good. Now will you *please* shoot this stupid farmer before he cuts someone?"

"Okay," I replied, cocking the piece.

"Hey, man . . ."

Virgil moved his coat. The sawed-off shotgun eyed the pimp.

"Oh, man. You remembered!" the Prof said. Like it was his brand of beer. He turned to the pimp. "You see how it is, fool. A knife don't make it right, but a gun can make it fun."

The pimp pocketed his razor, slid toward the door, his eyes filled with wonder. He'd seen guns before . . . but a tiny black man with a preacher's voice who used hillbillies for enforcers was science fiction. The legend of the Prophet was due for another installment.

We didn't block his path, letting him go. I tracked his face, making sure he knew I'd remember him.

Nobody had to tell him. Don't come back.

⚕ 158

IN THE LINCOLN, the Prof barked directions like he'd lived in that maze all his life. We parked in a row of garages. Cherry jumped out, opened a padlock. A shocking-purple car with a long, low hood and a black vinyl top stood inside. The Prof handed me a set of keys. We all climbed out.

"This is it?" I asked him.

"You can take that tank to the bank, bro'. It'll stop what he's got. Papers in the glove box."

"I'll meet you back at the house," I told Virgil. "Give me the scattergun, case you get stopped."

He handed it over.

Cherry turned to the Prof. "You not comin'?"

"You go back to the room, beautiful. Wait for me. Stay off the streets tonight." To me: "Give her a yard, pard."

I handed her two fifties. She took it, a reluctant look on her face. "You really comin' back?"

"Woman, have I said one word to you that has not been the truth?" the Prof snapped out at her; switching to his preacher's voice. "Do not confuse me with panderers and pimps, child. What I say shall come to pass, for it is written that children of the night shall forever find each other in the dark."

She turned, started down the alley to a grime-colored building. The Prof watched her walk, shifted back to his cornerboy's voice. "Ain't no fake in that shake, brothers."

She looked back once over her shoulder, waved once, and she was gone.

▼ 159

I UNLOCKED THE purple car. The inside of the door was covered with a thick slab of clear plastic right up to the windowsill. I dropped into the thinly padded bucket seat, turned the key. The engine crackled into life. I moved the pistol-grip shift lever into Drive and the beast lurched, straining against the brake.

The Lincoln pulled away. I followed.

The car was an old Plymouth Barracuda, a 1970s pony car. The hood went on forever, the trunk was tiny, the back seat just a padded shelf. The roof was lined with the same clear plastic, held up with cotter pins. I nursed the gas gingerly, getting the feel. The windshield was streaky, hard to see through.

At a light on Broadway, a maroon Mustang with a ground-scraper nose sloping down from gigantic rear tires pulled alongside. Revved its engine in the universal challenge. I ignored him. His passenger shouted across: "Is that a real one, man?"

A real *what?* The light flashed green and the Mustang peeled out. I stomped the gas experimentally and the 'Cuda catapulted forward with a roar, closing the distance in a heartbeat. I backed off quickly, hearing the exhausts pop and bubble. Quickly turned into a side street.

⚜ 160

INSIDE VIRGIL'S GARAGE, overhead lights on. I walked around the 'Cuda. Saw what had brought out the challenge from the Mustang. On the car's rear deck lid, chrome letters: Hemi.

"Why'd the Mole send me such a rocket ship?" I asked the Prof.

"Man said you packing mucho weight, you got to haul the freight."

He took me through the car, showing me how it worked. "See how this stuff is hinged against the hood? You just pull the pins and the panels slide right down."

"What is this stuff? Lexan?"

"The Mole said it was like that, only better. Only thing, you can't roll down the windows, they're too thick. Windshield's same stuff. So's the back window."

"It's beautiful, Prof. You know what I need it for?"

"The Mole said it was a shark cage. It ain't what you know, it's what you show."

"I never expected to see you out here."

"What was I gonna do with the ride, Clyde? Ship it UPS? The Mole paid the toll."

"I was going to fly back, bring it over myself."

"No beef, chief. It was a nice day, I felt like a drive."

"Thanks, Prof."

"Way I figure it, schoolboy, you and this hillbilly here, you ain't got a clue between you. What's the plan, man?"

∅ 161

DARKNESS SURROUNDED THE house, island of light in the living room. I told the Prof everything. Almost everything.

"It could play the way you say, 'home. You park that tank in the spot, the cops stake out the terrain, Virgil covers your back. The freak smokes the car, the cops move in, you take off. Virgil makes sure nobody cheats, right?"

"That's it."

"Where you gonna get the passenger, go parking with you?"

"One of those sex shops. They got them all over the place. Get one of those life-size blow-up dolls. He'll never know the difference."

The Prof lit a smoke, face a mask. "What if he don't show, bro'?"

"He will."

"Who told you?"

I looked in his eyes, not hiding it anymore. "Wesley."

"Yeah, I knew it would be true. The monster's in the ground, but he's still around."

"It's like he talked to me."

"Yeah, you goin' spiritual on me, brother? Talking to spooks? That's okay, if you can pay."

"There never was a better man-hunter, Prof. You know it as well as I do."

"You sayin' he taught you how to do it?"

"Yeah. Some of it."

"Wesley knows. This guy has to die."

"That's not mine. We're going to smoke him out, clear Lloyd once and for all. Then I'm gone."

The Prof looked around the room. Nodded.

"When that evil little baby-killer got on the train, he didn't know it stopped at Dodge City."

₩ 162

I DROPPED HIM off where we'd picked up the 'Cuda.

"You got enough cash?"

"I'm going back on the ground, ride the 'Hound. No problem."

"Prof . . ."

"It's cool, fool. Don't get sloppy on me now."

"Okay."

I took his hand, surprised as always by the power in the little man's grip.

His handsome face was calm, troubadour's voice a separate, living thing in the Indiana night. "Wesley may have showed you some things, schoolboy. But I was your teacher.

Wesley, he knew death. Up close and personal. Me, I know life. Stay right on the line, you'll be fine.''

⚓ 163

YOU LIKE THE blonde or the redhead?'' I asked Blossom.

The sex shop had a plentiful supply. Black, white, Oriental. Matching pubic hair, ''removable for washing,'' the dandruffy clerk told me. ''All three holes, too.'' The two faces were identically blank.

''I don't like either of them.''

''Yeah, okay. I know what you don't like. What I need is some clothes of yours, okay? They need to be dressed when I first pull into the spot.''

''It won't work.''

''Why not? You think he's gonna get that close a look?''

''Let's see.''

''What do you mean?''

''Let's try it. Look for yourself.''

''It'll work, don't worry.''

''You can't be sure.''

''Burke, we won't get another chance. I'll leave it up to you. Just take a look first. Please.''

''Get a suitcase,'' I told her as I pulled the plug on the inflatable dolls.

⑭ 164

VIRGIL AND LLOYD weren't home. "They went out somewhere," Rebecca told us. "Have some coffee with me—they
said they'd be back in an hour or so."

Virginia marched into the kitchen, pulling her brother by
one hand. "Mommy, can we get Junior a sailor suit? I saw
one on TV before. He'd look so cute in it when he goes back
to school."

"Junior, you want a sailor suit?" Rebecca asked him, eyes
dancing with joy at her children.

"No!"

"I guess that settles it, Virginia. Your brother's getting old
enough to know his own mind."

"He's just stubborn."

"Like his daddy."

"Daddy's not stubborn."

"No, Daddy's perfect, huh?"

"Well, he *is*."

"How come you're not practicing your piano, sweet-
heart?" Blossom asked the child.

"She don't hardly touch that thing unless her daddy's
around to hear her." Rebecca laughed.

"Mommy!" Virginia gave her a look I didn't think women
learned until they were grown.

I went into the living room. Watched a Monster Truck
competition on TV. Virginia sat down at the kitchen table

with Blossom and her mother, sipped her mostly-milk coffee with them. I lit a cigarette, drifting. Junior came inside, sat down in his father's chair, watched the trucks with me.

◗ 165

IT WAS ALMOST ten o'clock when I heard the door. The kids were in bed. Virginia came into the living room in her flannel nightgown, rubbing sleep from her eyes. Virgil picked her up, gave her a kiss, carried her back to bed.

"Got something to show you, brother. Outside."

The 'Cuda was in the garage, lights on. A neat round hole in the driver's door.

"Lloyd and me, we took it up to a spot I know. Off in the woods. I threw down on it from maybe fifty yards. Real close. Put one round into the door, one into the driver's window. From the thirty-ought-six. The bullets never got inside. That thing's a bank vault."

"You don't know the Mole," I told him.

His face was calm. "That's right, I don't. Thought I'd see for myself."

"Okay, it's time. We're set. Tomorrow night."

"What about the other test?" Blossom. Honey-voiced, thread of ice running deep inside.

"What test?" Virgil wanted to know.

"She wants to see what the dummies look like from outside the car. I got them in the Lincoln. I'll just blow one up, we'll take a look."

Blossom stood to the side, watching us, hands on her hips, jaw set. "Not here."

"What difference does it make?"

"Difference enough. Let's take it back, to where Virgil tested it. See what it looks like in the dark."

"This'll be good enough."

"No, it won't."

"Blossom . . ."

"She's right." Rebecca.

"Reba, you don't know what . . ."

Rebecca wheeled on Virgil. "What is it I don't know, honey? I don't know what you and Lloyd gonna be doing out there? What if this maniac sees a plastic dummy, figures out it's a trap, starts spraying bullets all over the place? Burke, he's inside this car, safe. What about you?"

Virgil held out his hands, palms up, surrendering. I caught the look between Blossom and Rebecca. Wondered why men ever think they run things.

ᐙ 166

BLOSSOM SAT NEXT to me in the 'Cuda's bucket seat, running her hands over the surfaces, gauging the weight. The coupe's tail slid out a bit as I gunned it around a corner, pavement-ripping power barely under leash.

"He would have just loved this car," she said.

"Who?"

"Chandler."

I watched the Lincoln's taillights through the dull windshield, following Virgil.

▌ 167

WE PARKED THE 'Cuda at the end of a dirt road. A few strokes of the foot pump (the one "optional extra" I bought from the sex shop after I passed on a great variety of cheesy negligees and garter belts) and the redhead doll was life-size. I positioned it in the passenger seat. Stepped back onto a rise, settled myself and looked.

The white body was only a dull streak behind the glass. Couldn't tell what it was.

"Look for yourself," I told Blossom, standing aside.

She stood next to me. Nodded.

"Let's get out of here," I said, taking her elbow.

She stood rooted. "Virgil, you got your rifle with you?"

"Yeah."

"Got a scope on it?"

He looked at me. I nodded.

I put the rifle to my shoulder. "Do it right. Play it square." Blossom's voice.

Or Wesley's?

I dropped prone, sighted in. He'd have a night scope of some kind. Infrared or luminous.

I put the cross-hairs on the passenger's window. This time, I didn't just look. I watched.

With his eyes.

The dummy sat stiff—I couldn't feel the heat.
The trap had no cheese.

☙ 168

IN THE LINCOLN, on the way back to Blossom's.

"Who else could you get to do it?"

I didn't answer her.

"You want to ask Rebecca?"

"Shut up. You're a smart girl, be smart enough to know when to keep quiet."

☙ 169

NO MATTER HOW many times I spun the wheel, it came up double zero—the house edge.

His house.

〰170

WHEN THE DARKNESS grabbed the ground, I pulled out of Virgil's garage. Blossom sat next to me, a man's white shirt worn outside a pair of blue jeans, her long blonde hair loose and free.

The padlock gave way. I stepped back inside the 'Cuda, drove slowly through the park until I found the spot, the dual exhausts bubbling like a motorboat, leaving a wake of power-sounds. I nosed the purple car into a pool of ink, the orange light from the mercury vapor lamps just brushing the passenger window. Where Blossom sat, profile to the rise where the rusting cross-ties made a perfect sniper's roost.

"What now?" she asked.

"Keep your voice down. I don't know how sound carries out here."

"Okay, honey." She ran her fingers through her hair, leaned back in the seat.

My watch said eleven-fifteen.

"You think he's out there?"

"Not yet."

"How long are we going to wait?"

"Long as it takes."

Waiting inside myself, I knew what the big cop had been thinking, the bargain we'd made. Homicide happens. They call it different things, depending on the uniform you're wearing at the time.

A night bird screamed. Blossom stiffened. "You think. . . ?"

"Probably heard Sherwood and his crew moving around."

"Oh."

171

ONE-THIRTY IN THE morning.

"Are we going to wait until light?"

"No. Couple of kids parking, they wouldn't do that. If he's watching, he's got to believe. It's got to feel right to him first. The way I see it, he probably stalks all the time. Maybe every night. But he doesn't go off until he sees the signal. Whatever that is."

I rotated my neck on its column, feeling the adhesions crackle as they parted. Too tight.

"Time to go," I told Blossom, lighting a cigarette.

"Burke . . . ?"

"What?"

"How come you . . . I mean, that's the first cigarette you've had since we parked here."

"I don't know what he can see, but the tip of a cigarette, you can see it for a long distance. That's why soldiers cup them in the field. He wouldn't expect to see a cigarette until it's over."

"What's over?"

"The sex. What he came to kill."

♨ 172

I GUNNED THE 'Cuda out of its spot, a young man pumped up on himself. Saying goodbye.

He didn't answer.

♨ 173

IT LOOK REAL to you?" I asked Sherwood later.

"Perfect. From where we were, we could see right into the front seat with the scope. Even without one, you could tell people were in the car."

"You up for a couple more times?"

"Yeah. I got two men with me. Good men. It jumps off, one of the boys'll radio for help while me and my partner move on him."

"Okay. I'm coming back tonight. A little later, closer to midnight."

"Burke . . ."

I looked at the big man, waiting.

"Last night, someone was there. Couldn't get a movement, but we weren't alone. You know the feeling?"

"Yeah. Jungle feeling."

"One difference, here."

"What?"

"Over in 'Nam, we didn't give Charlie the first bite."

◗174

THE CAR IS perfect, Mole.''

He didn't answer.

"The Prof get back?"

"Yes."

"Good. Tell him everything's okay."

The Mole stayed silent.

"Pansy's all right?"

"Sure."

"Give her a pat for me."

He hung up.

◊ 175

INSIDE THE 'CUDA, waiting.

"I spoke to my sister last night. After you fell asleep."

"Violet?"

"Rose. I told her we were going to find the man who killed her. Told Mama too."

I didn't say anything. Watching her fine profile, smelling her smell.

"Burke . . . our gull, the one we saved?"

"Yeah?"

"He's okay now. I let him go this morning."

Time passed. The sniper didn't come.

◊ 176

THE PHONE RANG at Blossom's the next afternoon. Answering machine picked up.

"Blossom? It's Wanda, girl. Get off your big fat butt and pick up the phone."

Blossom snatched the receiver. Pieces of the conversation came through as I dozed. "This better be right, now. You talked to her yourself, Wanda Jean?" Schoolgirl giggles.

I closed my eyes. She was a different person. Again. Another piece of the puzzle. Letting me see her essence the way a stripteaser shows you her body.

Keeping the G-string in place.

A red lacquered fingernail gently scratched my cheek. "Wake up, honey. We got places to go."

₩ 177

VIRGIL WAS HOME from work, sitting at the kitchen table drinking a beer, Virginia standing next to him, one hand on his shoulder.

"Where's my hero?" Blossom asked.

"Out in the back, playing catch with Junior."

Blossom went out to get him. I sat down, caught Virgil's eye.

"Virginia . . ."

"I know. Go practice my piano."

He gave her a kiss. She flounced out.

I told Virgil what Blossom had in mind. He sipped his beer, thinking it through. Nodded.

"Reba!"

She came in from the back of the house, scarf tied around her head, flushed from doing some kind of work.

"What is it, Virgil? Afternoon, Burke."

"We're going out for a bit. We'll get supper out. Be back after dark."

"Okay. Is Lloyd going?"

"Yeah."

"I'll let Virginia watch Junior. Be careful."

♨ 178

VIRGIL DROVE THE Lincoln over to Calumet City, me next to him, Blossom and Lloyd in the back seat. Talking low.

"Here it is," she said. A neat white frame house, dark green trim around the windows, driveway along the side.

I knocked on the back door. A panel about half the size of a man's face slid back. Blossom pushed past me. "We've got an appointment," she said. "With Crystal."

The panel slid closed. Door opened. A slim man wearing a black-and-white-striped shirt with red suspenders led us into a formal parlor. Matching love seats, easy chairs, all done up in a light blue pattern, dark blue Oriental rug on the polished hardwood floor.

We took seats. A woman came in, tall, subtle makeup burying her age, black hair done up in a beehive. Blossom got up, put out her hand. "Miz Joyce, I'm Blossom Lynch. My mother was Tessie Mae Lynch, from Weirton, West Virginia. She spoke of you often—I'm pleased to meet you."

The tall woman took her hand, bowed her head slightly, smiled. They walked off together.

Virgil looked around, shrugged.

"What'd you expect, pal?" the man in the striped shirt said. "A red light over the door?"

I laughed. It felt good.

Lloyd looked straight ahead.

Blossom and the madam came back with a curvy young woman, her small face almost buried under a toss of strawberry-blonde curls.

"Lloyd," Blossom said, "this is my friend Crystal. The girl I told you about."

"Pleased to meet you," Lloyd mumbled, his face scarlet.

We sat down in the parlor to wait.

After a while, Lloyd came downstairs, a goofy grin on his face. His chest was too big for his shirt.

⚊⚊ 179

TEN-THIRTY THAT NIGHT. I sat on the bed, smoking, watching Blossom dress, fresh from her shower. She stepped into a pair of tiny black panties, snapped on a matching bra. Looked at herself in the mirror. Took the bra off, tossed it on the bed. Slipped a soft pink sweater-dress over her head. It came down to mid-thigh. She checked the mirror again. Hiked up the skirt to her waist, pulled a sheer stocking over each leg, fastening each one with an elastic garter. A dab of perfume behind each ear, generous splash of fire-engine-red lipstick. Tied a black scarf around her waist for a belt.

"Those won't do," she said.

"What?"

"Those gangster clothes of yours. We're going parking, you can't wear a suit. Put on a pair of jeans, you can borrow a leather jacket from Virgil."

⬙ 180

THE INSIDE OF the 'Cuda smelled like Blossom. We talked softly, Blossom bragging about how she'd pulled it off with Lloyd.

"I figure, I owed him that one."

"You see his face? Anything you ever owed him in life, you paid off."

Her smile flashed. She leaned over, kissed me on the cheek.

Swamp darkness. The kind that rises from the ground.

Blossom bounced in her seat. "Come on."

"Come on, what?"

She turned so she was on her knees, leaned across the shift lever into me, tongue stabbing into my mouth, making her sounds. My hands on her back, stroking her.

"Pull it up," she whispered into my mouth.

"What?"

"My skirt, honey. Let go, let him feel it. Let him feel what lovers do. Let him bring his hate—have it out. Come on, baby."

Her skirt slid over the nylon, my thumbs hooking the

waistband of her panties, pulling them down to her knees. She reached back, pulled them all the way down, leaving the black silk hooked around one ankle. Then she crawled into my lap, facing me, reaching underneath her for my zipper, her coppery estrogen smell almost choking me. She pulled me free. "This is mine," she hissed. "Give me what's mine," fitting herself over me, her neck arched against my face.

I felt her magnetic wetness. "Come . . . come . . ." she whisper-moaned against my face. A machine-gun burst ripped open the night, devil's raindrops splattering against the windshield. Instinct threw her down against me as I frantically tried to turn, get my back between Blossom and the sniper fire.

High harmonic crack of the sniper's assault rifle. Virgil's carbine boomed out an answer. Bullets slammed into the car, rocking it on its tires. Spotlights beamed across the rise, bullhorn crackled: "*Police!*"

I shoved Blossom away from me, clawing for my pistol. Found the door handle. "Get outta here. Back to Virgil's. Go!"

And I was out the door, crouched behind the car, pulling up my zipper, pulling it together.

The gunfire stopped. Sounds of men thrashing around in the dark wood. I took off to my right, running hard.

⚑ 181

I COVERED THE length of the blacktop, crouching low. All the way to the end, watching the night above me, praying for the hunter's moon to show.

Plunged into the woods, over the fence. Grabbed a breath, belly-crawled my way up the rise toward the railroad tracks. Far to my left, the cops were still beating the bushes. I stopped at the top, shallow-breathing, feeling the ground against my cheek.

The guns were quiet. I stood up, worked my way over the tracks to the far side of the woods. I backed against a tree, antenna out.

The distinctive rumble of the 'Cuda's exhaust, growling along in low gear, somewhere behind me.

Something moving. To my right. Clumsy-sloppy, blundering. Fear-booted. I took off, feeling his trail, following the blood spoor.

A sapling branch lashed my face, warning me. I dropped to one knee, listening.

I felt the panic, heard him crashing down the back side of the hill, heading for the slough where he'd been born. Where it started. I stumbled onto a dog path through the brush. A black plastic sniper rifle lay discarded on the path, the night scope a blind eye now.

Sirens to my left, homing in, surrounding.

The only fear I felt was his. Then: a stick figure in camouflage gear, running, arms pumping, hands empty. I leveled the pistol, sighted in.

Wesley's voice: Make Sure.

I lowered the .38, took off after him.

He flew around a corner just as I reached the street. Sprinted up a dirt alley a block from the water, coat flapping behind him. I closed the gap. Did he have a mail-order killing knife strapped to his boot?

Kill-lust driving me at him, not mine.

Wesley's chill in me, patient.

I heard the 'Cuda again, its stump-puller engine throttled down.

A dog yapped fearfully.

My eyes picked up an image of movement. It disappeared. I stood, scanning, the pistol down at my side. The closest shelter was an aluminum house trailer sitting like a bloated mushroom in an overgrown patch of jungle, no lights in the windows. A high-pitched moan rode the air as he charged across my path, right for the trailer, never breaking stride.

He dove inside before I could bring the gun up.

The sirens closed in. The door to the trailer stood open. I flattened my back against the metal, dropped into a crouch, slid inside, head down, eyes up, the stubby pistol held before me like a divining rod.

Freakish wet sounds.

He was crumpled on the floor, holding his crotch, mewling.

"It's over, Luther," I told him, my voice shaking. "All over, now."

The sniper's eyes found me. Dry ice, burning cold. His face was a ravaged skeleton, claw marks on his cheeks from his own hands, clear fluid all over his chin. Wesley called to me. I cocked the pistol.

"Don't do it." Sherwood's voice, behind me.

The thing on the floor spasmed, making noises I never wanted to hear again.

❧ 182

THE TRAILER WAS a tiny, humpbacked thing, kitchen against one wall. I passed the closet-sized bathroom, heading for the back. His room. A TV set, twisted coat hanger for rabbit ears. Fast-food cartons, TV dinners. Empty Coke bottles. Rancid smells. Stack of magazines in one corner, as high as my waist. Newspaper all over the floor, like you'd put down for a dog that wasn't housebroken. Sleeping bag with a camouflage-pattern lining. CB radio. Cheap pair of binoculars hanging from a strap on the wall. Neat row of X's drawn above them in red crayon.

Six marks. There wouldn't be eight.

⚘183

WHEN I STEPPED back into the front room, there were three squad cars outside, bubble-gum lights rotating in the windows. Red and white.

A cop in a baseball hat and flak jacket pulled Luther to his feet, making a face at the smell. Snapped the handcuffs behind him. Walked him outside to the waiting cars, now bright with probing spotlights.

"You think . . . ?"

"It doesn't matter." Sherwood cut me off.

We stepped into the night air, watching. Luther was ducking his head to climb into the back of the squad car, the SWAT Team cop right behind him.

I lit a cigarette. A shot rang out, slamming the sniper against the squad car door. Blood flowered on what was left of his face.

"Down!" Sherwood screamed at the cops, hitting the deck. My eyes twisted to the left. A flash of soft pink in the darkness.

I moved away into the night, hearing tires torture rubber as a car took off close by.

Nobody gave chase.

✴ 184

I SHOOK HANDS with Lloyd. "Thank you. For everything," he said. He looked older, harder. Softened as Blossom kissed him goodbye.

"You always have a home here, brother." Virgil.

Rebecca stood just to the side. "Look at you men. You don't know how to do anything, do you?" She wrapped her arms around me, hugged me fiercely. Her face was wet against mine.

Virginia watched from the side, her hand on Junior's shoulder.

✴ 185

THE LINCOLN TOOK us through the steel city onto the highway. I parked at O'Hare. Carried Blossom's bags inside. We stopped at the gate. She faced me, her hands wrapped in the lapels of my jacket. Turquoise eyes glistened with secrets I'd never know.

"Listen to me, trouble-man. I don't know where I'm going, how long it will take me to get there. Maybe I'll be alone, maybe I'll live in a nice big house with a white picket fence, have a husband and four kids. I don't know. Wherever I'll be, I'll be a doctor. Follow the scent, you know what I smell like. You can always find me."

"Blossom . . ."

"Just listen to me—I know what's mine. Wherever I end up, I'll tell you one thing, I'm going to have a dog. A big, nasty killer dog who loves only me, protects me with his life. Every night, just before I go to bed, I'm going to let my dog out into the yard. Anybody comes after me, he's going to raise holy hell. You find my house, Burke. Wait until dark. When you come over the fence for me, that dog, he won't bar the way."

She turned and walked, her heels clicking, trailing mystery and promise behind her.

⚚ 186

THE PLANE DROPPED into La Guardia. I took a cab back to my life.

Back in New York City,
Burke confronts a crime
unlike any he has seen before.
And he's seen a few.
A missing infant leads Burke
into the horrifying world of
voodoo and witchcraft, Satanism and

SACRIFICE

by Andrew Vachss

Available in hardcover at your local bookstore.
Published by Alfred A. Knopf.

The first few pages will draw
you in to the galvanizing new novel
from an incomparable suspense writer . . .

☷ 1

WHEN YOU HUNT predators, the best camouflage is weakness.

The E train screeched into Forty-second Street. I got to my feet, pulling slightly on the leather handle of the dog's harness. She nosed her way forward, wary. Citizens parted to let me pass. A black teenager wearing an oversized blue jacket with gold raglan sleeves braced one side of the doors with his arm, making sure they wouldn't close as I walked between them. "You okay, man. Step through."

My dark glasses had polarized lenses. The kid's face was gentle. Sad. Someone in his family was blind. I mumbled thanks, stepped off the subway car onto the platform.

I pushed forward on the harness handle, like shifting into gear. The dog headed for the stairs, waited for a clear path, then took me up along the rail.

On the sidewalk, I turned my face toward the sun, feeling the warmth. "Good girl, Sheba," I told the dog. She didn't react, a professional doing her work. I shifted the handle and she went forward, keeping me in the middle of the sidewalk. Away from doors that might open suddenly, maintaining a safe distance from the curb. I closed my eyes, counting steps.

Sheba halted me at the corner of Forty-fourth and Eighth. She didn't watch the traffic signals any more than the other pedestrians did. It's the same rule for everyone here—cross at your own risk.

I made my way carefully along the sidewalk, counting steps, guided by the dog. Found my spot. Tugged slightly backward on the handle—Sheba sat down. I unwrapped the blanket from around my shoulders, knelt, and spread it on the ground. When I stood up, Sheba lay down on the blanket, made herself comfortable. I opened my coat. Inside was a cardboard sign, held around my neck with a loop of string. White cardboard, hand-lettered in black Magic Marker.

PLEASE HELP

I held a metal cup in my hands. Added a few random coins to sweeten the pot.

Waiting.

 2

HUMANS PASSED AROUND me, a stream breaking over a rock. They didn't look at my face. If they had, they would have seen a couple of rough patches where the blind man had missed with the electric razor. I was wearing high-top running shoes, loosely laced, denim pants, a gray sweatshirt. All under a khaki raincoat that came past my knees. A well-used black fedora on my head.

The local skells were well used to me by now. I made it to the same spot every day. Patiently collected coins from passing citizens, face held straight ahead.

I was a piece of scenery, as anonymous as a taxicab.

My eyes swept the street behind the dark lenses.

Sheba settled into her task. An old wolf-shepherd, mostly

gray, soft eyes watchful under white eyebrows. She had a warrior's heart and an undertaker's patience.

Hooker's heels sounded on the sidewalk. A bottle blonde, wearing a cheap red dress, short-tight, black fishnet stockings, a hole the size of a half-dollar on the front of one thigh, pale skin poking through the mesh. Low-rent makeup smeared her face. Getting ready to work the lunchtime crowd.

"Your dog's so pretty."

"Thank you."

"Can I pet her?"

"No, she's working."

"Me too . . . I guess you can't tell."

I drew a sharp breath through my nose, inhaling her cheap perfume as greedily as a cokehead. She laughed, bitter and brittle. "Yeah, I guess maybe you can. I seen you here before. Standing here."

"I'm here every day."

"I know. I seen you smoke sometimes . . . when someone lights one for you. You want one now?"

"I don't have any."

"I have some . . . " Fumbling in her red vinyl shoulder bag. "You want one now?"

"Please."

She stuck two cigarettes in her mouth, fired them with a cheap butane lighter. Handed one to me.

"It tastes good," I told her, grateful tone in my voice.

"Its menthol."

"The lipstick . . . that's what tastes good."

"Oh. I guess you don't . . . I mean . . . "

"Only my eyes don't work."

She flushed under the heavy makeup. I didn't mean . . ."

"It's okay. Everybody's missing something."

Her eyes flashed sad. "I had a dog once. Back home."

"And you miss her?"

"Yeah. I miss a lot of things."

"Go home."

"I can't. Not now. You don't understand . . . Home's far away from here. A million miles away."

"What's your name?"

"Debbie."

"These are bad streets, Debbie. Even if you can't go home, you can go away."

"He'd come after me."

I dragged on my cigarette.

"You know what I'm talking about?" she asked, her voice bitter-quiet.

"Yeah. I know."

"No, you don't. He's watching me. Right now. Across the street. I spend much more time out here, talking to you. I'm gonna get it from him."

Even with my eyes closed, even with her facing me, I could see the coat-hanger marks across her back. Feel them. I shifted my face slightly, let her hear the core to my voice. "Tell him you made a date with me. For later."

"Sure." Melancholy sarcasm.

"Put your hand in my coat pocket. Your left hand."

"Wow! You got some roll in there."

"It's mostly singles, two twenties on the inside. Take one. . . . Tell him you asked for half up front."

She glanced over her shoulder, hip-shot, leaned close to me. "I tell him that he'll be waiting for you later . . . when you go home."

"I know. Tell him the roll was a couple a hundred, it's okay."

"But . . ."

"Just do it, Debbie. You live with him?"

"Yeah . . ."

"You can go home tonight. Away from here."

"How . . .?

"Take the money, go do your work. Tell him what I told you."

"Mister . . ."

"Reach in, pull out the roll. Shield it with your body. Take the bill, put the rest back. Pat my dog. Then take off. Tonight, you go home, you understand? Stay out of the bus station—take a train. It'll be okay, Debbie."

She reached into my pocket, knelt down.

"Sheba, it's okay girl," I said.

The dog made a sweet little noise as Debbie patted her. She straightened up, looked into the lenses of my glasses. "You're sure?"

"Dead sure."

I listened to her heels tap off on the sidewalk. A different rhythm now.

3

IT WAS ALMOST two o' clock before he showed. I recognized him easily now. In his thirties, close-cropped brown hair, matching mustache, trimmed neat. Wearing a blue windbreaker, jeans, white basketball shoes. Youth worker from one of the homeless shelters. Last time he stuffed a dollar bill into my cup. I remember saying, "God Bless you."

Watching his smile.

This time he wasn't alone. The kid with him was maybe eight years old. Skinny kid, wearing a brand-new sweatshirt with some cartoon characters on the front, munching a hot dog. Having a good time. Probably spent a bunch of quarters in the video arcades first.

They turned into the electronic store a few doors in front of where I was standing—the same place he'd gone the last time. When he'd come up behind me and put the money in my cup. The same place he always went.

He was inside almost an hour. When he came out, he was alone.

))) 4

HE WALKED PAST me. Stuffed another dollar in my cup. "May the Lord follow you always," I thanked him. He smiled his smile.

The Prof strolled up to me. A tiny black man, wearing a floor-length raincoat, scuffling along.

"You got him?" I asked.

"Slime can slide, but it can't hide."

"Call McGowan first," I told him, holding his eyes to be sure he got it. McGowan's a cop—he knows what to do, but kids are his beat, not hijackers. "Tell him the freak made a live delivery this time. Tell him to go in the back way—Max is there on the watch."

"I hear what you say—today's the day?"

"The bust will go down soon—they're ready, warrants and all. You find out where the freak goes, where he holes up. They'll take him tomorrow, at work. Then we take our piece out of his apartment. Just the cash—the cops can have the rest.''

The prof took off, disappearing into the crowd. The freak would never see him coming.

 5

TIME TO GO. I gently pulled on the harness and Sheba came to her feet. I folded the blanket, wrapped it around my neck, and let the dog pull me forward. I turned the corner, headed down the alley where Max would be waiting. I spotted Debbie's owner lounging against the alley wall. Tall, slim, brownskin man wearing a long black leather coat and Zorro hat. Stocky white kid next to him, heavily muscled in a red tank top. A pimp: he needed reinforcement to mug a blind man.

I plodded on ahead, oblivious to them, closing the gap.

The pimp pushed himself languidly against the wall to face me. The muscleman loomed up on the side.

''Hold up, man.''